D1785621

SUMMARY

Snowflakes don't make any sound. Like a first kiss...

PART ONE: When Robert finds Ange bleeding in an alley, he employs him in his vintage toy store as an act of charity. Months later, as Christmas approaches, he still has many unanswered questions about Ange, but one thing is clear. The eccentric young dancer is determined to offer his thanks—and himself—to teach a brokenhearted Master how to open his heart to love again.

PART TWO: Yet even as Robert embraces Ange's eager submission to him, the mystery of Ange remains. Something nearly destroyed him and his ability to cope in the outside world. Robert resolves he will find out the truth. Ange brought light to Robert's life again; as a true Master, Robert will make sure the power of their bond heals them both.

∼

AUTHOR'S NOTE: Part One of Submissive Angel was released in 2012 in an anthology. This Story Witch Press re-release edition includes Part One (unchanged except for some polishing/minor tweaks), and a lengthy new novella, Part Two, where readers find out what happened after Robert at last claimed Ange for his own, and what fateful events brought the two of them together.

SUBMISSIVE ANGEL

A BDSM Romance Novella

JOEY W. HILL

ACKNOWLEDGMENTS

My great thanks to Sarah Frantz, who did a superlative job editing the Part One version of *Submissive Angel*. She reminded this veteran author of a vitally important lesson—no matter how many stories you write, you can always learn to write a better one. Especially if you remain open to feedback from people who truly want you to do so!

A special thanks to my readers, whose enjoyment of Robert and Ange's initial story led me to take a second journey with them and answer the questions the original shorter novella didn't give us the chance to explore.

One additional note: In Part Two, you'll meet a character named Charlie. While the character and his situation in the story is 99% fictional, he was directly inspired by my high school world history teacher. At that time, I already loved a well-told story with strong characters, but he deepened and expanded that love. So many of my characters and storylines have been affected by the way he taught history. Because he devoted an entire block of his curriculum to art history, he is also responsible for the love of art so often reflected in my books.

This teacher was the first gay man I ever met (knowingly, of course), and I credit that experience with broadening how I view love–as something that should be celebrated in all its wonderful forms.

PART ONE

CHAPTER ONE

*S*nowflakes don't make any sound. Like a first kiss. That must be why they feel the same against your skin.

Robert stared up at the thickly falling snow illuminated by the Victorian-style streetlight, the iron pole wrapped in a garland and red velvet bow. Earlier today, he hadn't thought to test Ange's assertion, but at this late hour, with no foot traffic and the storefronts cloaked in hushed silence, he found himself listening to the snow. Comparing how it felt, falling on his upturned face, to all the kisses he'd had in his life. As well as the kisses he might want in the future.

Even though they're silent, you can still hear something. The way you can hear somebody holding their breath.

It made sense that one of Ange's quirky observations would cross his mind right now. He'd collected a lot of them since the boy had started working for him nearly six months ago. After all, he'd made a hell of an impression, applying for the job while flat on his ass in garbage and bleeding profusely.

On that sticky June night, Robert had heard a noise behind the dumpster in the alley next to his vintage toy shop. Setting aside the trash he'd been taking out, he picked up the baseball bat he kept inside the back door. Not one of his 1920s Louisville

3

sluggers, just a made-in-China piece of crap, but still solid wood. When he peered around the steel container and saw a blood trail on the cobblestones, he followed it to a pair of legs in ripped jeans.

He was confronted with a shock of dirty white-gold hair atop a long, lean form in a thin T-shirt. Someone had worked the guy over—his nose was bleeding all over the fabric. But he was holding the broken skyhook Robert had reluctantly tossed after he'd knocked it off a shelf. It was a jockey on a horse, perched on the top of a stand. When it sat on a table, the counterweight ball made the horse rock, so it looked like it was running.

In Victorian times, people couldn't get enough of toys that used the law of gravity to do what seemed impossible, magical, and his modern-day patrons were no different. He had a whole shelf of balance toys from that era.

At Robert's appearance, the kid, mid-twenties maybe, had held up the toy as if he didn't have one eye swelling shut, a busted lip, and what was definitely a broken nose. Robert had done a couple tours in Afghanistan. Between that and boxing at the local gym for his daily workout, he was very familiar with the look.

"I fixed it, sir," the young man said earnestly. And he had. He'd hinged the arm back in place on the jockey's side, and fixed the snapped stand using tape he'd probably fished out of the trash. "It's temporary, but I can solder the stand and re-attach the arm with wood glue. No one will even know it was broken. I'm good at fixing things people don't think to fix."

Robert squatted on his haunches. Putting his fingers on the man's jaw to hold him still, he took a closer look at the damage. At his touch, his unsolicited applicant went quite still, except for a significant quiver that hit Robert in the gut, particularly when he lowered lashes as white-gold as his hair.

"What's your name?"

"Ange." Ange pronounced it in the French manner, so that

the *an* sounded like *own* and the *ge* a soft *ssh*, like a mother's gentle reproof.

"French for angel." Robert tried for a smile but failed. The harm to Ange's face must have been done with more than one pair of fists. Looking at the guileless eyes and sensitive mouth, he knew this kid had done nothing to warrant it except be what he was. "Come on. I'll drive you to the hospital."

"I'm okay. I don't need a hospital. I need a job. Sir." Ange held up the toy. "Since the North Pole layoffs, things have been rough. I'm just glad I found you before the other elves did."

Robert's lips twisted. Funny bastard. Odd fellow, obviously all in his head. Until he looked at Robert and said *Sir*. Then he was a hundred percent there.

"You have a lot of metal toys, trains, things where gears get stuck. I can unjam them. I can dust everything, keep it all looking good. Everyone hates to dust. You don't have to pay me much. A cot in a back room and enough to buy my lunch. Don't pay me at all until you're sure I'm worth a salary."

Robert put a quelling hand over his. The boy had slim, elegant fingers, like a pianist. Thank goodness whoever had beaten on him hadn't noticed that. The knuckles were scraped, though. Ange had fought back. That, and the stubborn jut of his jaw, told Robert he'd gone down fighting. It sent a twinge to his groin, because he liked a sub with fire. *Jesus.*

"We'll talk about that later. Hospital first."

"I don't—"

"You're going." Robert gave him a hard look. "Got it?"

He wasn't sure what made him test those waters. For Chrissakes, he'd almost said *You're going because I said so.* The vibe Ange put out was so strong he couldn't resist it. He'd hung up the paddle, hadn't taken on a new sub since...since everything had shut down. But apparently his desire to take charge, exert control, figure out the right combination to win willing surrender, wasn't as dead as he thought. And it was coming back to life with an injured homeless man. How desperate was that?

Then the kid delivered a sucker punch in return, making it even worse. Like a switch flipped, the green eyes skittered down to Robert's chest, focused on his dark blue bowtie. "Yes, sir," he muttered.

Robert gave his jaw a reproving tap. "What was that?"

"Yes, sir," Ange said more respectfully, with a quick glance up. When his fingers slipped out from under Robert's and caressed his wrist with a shy touch, a spark flickered, reminding Robert what it was to want.

That touch dared him to be a Master once more.

He'd gotten Ange fixed up, given him a fair wage and a cot in the back room. Crazy as risking all that was, he'd never dared taking his other feelings any further than they had gone that first night. Losing parents within seven months of each other had a way of shutting down body, mind, and soul. Everything became too tentative to deal with the aggressive joy of D/s play, which, when done with the right person, risked everything for the potential of gaining everything. For the past two years he'd been frozen in a fragile state of grief and loss. But during the last six months, he'd started to thaw.

Coming back to the present, Robert lowered his gaze from the snow-filled firmament to the city skyline. In the backdrop, he could see the lights of downtown Charlotte skyscrapers, but in this little SoHo-esque section, except for the Christmas lights edging the eaves of the buildings, the galleries, trendy cafés, and various stores were all dark. Well, almost all of them. His vintage toy store was lit up like the nativity star. The six Christmas trees placed at various spots inside the main showroom threw their illumination out onto the sidewalk, clouds of color against pristine snow drifts.

Earlier in the day, they'd forecast over a half foot of snow, but no one had believed it until it started to fall. Charlotte rarely had snow in December, let alone several days before the holiday. Despite the late hour, on the walk here he'd seen people his age and older making snowmen, having snowball fights, laughing like kids. Couples kissing as snowflakes fell upon their hair, their clasped hands. Christmas spirit, all the hope and wonder of it, had infected everyone. Including him.

There was only eight years' difference in their ages, Ange nearing thirty, Robert on the north side of that decade, but Ange seemed so young. Not in the no-right-to-be-thinking-about-touching way, though. More like in the submissive-just-begging-for-a-Master way.

It was close to midnight, a dangerous hour for a lonely man to be standing in the snow. Coming to the store in the middle of the night was outside their normal structure, leaving anything open to possibility, but Robert had made that conscious decision when he'd left his place, heading back to the store for no other reason than a desire to be where Ange was. When he crossed that street, opened the door, there'd be no turning back.

Oh, fuck it. He was a childless, gay, nearly-forty-year-old man who wore a bow tie and suspenders and collected rare toys. All he needed was a cranky little dog to complete the stereotype, but he was allergic. What was holding him rooted to this spot was fear of loss, and he knew how irrational that was.

Taking a breath, he crossed the street, pulling out his keys. When his heart started to beat faster, he had to stop a moment, close his eyes. He wanted to do this. He would do it. He couldn't fight it anymore. He wanted to be *alive*.

He'd told Ange to turn off all the trees except the small one in the display window when he went to bed. Robert didn't want the more valuable cast iron collectibles to be seen from the outside. But Ange loved those trees. He'd keep them turned on twenty-four hours a day, would probably sleep underneath them every night if he could. However, since he took Robert's orders very literally, if the lights were on, that meant he was still up.

Robert didn't like to think of a break-in happening while

Ange was there alone, so he'd be more specific, tell Ange the trees should be turned off at closing. Even as he had that thought, he was inundated with images of more punitive, provocative ways to impress the lesson on his only employee.

Unlocking and opening the front door, he also discovered Ange hadn't turned on the security system. Again. He was so going to kick his narrow ass.

Brad Paisley's "Silent Night" was playing, part of the Christmas playlist Ange had created, mixing old and new favorites. It was a balance the customers and Robert enjoyed, though Robert had never considered himself a fan of holiday music. Hanging up his keys, he moved out of the shadows of the foyer into the archway of the main show room. Since he'd come at the store from an angle that didn't give him a clear shot into the front display window, he hadn't seen what he saw now. If he had, he would have crossed that street with no hesitation at all, because no man with a pulse could have resisted the scene before him.

He and Ange had rearranged the main showroom so it looked like a late Victorian-era parlor at Christmas time, just waiting for the children to arrive and open packages. For Robert, it recalled the opening scene from the Nutcracker ballet, particularly with Ange dancing in the middle of it.

Ange was in the middle of a *fouetté*. Tight, in-place turns that brought him up on the ball of his foot on each rotation, like a Turkish warrior dancing. He was wearing his bedtime pajamas of a thin white tank and gray sweatpants, the former displaying the layers of muscles on his arms and shoulders, the latter the flexing of his ass. He'd wrapped red ribbon around his wrists, splitting them into tails and using scissors to curl them so they fluttered as he danced. He had them on his ankles as well, with tiny bells. Now Robert realized why he heard a pleasing chime buried inside the Christmas music.

It was like watching a male swan. That sense of restraint, the quivering desire to soar compressed in graceful movement that hinted at what miracles would be possible if the bird's wings weren't clipped. If he had the confidence to soar.

Until six months ago, Robert had forgotten that feeling, his heart bricked off to withstand the harsh realities of mortality. Now he felt a painful, final crack in the mortar as Ange finished the turn, his fingertips reaching toward the treetops, his leg a straight line behind him. When he went from that into a standing leap, as impressive as a Lipizzaner stallion, Robert's heart began thumping erratically again.

He pressed his fingers hard into the wood doorway, all the want and need he'd stored up pooling in his mouth and groin. Ange had landed, but his eyes were closed. As he tilted his head to the right, exposing the line from throat to shoulder, Robert had a vampire's craving to sink his teeth into that pale column.

Then Ange saw him. He straightened, chest heaving, eyes bright, uncertain. His hair was dark with sweat at his temples and nape. If Robert put his nose there, he'd inhale that sharp scent of exertion and Ange together.

"Come with me."

He didn't look to see if Ange was following. He knew he was, the same way he'd known Ange was waiting for him when he saw the tree lights still on. Hell, the boy had been waiting for months. He was a true submissive. As long as he could take care of Robert, he was happy, but that didn't mean he didn't burn the way Robert did. More than once he'd caught Ange giving him a look so hungry, it took everything in him not to pin him to the wall then and there. He'd gone home at night and masturbated like a fucking thirteen-year-old, imagining that taut, slick ass, feeling Ange's mouth on him...hearing him call him Master.

Ange often called him *sir*, as if he knew the way it made things clench inside of Robert. He made it clear he was Robert's, though Robert didn't encourage that. Of course, he sure as hell hadn't discouraged it, either.

When he returned to the front door and unlocked it, stepping out under the eaves, he found the snow was falling even thicker now. The street was covered in it, virgin and unmarred.

Glancing back, he saw Ange's green gaze fixed on him. "Dance for me, out there. Show me how a male swan soars."

He reached out, intending to guide him through the door, but Ange bent his head, brushed his lips over Robert's knuckles, leaving the electric tingle of moist heat on his rough skin. Then he leaped out into the night, almost hovering in the air for a brief moment, light as the snowflakes. The thickly curling red ribbon and bells made Robert imagine a reindeer in harness, awaiting the command to fly and the touch of the whip.

Ange had given Robert very little of his past, but it had been easy enough to figure out he'd been a danseur before he'd been on the street. When Ange was pulling down stock from upper shelves in the back, Robert had seen him lift up on the balls of his feet with an odd sense of weightlessness, like he was levitating. He'd stretch one arm upward, his body remaining locked and upright, his back leg leaving the ground to create a rigid line from the tips of his reaching fingers to the point of his toe.

If he thought Robert wasn't looking, sometimes Ange would whirl down an aisle rather than walk it. He'd spot his destination, his head whipping toward that fixed point, strong arms locked in a precise oval before him. When he reached the back wall, he'd stop like an expert swordsman executing a lunge.

Once, when a customer was waiting, Robert had asked Ange to bring him something from the back stockroom that would normally require a ladder. He'd followed him a moment later with another request, arriving in time to see Ange remove his shoes and execute a powerful spin in the air, catching the item on the turn. He came down into what Robert now knew was ballet's fourth position. He'd been wearing a pair of faded jeans that fit him just right in the crotch and seat when he landed. Robert's mouth had gone dry.

Taking a break from his auction browsing one night, he'd called up some ballet sites. What he'd seen Ange do that day was a modified *tour en l'aire*. He'd felt like he was surfing porn, lingering on pictures of male dancers in their nothing-to-the-imagination tights, which made him think of Ange in such an outfit. When he was in that swordsman lunge, his cock would be erect and long beneath the straining fabric, the imagined shape of the testicles making Robert itch to close his hand over them.

The tune now turned to Tory Amos's wistful "Have Yourself a Merry Little Christmas," and Ange changed the pace. He was dancing barefoot in the snow, in the thin tank and sweats, but his skin was glowing. When he spun toward Robert, he spotted on him, every whip of his head coming back to Robert's eyes, until he finished with one of those floating-in-the-air, bent-leg bounds that he completed on his knees at Robert's feet. Staring up at him, face flushed. Lips parted.

Robert reached down, intending to brush the long strands of hair from his forehead. Instead Ange pressed another kiss to his hand. Robert turned it, trailing his fingers over Ange's mouth, the moist lips, to his chin. Ange dropped his head back. As Robert moved down to his throat, to his chest, Ange kept bending backward. Robert dropped to one knee as Ange's head touched the snow between his cupped feet, the body in a perfect, severe arch for him. Ange's arms were out, like a cruci-fied swan. Or a man surrendering.

As he held the pose, eyes closed, chest rising and falling, the bump of his nipples against the cotton drew Robert's gaze. He'd given Ange that tank the first night. Ange had bought himself new clothes since then, but he still slept in Robert's shirt. Robert's burlier build made the armholes wider, inviting his fingers to creep beneath, caress naked flesh. He restrained himself, barely.

"Ange." His voice was thick, making him clear his throat. "Call me by my name."

Ange opened his eyes, his gaze a reflection of Robert's desires. "Master," he said.

Had he wanted him to say *Robert*? He'd made the decision to cross the street, unlock the door, but now the fear that he was opening a well of pain in himself returned, compounded with a fear that the pain could hurt Ange. He started to rise, but Ange put his hand on his thigh.

"Robert," he said quietly. "Master."

The music selection switched to the *a cappella* stylings of Straight No Chaser, crooning "This Christmas," one of Robert's favorites. It was more upbeat, more hopeful. Giving him courage. He laid his hand on Ange's chest.

A breath escaped from Ange, a shudder like the first time Robert had touched him. "Master," he breathed.

Robert dug his fingers into that firm flesh and then let his hand glide downward, over Ange's abdomen, waist, hip bone. The sweatpants made it easy to log Ange's response, altering the fabric in reaction to Robert's touch. That was no kid's equipment, but a man's thick and hard cock.

"You stay still," Robert ordered. He had to put himself on a short rein as well. He was testing the waters, still waffling on the block. When his hand closed over Ange's dick, his sub made a little spasm of movement, but that was all, obviously keeping himself still at Robert's command. Which brought him that much closer to making the dive.

He traveled back up the same pleasing terrain, over that arch of muscle and bone, back to the point of his chest. Then he slid down the opposite slope, tracing the sternum to the collar bone, curving his broad hand around Ange's throat.

He saw it so clearly, what he wanted from him. Until he'd lost his nerve, Robert had always demanded a lot from his subs. Ange tempted him to grasp his desires again, follow his instincts as a Master.

Once, feeling like he was taking advantage, he'd reached out to some of his acquaintances, set Ange up on a couple of dates. Ange came down with a twenty-four-hour cold the first time. The second time, he claimed he got lost and couldn't find the restaurant where he was supposed to meet the prospect. Ange's ingenuous expression had left Robert nowhere to go to call it an outright lie, but the little bastard had a stubborn side for sure. Robert didn't arrange any more dates for him.

"Let me be your Christmas present, Master. Wrap me up the way you want. And open me early." His green eyes glinted. "Please."

It would have made Robert smile, if so many other emotions weren't competing for the same constricted space in his chest.

Sliding a hand under Ange's neck, he brought him up into a sitting position on his heels, then kept going, compelling him to fold forward, to put his forehead on the welcome mat, flatten his palms in the snow. Robert cupped the irresistible butt revealed by the cling of the sweats. The cloth was damp from the falling snow, just like his shirt.

The tail ends of the ribbon on his ankles had enough slack to tie them to one another, a hobble that allowed a foot of space between them. Robert touched the soles of Ange's feet, noting he was too cold to be ticklish. Then he moved to his head.

"Keep your eyes down," he said. It was the same low voice he'd used to command Ange to come out here. He never shouted at a sub. He could deliver an order that resonated right down to the scrotum without lifting his voice a decibel. The power and pleasure of that skill washed over him now.

He tied two of the curling tails on the ribbons on Ange's wrists to each other, then grasped that line to bring him to his feet.

"Dance for me like this. Stay within reach of my hands, as if you were tied to me by a one-foot leash."

Robert guided him back out into the snow and Ange obeyed, doing measured circles and lots of sinuous upper body and arm movements that never took him outside Robert's reach. Though Ange might think it was a test of his dance skills with his hands and ankles hampered like that, it was to ensure Robert could catch Ange if needed. But he didn't fall, and the longer he danced, the more Robert burned to touch the body moving so close to him, run his hands over all that rippling, smooth muscle. He could tell Ange felt the same, the way he tailored those movements to simulate the contact he wanted with Robert. The connective heat in the small space between Ange's moving torso and his own increased like fanned flames.

But sexual heat, powerful as it was, couldn't overcome Nature's temperature. Ange started to shiver, and his feet had to be ice cold by now. Robert stopped him, bent his knees, and put his shoulder to Ange's midriff. He wasn't heavy, not the Irish brawler Robert was. He hiked him over his shoulder. Steadying his weight by sliding his hand into Ange's loose pants, he was pleased to confirm there was nothing under them. As Robert stroked the peach-fuzz on his buttocks, Ange clutched his belt, holding on as he was carried back into the store.

"Time to wrap my present," Robert said.

He let him down inside the threshold, closing the door and pulling the shade down, sealing in the warmth and privacy of the foyer. Ange stayed quiet beneath Robert's grip on his forearm, but his anticipatory stillness made Robert think about what Ange had said, that holding one's breath actually made a sound.

"Stay there." Moving to one of the lit Christmas trees, Robert brought back a sturdy wooden stepstool painted with a winter scene. Fishing out his pocketknife, he cut the ribbons hobbling Ange's ankles and wrists. "Step up."

They kept mistletoe hanging in the entryway, a touch of whimsy that sometimes inspired couples married for decades to snatch a fond kiss. Teenagers, with a giggle or shy look, would lean in and press lips together. Mrs. Fitzgerald, who went nowhere without her toy poodle Horatio tucked in her large fuchsia-colored handbag, had kissed the top knot of the gray fuzzy head.

Now Ange tilted his head back, studying the plant. When his chin came back down, Robert arched a brow at the hopeful expression. "You'll have to earn that."

A tiny smile appeared on those sensual lips, the green eyes

alight with something that made Robert want to kiss him sense-less right now. But this angle also showed him the faded scar under Ange's chin, an additional deep cut obscured that night by the blood of his busted lip.

"Are you ever going to tell me who hurt you?"

Ange's mouth set in that stubborn line, the one that made him look all of his twenty-something years. It also made Robert want to put him on forehead and knees and paddle him until his ass was red. "I fought back," Ange said.

"Yes, you did. Will you tell me why you dance like you do, here in my store, and nowhere else?"

"One day. Right now I just want to serve you, Master. That's all I need. To dance for you, work for you. The world is so ugly..." He pressed his lips together, met Robert's gaze. "Finding the right space is the only thing that matters."

Robert thought about that. "Ange, if you want me as your Master, you need to trust me to care for you. Understood?"

Ange nodded. "Why aren't you with anyone, Master? Not that I'm glad you're not with anyone... Right now, I mean."

"How do you know I'm not?"

The change in Ange's face was surprising, but Robert had a feeling it was the expression his attackers had seen, albeit right before they'd kicked the shit out of him. "Because...I feel it. You come here...to be with me."

You're mine as much as I'm yours. The ballsy kid didn't say it outright—he was too much of a sub to do that—but Robert saw it in the set of his chin, the way his hand reached out almost of its own volition to curl in Robert's shirt front, holding on. God, he really couldn't wait to plunder that defiant mouth, give it a workout.

"You better rein back that attitude, or I might find a way to deal with it."

Ange's countenance eased, even as his grip on Robert didn't. He had a firm, capable touch, one that never fumbled anything in the store, always sure and gentle in whatever he handled.

"No," Robert said. "I'm not with anyone. I was, for a year or so. When my parents got sick, it was more than he could handle. He bailed."

Freddie had turned out to be more of a bottom than a true sub. He'd talked a good game about wanting to be 24/7, but in the end, he hadn't wanted the two-way emotional exchange or the work of a relationship. He wanted to be topped, overpowered and launched into subspace through extreme restraint and discomfort, then go out afterward to Starbucks with his real friends.

Whereas, looking around his store, Robert saw a hundred things that proved Ange's care and service for him, despite the fact he hadn't so much as kissed him. Maybe that was why he'd just told him something he hadn't told anyone else.

Ange was staring at him, his green eyes warrior fierce.

"He left you alone to watch your parents die?"

CHAPTER TWO

*L*eave it to Ange to put it so directly that it was like getting punched in the face. Robert actually took a step back. Swallowing, he looked away. "Yeah, well, not everyone can handle..."

The reality was *no one* could handle it; he just had, because that was the way it was. For every moment his mom and dad had been there for him, through every tear, every lesson, every smile, every gift of time, protection, or love, his care had been that debt come due. Not a debt paid out of obligation or resentment, but one paid in fervent honor of a job well done. To "handle" it, the heart had to break, no help for it, shattered like one of his porcelain dolls.

His throat was too thick to continue. *Watch my parents die...* They'd each passed at home, under his care. When his mom had gone, seven months after his father, he'd sat alone, waiting for the hospice nurse to arrive, to confirm the death, to prepare the body for the funeral home. It was stupid to dress them up, given that they'd both wanted cremation, but when his father died, he'd put him in his dark blue suit. He'd dressed his mother in her yellow dress with lace at the collar. They'd worn those clothes to meet him at the airport when he'd returned home from his last tour in Afghanistan. His dad, a Vietnam vet himself, had saluted him, his mother hugging him like she'd never let him go again.

"Fuck." Those emotions he feared spilling onto Ange were threatening to swamp him. He shouldn't have come here tonight. On the stool beneath the mistletoe, Ange was taller than him by half a foot. The kid reached out. Robert started to draw back further, but Ange leaned forward and Robert extended a quelling hand, concerned that he might overbalance the stool. Ange ended up touching his face, his fingers sliding along Robert's cheekbone, his temple, up into his hair, stroking it. His other hand caught Robert's outstretched one, linking fingers, then moved up his arm, to his shoulder, bringing them closer once again.

I fix things people don't think to fix...

Ange made a soothing noise. Robert thought of him dancing in the snow as those still-cold arms enclosed him, brought him against his chest, his beating heart. Michael Bublé's "I'll Be Home for Christmas" had to be playing now, right? *Shit.* "Ange—"

He really did have incredibly strong arms, because he wasn't letting Robert budge, not without a struggle. "It's all right. No one sees, Master. It's okay. Just hold on until it passes. You can't survive an ocean storm without a boat."

Another Ange-ism to file away. He had his face pressed between Ange's pec and biceps, which meant he could smell the sweat he'd worked up with his dancing, but that was okay. It smelled real, earthy. The snow that had melted on his shirt was damp against his cheek. Robert realized his shoulders were tense, his hands closed into tight fists at his sides. Ange had wrapped both arms around him, one around his back, the other bent between his shoulder blades, fingers stroking the short hairs on his neck. Robert closed his eyes, a hard shudder running through him. He needed to set Ange back on his heels. He couldn't open his heart. It had been shut too long. Prying open the doors would be too painful.

"I'm sorry I wasn't here sooner," Ange whispered. "I should have been here when you needed me."

For some reason, Robert recalled Ange getting on the floor with Mr. Dixon, an octogenarian and one of Robert's premier collectors, as they raced 1953 "cars of the future," friction motor drive cars that roared and had sparks shooting from the exhaust. His clients gravitated toward Ange and his childlike delight in the store's offerings. Ange played with the toys—albeit carefully—showing people how they worked so they'd fall in love with them as well. Much like Christmas itself, the toys helped people rediscover a feeling or memory that had been lost. Watching Ange open up the hearts of his customers had performed the same magic on Robert. He'd felt outside the world, detached from it, but Ange had started to connect him again.

Ange thought he should have been here sooner, but maybe he was right on time. For so long, Robert had had a perilous sense of falling, and yet Ange's arms gave him solid ground again. It was okay for that door to his heart to open; Ange could handle what would come through it. Robert put his hands on the other man's hips, fingers digging in.

"You're going to tell me who hurt you one day."

"Tell me the address of the bastard who abandoned you, and we'll call it even."

Robert chuckled at the pugnacious note and pressed his face into that surprisingly solid body for one extra second before he lifted his head, pulled back. He could only do so much of that, but it had felt good. Maybe too good.

"I want you to take off your shirt and reach above your head. Grab hold of the mistletoe hook."

Light burning in his green gaze like the electric candelabras they had in the store's side windows, Ange slowly obeyed, stripping off the tank and putting it in Robert's outstretched hand before reaching above him. The hook was a heavy grade, screwed into a support beam so he could tether the oak front door to it on windy fall days, when Robert liked to inhale the scent of seasons changing.

With the footstool, the hook was just above easy reach, so Ange had to stretch out that incomparable body, showing off the upward tilt of his rib cage, the golden down on his chest that arrowed along his flat belly toward the now lower-hanging sweat-pants. Robert's command had brought his erection back to life beneath them.

As distracting as that was, Robert's attention was caught by something far less appealing. Gunshot scars, two of them, right in the gut. Six months ago, they hadn't let him into the exam room at the ER, needing to make sure he wasn't the one who'd worked the kid over, so he hadn't seen Ange shirtless. He'd imagined it countless times, but this hadn't been part of those fantasies.

"What the hell... Ange?" When he put his hand on the scars, the two entry points close enough that his palm could cover them, Ange started to tremble, and not the kind of trembling Robert was trying to inspire. He recognized it, that panic that could grab hold of a grown man, drench him in sickly sweat, and make everything disappear except that moment of horror. "I can't. Please, Master...don't."

"Okay. Shhh. This isn't about that. Like you said. Another day. Stay with me, Ange. I mean it. Listen to your Master."

It was the first time he'd referred to himself directly as such. The power of it was enough to bring Ange back to him. He settled, breathing slower, the trembling easing.

From the beginning, Ange had related well to the people in the store, but he'd been hesitant about going out on errands. He tended to get distracted, or even disoriented. Robert had worried he might have sustained a head injury that first night, but over time he'd realized Ange merely lived in a special place in his head, elevated above the practical day-to-day, like an angel in truth. However, Robert had started taking him for supply runs and meets with vendors, encouraging him to do the talking while acting as his backup. It worked—Ange sent him a dazzling smile when he did well, and Robert got a kick out of boosting the man's confidence. But the question remained of what had pushed him into such a detached state, or put him on the street. Those two wounds, and Ange's reaction to him asking about it now, gave Robert a clear hint.

He had been fortunate in his military service, getting away with some shrapnel wounds, but in the VA hospital for follow-up care after his discharge, he'd seen soldiers injured far worse, physically and mentally. Some of those who couldn't shake the trauma lost their connection to everything else, so out of sync with the reality they'd once shared with the rest of the world that the street became home. While Ange's gunshots weren't from military action—nothing about him suggested military training—unfortunately a person didn't always have to travel thousands of miles away to see that level of violence.

However, as he'd said, tonight wasn't going to be about that, for either of them. If the demons couldn't be laid to rest on this snow-filled evening, they could at least take the night off.

Robert moved behind Ange to run his hands down his back, broad compared to the nipped waist, tapered hips. The boy was five-foot-ten of lean muscle. Reaching around him to pull the drawstring of his sweats, Robert loosened them so the waistband caught on the upper rise of his buttocks, revealing the dimple between. When he returned to Ange's front, he saw the pants had fallen low enough to show off the intimate muscles angled to his groin. That pale blond down thickened there, revealing the top line of the pubic pelt still hidden beneath the cloth. Ange's breath clogged in his throat as Robert traced it.

"Master..."

"Shhh. No more talking unless I give you permission or ask a question." Robert arched a brow. "Unless you want me to put one of our ball ornaments to creative use?"

He could imagine that vividly, testing which size of the satiny thread-wrapped foam balls would fit Ange's mouth just right, make him work his jaw hinge hard before it popped in behind the teeth. Robert could picture the gleam of the silvery sapphire curve behind Ange's stretched lips.

Right now, though, he decided to leave it as a pleasant possibility. Going to the register counter, he looked behind it. Ange kept everything so well organized, Robert found the box he was seeking right where he expected it.

As he straightened, a movement outside the display window caught his eye. A group of women, probably coming from a late show at the independent theater down the street, had paused on their stroll past his shop to look at the lit trees, the toys grouped around them. If any of them chose to strain their gaze to a forty-degree angle, they might make out the stretched, pale silhouette of a mostly naked man on a stool, his arms held on a hook above his head. Ange's back muscles vibrated, his recognition of possible exposure, but he didn't move. His Master's command held him where he was.

The women were laughing, chatting, oohing over the things they saw.

"I need to come here..."

"Look at that doll, it reminds me of my aunt's..."

"I bet Celia would love this..."

"There's a blond guy working here who is so hot—we should come back at lunch on Monday just to get an eyeful."

"But that's all you'll get," Robert murmured. Ange's shoulders twitched, registering the comment. As the women strolled onward, Robert returned to him, putting the box down and then laying his hand on the channel of Ange's spine, teasing the rise of his buttocks with his knuckles. Then, because he couldn't resist, he dipped into the cleft, fingers furrowing down to stroke the soft hair between, finding his rim. He savored the noise Ange made, the jerk of his hips as he explored him there.

"They'll never know what they missed tonight," he observed, well aware his voice was a satisfied rumble. Gooseflesh rippled across Ange's skin, his lips parting to let out an uneven breath at Robert's invasive touch.

Robert skinned Ange's sweats to his ankles in one fluid movement. As he made Ange step out of them, he kept a steadying hand on his hip. Maybe overprotective, since the boy could twirl on top of the stool, but Robert didn't cut corners on those kinds of things. From the first time Ange had called him *sir*, it was as if he'd handed Robert the key to an imaginary collar. Which meant Ange's well-being became Robert's top priority, the Master side of him too strong to ignore that responsibility.

Pale hairs dusted Ange's legs. The quivering, cold ass on display just above them tempted touch, taste, and paddle. Robert took a long, satisfying look at the firm buttocks, the slim, muscled thighs, the tender backs of the knees. When he pressed a kiss to Ange's hip, Ange vibrated like a musical instrument.

"Beautiful." Coming around to the front, Robert found him fully erect, the shaft thick and long and already wet at the tip. "Eager for it, aren't you? Naughty elf."

Despite the weak joke Ange had made that first night, the description matched. Not the short, cupid-like elves of Santa's workshop, but the mesmerizing beauty of the Fae.

Pulling the box over with his foot, Robert withdrew the Christmas lights. They were 1950s vintage lights, like those on the shop trees. The bulbs looked like small, lit fruit, rather than stars hiding amid the branches. They had more heat as well. Not enough to catch anything on fire, but they'd warm the skin on contact, enough to make an angel squirm a bit.

He started at the ankles and worked his way up, tying Ange's legs together. When Robert adorned the trees, he made sure the lights had the proper distribution for that artful random look. For Ange, his focus was on optimal placement of each bulb upon flesh. Ange's muscles quivered as he reacted to the gradual restraint. Robert paused when he reached his cock, relishing the moment, then closed his fingers around it for the first time. Heated steel and velvet, pulsing with life and need. It made him want to taste, to suck, to grip and pump until he saw come jetting from the slit.

Stretching out his unoccupied fingers, he captured the testicle sac pushed forward by Ange's closed thighs. He held the entire package in a possessive, sure grip as he wrapped the base of the cock several times, creating a collar. That put a bulb on either side of it, the smooth glass pressed into the crease between thigh and testicles. He gave the strand an extra cinch when finished, so Ange's cock was kept bound close to his balls. Robert had done some Japanese rope-tying at one time, enjoyed it. While he couldn't take advantage of the knots that art form provided right now, the wrap skill helped.

"Keep breathing, Ange. Don't want you to get dizzy up there." The kid had gone still as a statue, doing that submissive intense energy build that could absorb Robert's full attention, make him a little lightheaded himself.

Robert brought a stepladder over to handle Ange's upper body, using the bottom rungs for better access to his shoulders and arms. He could tell Ange was disappointed when Robert did a wrap over the shoulders and bypassed the throat. Ange's obvious desire for some type of collar was enough to get Robert even harder. Even though his jeans were killing him, thank God he'd worn them instead of slacks. If he hadn't, he and Ange would be fencing swords. As it was, the broad head of Ange's cock was bumping his upper thigh. It took great effort to focus on what he was doing.

He wrapped Ange's wrists, tying off the strand on the hook. Now Ange was bound to it by the cord, not just his willing handhold. Robert met Ange's eyes then.

"Not around the throat," he said. "I know you want that, but it's not safe. If you start moving, it could constrict."

Ange gave him a look that would've melted the toughest Master's resolve. "I'd only move if you told me to move."

"If I work you up so hard you can't control your own body,

you'd break that promise. All control, all decisions, your safety—it's all in my court. Got it?"

Ange nodded, lowering his gaze again. "Yes, Master."

Stepping off the ladder, Robert moved it out of the way, then found an outlet. "If this string has a bad bulb, I'm going to enjoy the hell out of testing each one."

The strand worked, however. Robert rested his ass on the top of the step ladder, enjoying what he'd created, the treasure the oblivious women had missed.

The multicolored lights threw red, green, and blue hues over Ange's fair skin, as reflective as a screen. Every muscle layer was tense, pronounced. He'd kept his eyes down, his mouth pressed closed, but Robert could see the pulse dancing in his throat. His cock, highlighted by that triple wrap and those two bulbs, was stiff and straight as an arrow. The cinch to his balls kept his cock away from his belly, but it was turgid enough to be pointing north.

"Fuck," Robert muttered. He wanted to touch, but the time wasn't yet right. Watching Ange get more aroused by his detached appraisal made the self-denial worth it. "I should put you in the window. Every wealthy gay man in the Charlotte area would be here tomorrow. We'd make our annual profit goal in one day."

Except they'd be ogling what was his. And that wasn't going to happen. The women maybe seeing Ange had been titillation. The reality was something far different.

The kid was starting to feel the burn of those bulbs. Robert could see it in the slight twitches of his body, the uncertain stretch of the fingers. "You feeling that, Ange?"

"Yes, Master."

"Too hot?"

"No... Feels...right."

"I like to give out pain to my subs, Ange. Do you have a problem with that? As long as you answer me honestly, you won't disappoint me. You lie, we'll have a problem."

Ange shook his head, a jerky motion. "When you've corrected me about things, in the store..." His voice was a thick rasp. "I've dreamed of you...tying me over the manger in the nativity scene. Pulling my jeans to my knees and using your belt to punish me until my ass is black and blue."

"But I wear suspenders, not a belt."

Ange gave a strangled half-chuckle. "It's a dream, Master." His voice got very soft. "And you're wearing a belt tonight."

So he was. He didn't need the suspenders to hold up his pants, but they went well with the bowtie, and the customers enjoyed the antique pins he tacked to them.

Robert liked Ange's low tone, making it clear it was a desire, not a demand. He wasn't a topper, not in any way. Robert had no use for the independent, smart-mouthed fuckers who didn't have a clue what he was seeking in a submissive. Yeah, he liked a fighter, but the kind of fighter Ange was, his breath elevating from the burn of the bulbs, his muscles bunching, proving to his Master he had a capacity for turning pain into pleasure and only asking for more.

Robert moved back to Ange's perch. Sliding his fingers under the strands of lights wrapped around Ange's waist, Robert let him feel the resulting constriction around his balls.

Ange moaned, rocking into him. Robert gave him a rough tug, enough to pinch, and the man went still again, though he became like a bowstring, everything straining toward Robert without actually doing so. Robert bent, propping his knee on the stool in the small space between Ange's feet. Gripping those lean hips, he went down on the jutting cock with a hot, demanding mouth.

Another noise from above, a suppressed shudder of motion, made Robert's blood heat like the bulbs. Ange had a sweet-salty taste, reminding him of those pretzel M&M snack combinations. Ange liked them so much that Robert bought them for him by the one-pound bags.

The kid never looked like he ate enough, but then he was

never still, either. Like a restless squirrel, Robert told him. Since Ange didn't like going out for lunch without Robert, and the art district's food prices were too high for Robert to indulge every day, Robert had started bringing enough homemade lunch to feed both of them. He wasn't a great cook, but apparently Ange was, because he'd suggest things, a little more paprika in this dish, some cilantro for that one. He'd started an herb garden in a sunny spot in the back alley, introducing Robert to different flavors.

Robert remembered the day he'd been checking it out, squatting next to the garden while Ange explained what he was doing. Ange had gripped the stalks of the basil, directing the leaves to Robert's nose. When Robert laid his hand over Ange's forearm to steady his grip as he sniffed, he felt the current between them again. Just like that first day, Ange held his gaze for a blink, then swept his down, which had tied Robert's gut in knots. And sent him into full retreat.

He wasn't retreating now. No way in hell. He had his own hunger to sate. He filled his mouth with Ange, closing his eyes at the sheer pleasure of tasting him, sucking him. The organ jumped in his mouth in response, Ange making panting breaths above him. The femoral pulse thundered beneath the press of Robert's thumb. He took Ange deep, then slid back up, working the suction on him like he would one of the everlasting suckers they sold in the old candy shops, the kind that seemed to last forever and tasted as vibrant with the last suck as the first one.

"Master...." Ange had his fingers clenched around that hook, making it obvious the support beam had been a good idea. The lights cast from the bulbs were dancing over Robert's vision, thanks to the force of his captive's trembling. There was something about seeing a strong man in bonds like this, all his muscles working against the instinct to bust free, that never failed to stir Robert. The conflict. The desire to surrender warring with the desire to fight.

"Sshh." Robert went back down on him, working him in his

mouth, flicking the head with his tongue, the pulsing vein beneath. He wrapped his hands over Ange's thighs and buttocks, digging into that choice area to ensure he stayed steady on the stool.

When he pulled off him at last, Ange had his head thrown back, his eyes shut. The bulbs on either side of his cock were heating Robert's knuckles from proximity, telling him it was time to turn them off. "Steady now," he warned, letting Ange know he was stepping back. He waited until Ange lifted his head, tightened his grip on the hook. When he went to the wall, he unplugged the lights, but he also hit the switch, turning off all the Christmas trees. The shop went dark, except for the dim glow provided by the streetlights outside.

Robert came back to Ange and pulled the stepladder closer, using it to get high enough to free Ange's hands from the hook, though he left his wrists wrapped in the lights. Ange had behaved when Robert was focused on the wrapping, but now his cheek brushed Robert's chest, his rigid cock alongside Robert's hip. Robert tangled his fingers in his thick hair, gave it an affectionate tug, then stepped down, bringing Ange's bound arms down before his body. He adjusted the lights along his shoulders as necessary to accomplish it and keep circulation flowing.

Wrapping an arm around his back and ass, Robert lifted and brought Ange safely to the floor, since his legs were wrapped too close to allow mobility. When Robert straightened, they were almost eye to eye, since he was six feet.

"You're strong," Ange whispered. "I felt it in your hands, that first time you touched me. That's why I won't tell you who hurt me. Because I don't want you to go fight them. I don't want you hurt."

He couldn't resist the call of that mistletoe any longer. Robert caught Ange by the nape, brought him close to his mouth. Sugar cookies. Ange had a weakness for them, such that they flavored his breath now. "Stay still," he reiterated, not knowing if it was a deliberate move of a Master, or the desperate plea of a man in too deep. Either way, Ange obeyed, trembling as Robert put his lips fully over that sugar cookie sweetness.

The kid sighed into his mouth, a sound of pleasure, and Robert plundered, tracing Ange's tongue, his teeth, coming back out to his lips, holding Ange's naked body against his clothed one. He could feel Ange reacting to that, all the evidence of a Dominant gathering up the reins, taking full control. As his sub became more pleasurably frenetic, making sexy little noises under the manipulation of Robert's mouth, he himself growled like a territorial animal. He wanted to wrap Ange up in his embrace and hold him there for a few decades. All the need he'd sat on these past months was ready to explode, take over everything. It wasn't Ange he needed to restrain, but himself.

Taking a firm hold of one buttock, he squeezed and explored. As he pushed his cock hard against Ange's hip, the other man's body rippled, Ange clearly struggling with the desire to hump against him. It told Robert that Ange had paid close enough attention to know his Master appreciated self-restraint until he ordered otherwise. Of course, with a submissive this delicious, Robert might welcome Ange losing control so he'd have an even greater excuse to bind and punish. To enjoy.

When he broke the kiss, Robert ran his hand down Ange's forearm. Something was tangled with the lights and red ribbon, something he'd missed when wrapping Ange's wrists because of the profusion of ribbon curls, and because his focus had been on other things. Now, though, he saw a bracelet, a chain of construction paper and glitter, like they had on the tree decorated with homemade ornaments.

As he noticed it, Ange flushed to his blond roots. If his arm had been free, Robert suspected he would have tried to hide it behind his back.

"It's nothing. One of the kids got the idea for making Jesus bracelets during the craft hour today."

It had been Ange's idea to turn the spare storeroom into a place to hold weekly one-hour craft workshops, teaching children and adults how to make their own old-fashioned toys out of inexpensive materials. Robert had picked up books on it and Ange brought the designs to life. It was a good way to highlight the store's toys as well, since so many of them were made by craftsmen with nothing more than raw materials and creative minds, no dependence on computer chips or batteries.

"It's okay. I'm not opposed to the idea." Robert raised a brow, puzzled. Ange knew Robert was Christian, though he was more spiritual than religious. "So you made your own with the kids. Show me."

Ange hesitated. "It was stupid."

"No." Robert studied his uncomfortable expression. "You think *I'll* think it's stupid. Show it to me. Now, Ange."

Robert could simply lift Ange's wrists, holding onto the bonds the Christmas lights formed, but he was making a different point. His sub wouldn't hide anything from him.

A muscle jumped in Ange's jaw, then he held out his arms. Now Robert put his palm beneath Ange's elevated wrists, giving them support, his fingers closing around Ange's hands as he studied the bracelet.

The links were smaller in diameter than the chain on the tree, but large enough he could make out what was on them. Each link had a word on it, embellished with some glitter. Savio<u>r</u>. <u>L</u>over. <u>B</u>est F<u>r</u>iend. Mas<u>t</u>er. Hi<u>s</u>. The precise yet innocuous underlines formed a word. *Roberts.*

Robert stared at it, then lifted his gaze to Ange, who was squirming without obvious movement. "I couldn't think of a word that had an apostrophe," Ange said lamely. "It was something to do while the kids were making theirs. I know it seems kind of juvenile."

Robert stepped into him, his arm snaking around to grip three rows of lights that crossed his back. The bite of the lines into Ange's chest and hips brought his eyes up to Robert's face.

"Yeah, it does." Taking a firm grip on the kid's hair, Robert pulled his head to the side so he could put his mouth to Ange's jaw, then his throat. When he started laying hot, sucking kisses there, Ange let out a whistling, unsteady breath. Dropping his hands to Ange's ass, Robert pulled him flush against his cock, holding him there with a bruising, kneading grip. It broke Ange's control, had him undulating against Robert in a fucking irresistible way, those wild movements increasing as Robert kept sucking, biting harder on his neck. Ange breathed expletives, bound hands opening and closing against Robert's shirt where they were pressed against his lower abdomen. Robert bet his jeans were marked with the viscous fluid leaking from the slit of Ange's cock. He'd enjoy making him pay for that.

When he lifted his head, studied his handiwork, he nodded, satisfied. Then he met Ange's dazed gaze. "That's a hickey. Everyone coming to the store will know someone's marked you. That's juvenile, too." His lips curved. "Every time I see it, I'm going to get hard and want to do it to the other side of your neck. At lunch, I'll probably make you take your pants down and I'll do it to both your ass cheeks."

Ange blinked, then his green eyes shone with such an eager response, Robert knew he might be in danger of an involuntary reaction of his own if he let Ange's arousal build fast, too soon. So he straightened.

"Be still, love." He began to unwrap Ange, starting at the wrists and working backward, noting the grooves the cords had put in his tender skin, the reddened spots of heat where the bulbs had pressed against him. When he was done, he balled up the string of lights, tossed it in the box. He'd untangle it later. Or his very helpful employee would.

"We're going to the craft room." Taking Ange by the elbow, he guided him, sensing his dancer was not as steady as he usually was. Robert savored the look of Ange naked as a newborn, the heavy bounce of his enormous erection against his testicles as they crossed the main show room. He took the hallway that led to the space they'd carved out for the craft room between the storage and office areas.

He saw evidence there of Ange's work on the tree of home-made ornaments, the task he'd probably been doing before he'd had the urge to dance. Tape, glue, glitter, and paper were scattered over the worktable. They kept a handful of vinyl mats stacked in the corner in case younger children required naps while their older siblings created. Robert pointed to them. "Put two of those on the floor."

Ange obeyed, his handsome bare form moving without self-consciousness before Robert's appreciative gaze. When he returned, Robert put a hand on his shoulder, pressing him down to his knees. "Lie down on your stomach."

If the statue of a young Roman god stepped off his pedestal and stretched out his marble body as fluidly as water, he'd look like this. Ange had no tattoos or piercings, a rarity these days, but Robert was glad of it.

Moving to the bin of toys and craft supplies Ange collected from various sources, Robert pulled out two scratched and faded wooden hobbyhorses. He unscrewed the heads and set them aside, gauging the riding sticks to be between three and four feet long. Beneath the workbench he found a handful of Lincoln Logs and a coil of half-inch nylon rope.

When he saw Ange watching him, hands folded beneath his cheek, he set aside his supplies, dropped to his heels by Ange's head. Those green eyes tilted up toward his face, his gaze so attentive, expression so...open. "That frog move you do. Where your feet are spread, and you squat until your knees are ninety-degree angles."

"*Grand plié*, second position." There was a smile in Ange's voice. Robert ran his fingers through the blond hair, ruffling it.

"Yeah, that. Do it now, while you're lying down."

Ange's legs parted and then slid upward as he'd been commanded, showing Robert the smooth ovals of his testicles, shifting inside the sac. He also got a good glimpse of Ange's anus, a quivering pucker he imagined lubing up for his penetration. God, when was the last time he'd held onto an erection this long? Between that and the hickey, he really did feel like a teenager.

Focus. He'd told Ange he wanted to wrap his gift. The Christmas lights were just the beginning. He remembered now what it was like, having all the time in the world to do things like this, as if time stopped when the click happened, that key connection between him and the sub dependent on his demands. Except he'd never felt this quiet inner warmth with Freddie. There'd been more of a raw urgency to it then. Like the acceptable side of violence, fucking passionate. But this had a quiet, peaceful core, orbited by an extraordinarily intense arousal. Not only could Ange trust him, he could trust Ange. It was a revelation, the vital difference in the two men.

Ange's fingers curled, a tension in his shoulders. Robert also remembered what it was to notice those things, all the subtle emotional and physical details that told him the state of someone under his care. Under his command.

With Ange's legs bent in that "frog move," his hips open, pressed to the floor, he'd created an impressively horizontal line from one knee to the other. Pressing the sticks against the underside of his open thighs, it was easy for Robert to use the exposed testicles as the center point. As he put the sticks in front of and behind that appealing, heavy sac, he used two of the Lincoln Logs as spacers on either side. Then he began to wrap the improvised ball clamp and spreader bar to Ange's thighs.

He made it snug enough that his subject would get the anxious, titillating sense of compression, but not so snug that it would pinch Ange's balls off. He had uses for them, after all.

"You tell me if it hurts too much, Ange. You promise."

"Yes, Master."

He ran his knuckles over a cold butt cheek. "I like hearing you call me that. Too much."

"I wanted to call you that the first time I met you."

Robert lifted his gaze to find Ange staring at him with that hungry look again. "Close your eyes," Robert said gruffly. "I want you to feel. Jesus, I'm going to turn the heat up. Your ass is too cold."

"There are other ways to warm it up. Master." Ange said that to the mat, in that docile, I'm-not-trying-to-tell-you-what-to-do-but-here's-a-helpful-suggestion tone. Robert had to bite back a smile.

"I'll see about that after I finish this. For now, shut up."

When he was done, the two poles were against the back of Ange's thighs, the rope holding them all the way from the tender inside of one knee to the other. His testicles were clamped between them, spacers aligned all along the sticks in case one set failed. The rope's snug wrap kept the spacers in place. Ange was helpless, immobilized, and totally vulnerable. A hugely arousing state for a sub who trusted his Master. An even more arousing one for the Master himself.

Robert finished with an intricate series of cross ties around Ange's hips, leaving his ass open for whatever he wanted to demand from it. Ange's chest was expanding and contracting with shallow breaths.

"You're pretty hard right now, aren't you?"

"Yes, Master. Oh God..." Ange groaned as Robert tightened the sticks one more degree. "No more. Please."

"That's as far as we go. But it reminds you whose gift you are, doesn't it?"

"Yes. Yes, Master. Yours."

"I'm not sure. You don't listen as well as you should. I'm thinking we need a lesson about that."

His words gave Ange that sexy all-over quiver again. Still, Robert paused, thinking it over. The case he needed was in the store's safe, and he hadn't pulled it out since...Freddie had left? *Jesus.* Had it really been that long since he'd had sex with anything other than his own hand? He'd had a couple dates, set up by those same acquaintances he'd tapped for Ange, but he just couldn't seem to get anything from it. Once Ange had started working for him, he hadn't had any interest. Guess his heart and dick already knew what it had taken his fucked-up brain too long to understand.

Whoa. Getting ahead of yourself here, lad. Even so, Robert rose. The safe was in the back office, adjoining the craft room, so Ange didn't have to be out of his sight. Flipping the dial for the combination, he popped open the door, slid the case out. As he stared down at it, he realized it represented everything that was *before.* Before his parents died, before Freddie disappeared... In short, it had belonged to a man with a wholly different view of life.

His initials were engraved in the top, and there was a strap so he could carry it to the club he used to frequent, the one that held no appeal to him now. But the craft room, with its scents of childish creation, the man naked and bound on the floor, made him want to open it.

Squatting by Ange's side once again, Robert saw his green gaze course over his own thighs, linger on the groin area revealed by his splayed leg position. Ange pressed his lips together, moistening them. It was impossible not to imagine his mouth on Robert, and from there Robert took it even further. He saw himself boxing Ange's arms behind his back with another rope wrap, then putting him on his knees under the register counter. Throughout the day, whenever, however Robert had the urge, he'd just open his trousers and make Ange suck him off. His sub would get so hard and greedy his cock would leak onto his thighs, because of course Robert would keep him naked and wanting.

Probably not a good reality, given that Mrs. Fitzgerald and Horatio might keel over in co-dependent shock, and the strain on Ange's joints for an eight-hour workday would be extreme, but as a fantasy, it was a hell of a good one.

"Is that your box, like in *The Littlest Angel?*" Ange started to lift his head, but Robert put a hand on it, held it down, a command to be still. Ange settled, though his gaze remained curious.

Robert took out the pair of padded cuffs, the matching collar that went with it. Ange's expression was immediately swept by that same yearning look he'd had when Robert had been wrapping the lights. The boy was fair starved to be collared. It made Robert think of what was tucked in the bottom of that box, but that was going way too fast. If not for Ange, for Robert himself.

"Lift your head." He ran the collar around Ange's throat, buckled it closed, and ran two fingers beneath it to be sure it wasn't too tight.

He put his hand on the construction paper bracelet on Ange's wrist. "I'm going to remove this so it doesn't get damaged."

Robert un-taped one of the cuffs, reconnected it and laid the bracelet on the table, aware of Ange's attention upon how reverently he treated the evidence of his sub's devotion. Then he put the padded cuffs on Ange's wrists and guided his hands behind his head, snapping the cuffs into a lock with each other before he hooked them to the back of the collar. Now Ange's cheek was pressed to the mat, elbows bent and dropped on either side of his head. "I want those hands out of the way."

Rising, he put his foot on Ange's bare backside, bearing down so his pelvis was pushed down further. From his dancing, the boy had a mouth-watering flexibility. Plus, the pressure increased the hold of the ball clamp. Ange let out another groan.

"I'll be back. I'll just be in the next room." In fact, he wasn't gone long, knowing what he was seeking. It was a wall decoration, an ornament from Victorian times, but a very functional one. Ange jumped at the crack of the buggy whip, though it happened about two feet above his body.

"We were talking about ways to warm that cold ass of yours," Robert said pleasantly. "How many times have I told you to alarm the store when you're here alone at night?"

He could tell Ange hadn't expected that. "When I'm awake, I don't need—"

It had been a while since he'd used the whip, but at one time it had been an extension of his hand rather than a fixture on the wall. That first crack had re-familiarized him as much as necessary. He landed the pop right on the meat of Ange's ass and won a satisfying yelp. Ange's fingers flexed against the back of his head, his ass rising and then jerking back down in reaction.

"Not what I asked. How many times?" Robert repeated patiently.

"A lot."

"Hmm. Tempting. But I'm going to say it's been eight times. Why don't you count that off for me, prove you remember? If you're not screaming like a little girl when I'm done, we'll talk about what you need. And why you keep leaving that system off when you follow every other command I give you like it's the word of God."

He thought he heard Ange mutter "Fuck" into the mat, one of the few times he'd ever heard the boy curse, but those gorgeous buttocks flexed, ready for the punishment. Robert let him have it.

"One." Ange didn't scream, but the word had a strangled, strained sound to it. On the second one, he sank his teeth into the mat, leaving some interesting teeth marks for the kids and their parents to ponder.

"Three...four..." Every muscle from shoulders to thigh rippled, shuddered, constricted, and then his backside rose to take even more. Robert practically had to wipe the drool off his own chin.

"Five...fuck. Six!"

On that one, Ange was in danger of biting through the mat to the wood floor. Whether he knew it or not, he'd had enough.

For now.

CHAPTER THREE

Setting the whip aside, Robert squatted down next to
him again. It wasn't in everyone to react with pleasure
to what he'd just done, even Ange. For that reason, he gave the
next order with the anticipation and hope a kid carried on
Christmas morning, wanting to know what was under the tree.

"Lift up. Let me feel that cock that belongs to me."

Ange obeyed, his avid gaze on Robert's face. Robert reached
under Ange's body, closed his hand around the boy's dick. Holy
Mother of God. Like the Grinch, it seemed something on his
sub had increased three sizes, but it hadn't been his heart. Ange's
heart was already bigger than the rest of him, though, so Robert
had no problem with this. No problem at all.

"Please... Master."

Robert saw the glisten of tears. Yeah, a hard whipping did
that to some subs at first, even the strongest ones. Over the past
few months, he'd learned Ange was an odd mixture of fragile
sweetness and street tough. So seeing those tears wrenched his
heart like nothing else. Sliding to his hip, he stretched out next
to Ange, covering his trembling hands with one of his own.
Ange's attention riveted on his mouth, his eyes begging for it.
Robert denied them both, though it was hard as hell to do so.

"I'm not a kind Master, Ange. I make my sub beg, and beg hard, before I give him relief."

"Even at Christmastime?"

"Scrooge had nothing on me." Robert caught a finger in the collar wrapped around Ange's throat and tugged on it. As he did that, he wrapped two fingers over the connector between the cuffs on Ange's wrists. He swept his thumb along Ange's jaw.

"You think you don't need that security system because you're a grown man. A fucking gorgeous, one-of-a-kind man. But you're also mine. If you don't want me to go to prison for killing someone, you'll take preventive measures to protect the ass that belongs to me. Because if anyone ever broke in here and hurt you, I would kill them."

He knew Ange could tell he meant it. "I didn't go overseas and fight for my country to have some assholes here harm or take my property. And I'm not just talking about my inventory. Got it?"

"Yes, Master." Ange sounded like his throat had gone dry, a pleasing effect, but Robert wasn't satisfied yet.

"Tell me why you keep leaving it off."

Ange wanted out of that one, he could tell, but Robert tightened his grip, gave him a steely-eyed look that said he wouldn't have a problem giving him a few more tastes of that whip.

"Because I kept thinking of you coming to me...like you did tonight. Just suddenly appearing. And...all these months, it was like you were treating me like yours, but not. I thought...if I gave you one thing to punish me for...it would help."

Ange stopped, flushing. Despite the stumbling explanation, Robert understood immediately, enough that his mouth tugged wryly. Subs sometimes did that, if their Master wasn't paying close enough attention. While Ange was a pure service sub, a pleasure to a Master like Robert, he had the need all subs did at times: to feel the pull of the reins, the cut of the bit against the mouth. Robert was protective, and Ange had picked up on that. He'd chosen the one thing that, when the time came, would most likely inspire Robert to dish out the punishment he craved.

"I wish I could touch you," Ange said softly.

"You will. Eventually." Robert ran his hand down Ange's back to his abused ass. He straightened only to bend over it, pressing his lips to the first red area. Then to another. He traced them with his tongue, slid his fingers along the crease between Ange's buttocks to the compressed testicles and caressed them as well, testing the spacing. He also checked the coloring and temperature to make sure blood was still circulating.

Watching Ange's fingers was like viewing a ballet, the twisting and turning, gripping and releasing against his neck and hair. "The ones who beat me up...that first night. They wanted... I wouldn't let them take what's not mine to give."

Robert stopped. As he leaned back and Ange met his gaze, he remembered the scraped fists, the bloody nose, the bruises where he'd taken a hammering from multiple body blows.

I wouldn't let them take what's not mine to give. The words implied that his body belonged to his Master, to Robert, even though they hadn't yet met.

Robert lay down beside him again, stroked his hair. He learned Ange's face by touch, the precise cheekbones, straight long nose. Ange pressed his lips against the side of Robert's hand when it came close enough to allow it. Unhooking the cuffs from the collar, Robert then unlatched them from each other so Ange could bring his arms down. While he continued to play with Ange's hair, enjoying the soft blond hair passing over his knuckles, he closed his eyes, waiting to see what Ange would do.

Those elegant, strong fingers touched him, the pocket of his throat above the open collar of his shirt. Since it was afterhours, he hadn't worn a tie. Ange slipped several buttons, his fingers questing down the mat of Robert's chest hair, tangling and tugging, caressing, then he had his palm over Robert's heart, gently flexing, as if massaging it. It felt better than anything Robert had ever experienced. He found Ange's shoulder, covered the back of the collar, holding on. At length, though, Robert moved his hand over Ange's, trying to regain control of the situation. He opened his eyes.

"I'm not done with you, Ange. Not by a long shot. Is it too much?"

Ange shook his head. "No. God, no. I want...more. Everything."

That made two of them. Robert rose to his feet. "Good. Tell me the story of *The Littlest Angel*. And keep your eyes closed from here forward, unless I tell you that you can open them. I mean it this time."

Sensory deprivation increased nerve sensation, and he wanted to make the most of that. While Ange gathered his thoughts, Robert moved back into the stockroom. Finding the paraffin candles they used for the street candlelight ceremony on Christmas Eve, he pulled them out, along with a paintbrush, a potpourri burner, and a lighter.

"I've never told it from memory, so I may get some parts of it wrong."

"That's fine. I'll correct you later." Casting a fond look at the buggy whip, Robert bit back a smile at Ange's reaction to his words, obviously torn between apprehension and the arousal the punishment had provoked.

"A little boy dies and goes to Heaven, but he doesn't fit in anywhere. He tries, but he loses his halo in the hallowed halls, sings off tune in the choir. Eventually he's brought to one of the older, wiser angels, and he asks the boy what would make things better for him in Heaven. The Littlest Angel says if he could have this box that was under his bed at his home on Earth, he'd be okay. So he gets this box, and he's so happy about it, because it contains all the types of things a boy would love. A bird's egg, a special rock, his dog's collar...

"Then comes the night of the Christ Child's birth, and the Littlest Angel is agonizing over what gift to bring to the new baby. Finally, he decides to give him this box. But when he sees it sitting among all the other amazing gifts, he's sure that his poor little box is a terrible insult."

Robert checked the candles he'd put in the pot, saw they were melting down into liquid form. Ange's nostrils flared, taking in the scent, the heat. For his part, Robert was caught up in the story, in the parallels between that and the man at his mercy now.

"Just when he thinks he's done something too bad to be forgiven, God chooses that box above all the other gifts. The Littlest Angel loved what was in that box so much, but he was willing to give it all up, so that made it the greatest gift of all. God set the box in the sky and it became the star over the stable." Ange paused. "I thought you knew the story."

"I do. It doesn't mean I don't like hearing you tell it. I was thinking about the day you read it to Mr. Oglesby, who lost his sight last year. You were sitting in the corner with him, not reading very loudly, but by the time you were done, every person in the store was still and quiet as if they were in church. They were caught up by how you told it, like you believed every word. That's your magic, Ange. You *are* Christmas."

Ange opened his eyes at that. Robert brought the pot and brush to his side, along with a cardboard box containing the other key item he needed. "I thought I told you to keep your eyes closed," he reproved, but when he brushed a gentle finger over each of Ange's eyes, the boy's lips curved in a sweet smile.

Robert ran his hand over Ange's shoulders. "Arms out to your sides. Like you're making a snow angel."

When Ange complied, Robert shifted. The young man gave a surprised grunt as Robert knelt over his ass, one knee planted on the floor between his spread legs, the other foot braced on the outside of his hip. Since Ange was probably about a hundred and forty pounds, and Robert's burly Irish build was an easy two hundred, Robert didn't put his full weight on him, but he did brace his thigh against Ange's buttock, putting a little pressure on that sore ass, knowing it would constrict the clamp on Ange's balls once again. When he released his testicles, Robert would take great pleasure in a not-so-apologetic soothing rub of his privates.

He turned his attention back to the melted candles simmering in the burner. Swirling the brush in the hot paraffin, he lifted it free, held it poised just a second above Ange's flesh before he painted the wax in a short stripe outside his shoulder blade. From his own tests with it, Robert knew it felt like a teasing tongue, the tip of an aroused cock, the moisture of a kiss. Ange quivered, confirming the sensual experience, then stilled as Robert placed something in the wax.

"Feathers," Ange breathed, recognizing the light brush of sensation where the object touched his unwaxed flesh.

"White feathers," Robert agreed. "My angel."

The box was full of them, the leavings from a pair of broken angel wings Ange had picked up as castoffs from a school play. Though Ange would have used them for the kids' crafts, or to repair any feathered inventory they had, Robert liked his use better.

With every stripe of the paraffin, Ange let out a little breath at the sensation. Robert kept pressing feathers into his back, starting on the upper curve of his shoulders and then working down the inside lines of his shoulder blades, creating wings. As he reached the lower part of his angel's back, he shifted to Ange's side.

Ange's legs spasmed in their spread bondage, and when Robert painted some of that paraffin over his constricted balls, he moaned in ecstasy. Robert felt like doing the same, watching him. He left the small of Ange's back clear, so when he was done, he kissed his way down that track, toward the ass that was humping the floor in tiny, helpless movements. Even though the sticks compressed his testicles and cock every time Ange bore down, he was obviously too aroused to care.

Robert parted his cheeks and put his mouth there, giving Ange a teasing, warm lick like the paraffin. Ange cried out in recognition of the difference, however, shuddering at the contact from his Master. Robert penetrated his rim, exploring, teasing, running his tongue along the crinkled outside while Ange gasped, fingers clutching the floor.

Sliding to Ange's back, Robert put his face there, his cheek in the feathers, imagining how they would feel as he fucked Ange. Would he find possession, absolution, release... His own surrender? It was a complex thing, mastering an angel.

"Please..."

"Please what, love?" Robert moved up, lying on his hip once again, Ange's arm trapped in the tunnel between his upper body and propped arm. While he trailed his fingers down Ange's back, those green eyes sought his, wild, needy.

"I want... Please let me serve you, Master. How can I...give you release?"

"Nothing for yourself? You don't want to be fucked? To come?"

"Yes...but to serve you. It doesn't mean anything otherwise."

Robert passed his hand over Ange's head, stroking back the white-blond hair. "Do you ever brush this, and why does it always look so sexy, even in this shocking disarray?"

Ange blinked, then gave a desperate chuckle. "Hair. You want to talk about hair. I *knew* you were gay."

It startled him. Then something broke loose. Robert threw his head back and laughed. As the sound of it filled the room, he found Ange staring at him in wonder.

"I never... You've never laughed like that, Master."

"It's been a long time since I've felt like I could." Since it had felt right. He put his hand on Ange's face. "You want to serve me, and I want to care for you. I think there might be a way to take care of both of those things." He leaned in, breath close to Ange's face, lips almost touching. Ange was paralyzed by his own need, a state that a Dom loved to see happen. He was looking for direction, a command to serve his Master's desires. "Beg me to fuck you, Ange."

"Please, Master. Please fuck me. Please..." Ange swallowed hard. Abruptly, he groped for Robert's hand, clasping it in that upright angle like brothers-in-arms, and perhaps they were, for Ange had had his battles as well. "I mean no disrespect. I do want to be fucked, but could you also...love me?"

Jesus. The kid knew how to squeeze his heart like a vise. Robert pressed his forehead to Ange's, caressing his shoulder, the collar. The wrong kind of collar. Lifting his head to look around, he found the case he'd brought out of the safe. It was on the other side of his captive. As he leaned over Ange to pull it closer, Ange caressed his thigh with his mouth, hot and wet. Robert's balls reacted as if Ange had stroked a long tongue over them. Ange's hand slid along Robert's thigh and behind to cup his ass, brushing the seam. It made Robert shift, and the kid's mouth was right on his groin, the moist heat coming through the denim.

"Behave," he said, though his voice was ragged. Ange nuzzled him, but moved his mouth and hand back to Robert's thigh. The pressure of his fingers continued to convey his urgent need, however, his desire to serve, to have his mouth on Robert, to take Robert's release down his throat. Christ, the boy was fucking up his concentration. He was out of practice dealing with a sub.

No, that wasn't it. He had no practice handling a sub who was so much of everything he'd ever wanted, one who wanted to give as much as Robert did.

He didn't let himself hesitate. He pulled out the velvet bag pushed to the very bottom of the case, out of sight, but never out of mind. Sitting back on his heels, he gave Ange's cheek a reproving tap. "I mean it. Behave. Remember who's in charge."

"I do, Master. I'm sorry. I just want you so much, it's hard to hold back."

Simple, sweet honesty, and a mirror image of the feeling swamping him. It was time to get rid of the spreader bar and ball clamp. Robert wanted to take his sub closer to where they both wanted to go.

Setting aside the velvet bag for now, Robert shifted to the lower part of the mat and began to remove the rope, holding the poles and lifting the top one off when the ropes' steadying pressure disappeared. Lincoln Logs tumbled to the mat and he picked them up, laying them to the side with the sticks.

"Lift up your ass," he commanded.

When Ange complied, Robert closed his fingers over his testicles and cock once more, rubbing gently over the wax he'd painted on his balls. The friction elicited a whimper of arousal and relief both as he soothed the compression. Ange's cock was still just as tumescent, his balls drawing up beneath Robert's manipulation, making it difficult not to start rubbing in a far more aggressive and purposeful manner, but he hadn't forgotten what he wanted to do with that velvet bag. He indulged his desire to rub Ange's ass with the other hand, though, idly squeezing and stroking as he massaged the kid's enticing equipment. At length, he forced himself to let go.

"Sit up on your heels," he said gruffly.

Ange obeyed, putting his hands in a laced position behind his head without being told, back straight, knees open, cock out there for whatever Robert wanted to do with it. A few of the feathers floated to the floor, but the tips of others haloed his shoulders. His pale cheeks were flushed. Whenever Robert had corrected him about something in the store, however mildly, he'd noted that earnest blush of color, the fair skin unable to hide it. He never had to correct Ange on the same thing twice. Except the security system.

When Robert picked up the velvet bag and loosened the drawstring, he knew Ange was watching his every move. The tremulous breath he heard when he removed the contents proved it. The bag held a custom-made collar. It was a thick braided black band, bound every couple inches by sterling silver triskelions. The pewter buckle was boldly engraved with an angel's wing. The designer had recommended it, a symbol to suggest Robert was putting a guardian angel over his sub, but he'd never associated Freddie with an angel otherwise, even before things had gone sour.

"No one has ever worn this." He wanted Ange to know. "It was going to be a Christmas gift for the man I was with, but he left me before then. I think it was never meant for him. Will you wear it, Ange?"

For this, he would ask, because this wasn't a play collar like the one with the cuffs. He was taking the leap. He wanted Ange to belong to him. He wanted Ange to accept him formally as his Master.

When Ange lifted his gaze, his eyes were brilliant, his voice firm and steady. A man's voice, not a kid's. "Yes, Master. Please."

Three simple words, but then "I do" were two simple words, weren't they? Okay, maybe he was getting a little carried away. His father's Irish sentimentality was trying to overtake his mother's German practicality. Even so, his fingers shook a little as he removed the cuffs and the other collar before he wrapped this one around Ange's throat, buckled it in the back. His throat was one hole slimmer than Freddie's, but that notch made it a perfect fit. Robert lingered over the tracing of the angel wing, then ran his fingers along the heavy braid, the silver triskelions. "Mine," he said. Fiercely.

With that dancer's suppleness, Ange bent all the way over, leaving his hands clasped behind his head as he pressed his cheek to Robert's thigh. Robert caressed his back, tracing his spine between the array of feathers. Then he fanned out to follow his rib cage, before returning to Ange's neck. Placing his hand on that angel wing buckle, he tugged. "All right, enough of that. My property has a fantasy about a manger. So do I."

As Robert got to his feet, Ange straightened, but kept his fingers laced behind his head until Robert reached down. Then he put his hand in Robert's. Robert brought him to his feet, sliding an arm around Ange's waist to steady him. He'd been on the floor awhile and, flexible or not, a lot of blood was obviously, deliciously, in his cock, especially after that last announcement. Robert moved them out of the craft room, running a callused palm over Ange's buttocks. At Ange's involuntary flinch, Robert gentled his touch. "Don't worry; you've had enough of that for tonight. I have another idea in mind."

The store had six display rooms, and the life-sized nativity, a nineteenth-century carved set from Germany, was in the back left. The wooden faces were noble and dramatic, even the animals'. The creatures were in tranquil repose around the human characters. An angel was carefully mounted atop the wooden frame representing the stable cover.

They'd positioned the nativity scene so that, as a customer entered that nook of the store, it spread before them as if they'd stepped out of their world and into the Bethlehem stable. The old wooden floor added to the feeling, as did the scent of hay from the scattered handfuls and bales Ange had placed around the area. Shoppers could sit on them, contemplating the display of Christ's birth while they enjoyed hot cider and sugar cookies offered at a refreshment table in the corner. Ange had rigged a separate sound system in here so, at the touch of a switch, their visitors would hear the various messages of the angels to the shepherds and Mary, good tidings of the hope and love the Child would bring.

So it wouldn't get too repetitive, Ange had suggested adding other things to the recording, quotes from Jesus's teachings and relevant scripture passages. Robert remembered Ange sitting with his back braced against the manger, going through a children's book about Jesus because Ange said it had the purest understanding, the quotes that spoke directly to people's hearts.

Adults often don't say what they mean, but they feel the important things the same way a child does.

Once they'd agreed on the quotes, Ange wanted Robert to do the recording, but Robert told him he was the only one who could do it right. After hearing his reading to Mr. Oglesby, it was obvious to Robert that Ange's voice was best suited to conveying an angel's message of joy and wonder. That, and the genuine emotion he put into the other passages he'd chosen, made the nativity room a favorite with new and return customers. Mrs. Fitzgerald sat through the full recording at least once a week, her eyes often moistening as she cupped her cider to warm her hands, Horatio dozing in the nest of her purse.

Inasmuch as ye have done it unto one of the least of these my brethren, ye have done it unto me. The least of these shall have my love...

Ange added little improvs like that to the original quotes, adding to the spirit of the recording. Now Robert put his hand on Ange's shoulder, gazing at the nativity scene. "You did a great job with this."

When Ange fairly glowed, Robert felt an answering warmth spread through his chest. The boy treated every compliment like gold. It could make a Master ridiculously devoted to him in no time. Hell, he was already there, wasn't he? The collar proved it.

"You did, too." Moving forward in just the collar and angel feathers, beautiful in his nakedness, Ange knelt at the manger, studying the occupant. "It's nearly two hundred years old, but that's not why you arranged the hay just so, with the blanket over it. You made it soft and comfortable, the way Joseph and Mary would have done." He ran a long finger over the blanket. "You believe in the spirit of things. You understand what things to care for, and you care for them well, Master."

Emotion swelled to a painful pressure in Robert's chest. "Stay there," he said. "Kneeling in front of the manger is right where I want you."

It was a solid thing, bolted to the floor because, as Ange had noted, the doll was quite valuable. Robert didn't want a shopper accidentally knocking it over. But as Ange had also noted, that wasn't why Robert lifted the babe out so gently now, under Ange's close regard. He moved it to the extra cradle tucked to the side, used when Ange needed to rearrange the hay or shake dust out of the blanket. As Robert lowered his burden, he automatically said a simple prayer, like his mother had when she'd assembled and disassembled the nativity scene each Christmas.

He checked the carafe of hot cider. There was about a cup left in it from earlier today. After he plugged it in, he turned. Ange was watching him still, but now there was a pensive look on his face. He glanced down at the manger with serious green eyes. "This is okay, right, Master? It's not...blasphemy to you?"

"No. Not if we respect what's here, and if what we do, we do in love." When Ange's expression transformed to astonishment, Robert came to him, put a hand on his face. "Religion murdered Jesus, but faith kept his message alive for those who care to hear it. Do unto others... Love one another... Cast no stones..."

"Love one another." Ange touched Robert's thigh. "I've wanted you to love me for a long time."

"I've been in love with you for quite a while." There, he'd said it. The look on Ange's face made it worth hurtling over every fear to form the words. "But I lacked the courage to say it aloud."

"No, Master." Ange's expression revealed that streak of determination, the one that intrigued and aroused Robert at once. "You just needed time to hurt, to grieve. Everybody deserves that."

He paused so long that Robert could tell he was struggling with something. Robert tapped a gentle finger on his cheek. "It's all right. What is it?"

Ange looked up at him again, hope and desire wrapped up together in an expression so mesmerizing Robert couldn't look away. "When we were talking about *The Littlest Angel*, this store and you...you're that box for me. The star over the stable, guiding me home. Do I have a home here, Master?"

Robert gripped the side of Ange's face, fingers biting into his neck. "Yes, Ange. You made it a home for me again. When I thought I'd lost what home was."

Ange had said the world was ugly, and it could be, but he'd made it beautiful again to Robert. Love could do that.

Hooking a finger under Ange's collar, Robert brought him up on his knees. The kisses he'd taken before had been rough, demanding. This time it was tender and excruciating, like drawing a knife gently across flesh begging to bleed for him. He caressed with lips and tongue, held Ange's head still so he could tease and stroke, savor every single reaction. When he was done, Ange was holding onto his arms for balance, breathless with pleasure.

"I'm your Master, Ange. When we're done tonight, you're not going to doubt for a moment where you belong. Or to whom. Now, bend over the manger."

To his satisfaction, Ange looked a little dazed, but Robert helped him, guiding him to hold onto either corner of the manger. He thought about tying him there, but decided against it. Ange would stay still if Robert ordered him to do it. Robert switched on the decorative light that made it look like stars were swimming across the walls and ceilings. He also turned on the spotlight that framed the angel and Mary's gentle face. Ange's playlist was still going, and he could hear the bittersweet strains of Sarah McLachlan's "River." When he'd heard the song last Christmas, he'd wanted to skate away on that river as well. Now he just wanted to be on it with Ange, gliding through those white snowflakes, silent and perfect, like first kisses.

He checked the cider. It was warming fast. Ange usually rinsed the carafe out at night, so Robert expected he'd gotten distracted with his paper chains and dancing and hadn't had a chance to do it yet.

"Do you ever sleep?" Robert asked, coming back to Ange. Trailing a finger through those feathers, he made Ange's skin draw up with gooseflesh, his thighs shift out wider. Robert knelt behind him, putting his hands on his waist, pressing a kiss to his shoulder. Ange let out a soft sigh, fingers tightening on the manger, while Robert put his knee in between the spread legs, pushing his hip bone firmly against the seam of Ange's buttocks as he held him.

"Sometimes. I don't sleep that well. Haven't for a long time. On the street...you stay alert."

Robert brushed his jaw against Ange's neck, the cool press of the collar buckle against his chin. "You'll tell me how that happened one day. You'll trust me with all of it. It won't make me love you less."

Studying the hickey he'd put high on Ange's throat, Robert laid his mouth on the joining point between Ange's throat and shoulder and bit down to give him another. The hard, suckling pressure took away the tension his casual statement had caused his sub. Ange groaned, his ass pushing back against Robert.

"Un-unh." He backed off, gave him a smack for that, making those whip marks sing, he was sure. "You stay easy and still. Think about what's coming."

Ange let out a huff, a half-chuckle that said what he thought of the likelihood of those two ideas going together. Robert found himself smiling. He rose to pour the cider in a paper cup, picked up a plastic spoon, came back to him. "Put your forehead on the manger. I want your back like a sloped table."

When Ange obeyed, Robert stirred the cider, took a sip. Just hot enough. When he dipped the spoon, dripped some on the small of Ange's back, below the feathers, the boy shuddered, fingers gripping the manger harder. It was hot enough to burn, but too little of it to do damage, just roll that feeling down his spine, to his crack.

"Master... Oh God..."

The starlight fell on his skin as well, like snow itself. Robert did it again, loving the way Ange jumped from the burn, but then wiggled at the residual sensations. His hips lifted, lowered. He was trying hard not to get into a coital rhythm, but Robert could see it developing anyway, and his own cock pulsed with the same composition. "Lift your ass up to me, Ange. Take the burn."

He did, several more times, until he was making small, needy grunts. Robert knelt, putting the cider aside to reach between

Ange's spread thighs. When he took hold of his balls, Ange made an animal sound of lust. "God... Master..."

"Don't you move. Don't you be bad and thrust into your Master's hand. Be still." Robert let his touch move up to Ange's cock. As Robert bent lower to follow the cider's track with his mouth, Ange shuddered with the effort to obey. Robert took his time with it, pumping his grip on Ange's cock as the kid fought with all he had not to fuck that teasing hold. When he ran his tongue down between Ange's buttocks, lapping at that spiced sweetness, Ange made a strangled noise of torment. His cock pulsed alarmingly under Robert's grip, but he squeezed the base, making it clear his sub wouldn't come until it was okay with him.

"I told you I could be ruthless, Ange. I want my subs to beg."

"I want to please you, Master... I want you. Please...please... I want you inside me. Please."

His eyes never leaving Ange, Robert stood. He unbuttoned his shirt, shrugged out of it, then pulled the white undershirt over his head. When he started to unbuckle his belt, he could tell Ange was listening intently.

"Imagining me undressing?"

Ange nodded, a quick twitch. "I always wanted... I could tell you were in shape...fit, but you always wear so many clothes." The frustration in his voice surprised, amused, and flattered Robert all at once. "That day the air conditioning broke, you rolled up your sleeves and pulled off your bowtie, opening the top button of your shirt. Then you took it all the way off to work on the shelving in the back. You were wearing a white T-shirt beneath, and I came back to give you something. You were standing on the ladder, your biceps flexing with the hammering, your ass at eye level. You had your knee pressed to the inside of the ladder's frame, one step up from the other foot. God, I went into the bathroom and came like a fucking wet dream, not able to stop myself. It was like a striptease."

Robert had stopped undressing, stunned by the stream of words, the images Ange painted. He didn't think much about his body. He did keep it in shape, but he'd never thought of himself the way he thought about Ange: flawless, something any man or woman would crave to touch. Ange made Robert's body sound like that and more. He was almost afraid to let him look now. But he wouldn't be a coward. Ange deserved to see what he was getting.

"Look at me," he growled.

Ange lifted his head. Robert stepped to the right so Ange didn't have to remove his hands from the manger, making it clear he wanted him to stay in the subservient position. However, now he was the one who felt most vulnerable. His upper body was bare, his belt unbuckled, the top button of the jeans undone. As Ange watched, he toed off his shoes, stepped on his socks to pull them off, then removed the jeans and boxers beneath, leaving himself even more bare than the man kneeling before him.

Ange looked like he was holding his breath. His gaze moved from Robert's face down over his chest, lingering over the shrapnel scars he had, then down to thighs and cock. It was a decent length, thicker than most. He'd never had any complaints about its size or how he used it, but under Ange's attention, it seemed as if it was trying to outdo itself. Fuck, the kid affected him.

Ange did that lip moistening thing that could make Robert lose his mind. "Eyes down now. You've looked."

"Never enough," his sub murmured, though he obeyed, those white-gold lashes sweeping down in a way that was almost coquettish. "You're beautiful, Master."

"Yeah, right." But he couldn't help the curve of his own lips, the warmth he felt from the sincerity in Ange's words. "You're the beautiful one."

It hit him then, the immenseness of all of this, of the past, present, and future rolled together. He moved forward, putting a hand on Ange's shoulder. However, when he slid his thumb under the collar, he found he couldn't go any further. His grip tightened, that feeling rising in his chest, overwhelming him.

Ange stilled. "Master?"

"I'm all right."

Ange knew him too well. The kid straightened, a gentle, insistent push against his hold. Robert had been standing between his spread knees, but he gave way as the young man turned, looked up at him. Then Ange lowered his chin and pressed a reverent kiss against Robert's lower abdomen, just above his pubic area. His cock jutted over Ange's shoulder, but his sub didn't break the inviolate rule about not touching a Master there directly, bare skin to bare skin, without express permission, even though he was breaking some lesser rules by touching him elsewhere. Ange ran his hands up the back of Robert's legs, learning the musculature, tugging on the short hairs, then glided them up to his ass, molding over him.

"You're perfect, Master," he hummed against Robert's flesh. "A fighter, so strong and hard everywhere. Except your heart."

Robert dug his fingers into Ange's hair, held there as Ange worked his mouth across that pubic line. "Hell with it," he groaned, and angled his cock. "Suck on me."

Ange took him all the way to the base, a skill so impressive Robert might have come right then, except he knew exactly how and where he intended to do that. "Stop. Keep it in your mouth and look up at me."

He loved that image, a sub gazing up from that position of service. Ange's green eyes glittered beneath the fall of hair, his mouth stretched over Robert's girth, his own cock hard and ready, dripping pre-come on the floor below. It was the best Christmas card ever.

"Lean back over that manger. Now."

Ange complied, sliding off him slow and teasing, but not in a bratty way. Just savoring his cock in a way that made Robert think his inappropriate under-the-counter fantasy might become way too tempting. When Ange resumed his position, Robert pulled his jeans up off the floor. He'd slipped a tube of lubricant into his pocket from the case, so now he uncapped the lube and worked it over himself. He found he had to be careful about it, in danger of going off like a rocket.

Ange had his forehead pressed to the rough wood again. "I love you, Master."

Robert knelt behind him, put his palm on those angel feathers. Quite a few of them had fallen off now, the cracked wax making patterns over Ange's flesh. He looked forward to sponging that off afterward. With pleasure, he remembered he'd also brushed it over Ange's balls. At his place, he had a huge cast iron tub, big enough for two men. He'd clean him there, fuck him again.

"You'll sleep tonight, Ange. With me, in my bed. And that's where you'll wake up Christmas morning, too. We'll help each other sleep."

When Ange briefly turned his head, Robert thought he saw tears in those eyes again. He couldn't bear to wait another moment. Gripping Ange's hips, he put the head of his cock to that puckered hole, began to ease in. The kid knew the way of it, sphincter muscles pushing back against him, but Robert still took his time, wanting to feel it, wanting it to be right for both of them. For the first time, Robert was glad he'd been celibate for so long, so he didn't have to worry about a condom. He knew Ange was clean. Ange had given him his blood test results to file with the ER bill Robert had paid that first night. It was a move he now figured had been as deliberate as Ange blowing off those two dates he'd set up for him.

Thank God.

As Ange's muscles gave way, sucked him in, he let out a reverent expletive. *Holy mother of all that's good...*

When he glanced at the Mary statue, she was as serene as ever, which was reassuring. Though he'd said this wasn't blasphemy, he was pretty sure his own mom might say differently.

Yet sex had never felt so sacred to him as it did right now. What had Ange said? This wasn't fucking. This was loving.

He stretched out his arms, aligning them with Ange's, and

overlapped their fingers, putting them in the spaces between the white knuckles. The action pressed his body closer against Ange and he pushed in deeper, earning a grunt, a longing sound from Ange's throat. The stems of the feathers scratched Robert's chest, a pleasant friction contrasting with the tease of their soft fronds. "Tell me what you're thinking, Ange. All of it. No filter."

"I'm thinking... I knew you'd feel like this...thick and hard. You take care. You're so rough, so mean, but so gentle, too. I love it. The hard and the soft. The way you whipped my ass, but how you made sure the collar wasn't too tight, how you kissed me, hard and rough, but you also took your time pushing your cock into me, making sure I was okay every inch of the way. Every blessed, fucking inch." Ange groaned as Robert withdrew, thrust back in. "Make it hurt, but make it feel good, too, Master. Please."

Like love itself. Pain and pleasure, sorrow and remembrance, joy and memory-making. Robert slid his arm around Ange's waist, his hand pressed to his chest to hold Ange against him, the scattering of angel feathers between their bodies. Putting his face back against Ange's neck, against the collar, he set his teeth into Ange's shoulder. Mine. Always.

"You don't come until I say," he demanded. "Hold it back."

"Yes...Master." Ange's ass and shoulders were rippling in rhythm with their movements. The lights passing over them both became the streaks of shooting stars as Robert went faster, harder, testing the bolts on the manger. He was a strong bastard when he wanted to be, and Ange had told him he wanted it, wanted the power and demand with the pleasure. Ange grunted in exertion, telling him he'd hit the right note. "Yeah, you feel me," Robert muttered. "You take all of me."

He was channeling all those things he'd felt, every day he'd gone home wanting and aching, thinking about Ange's lean body, the watching green eyes, the sinful mouth, the gorgeous ass, and sweet smile. The generous and pure heart.

"Come now. Come for me."

Though he catapulted over that same delicious edge, Robert managed to reach beneath Ange to work him hard in his fist. The two of them moved in tandem, that instinctive rhythm that had their knees pressing hard into the wood floor. Robert's arm was a band of steel around Ange. The kid let go of one corner of the manger to clutch it. When Robert shifted so their hands became a knot high against Ange's chest, Ange set his teeth to Robert's knuckles, groaning out his release. His seed fountained over Robert's grip and wet the straw on the floor beneath the manger.

Robert had never felt anything so good in his life. He worked Ange until he was well beyond done, milking him, seeing how he handled himself when his nerves became so sensitive. Ange took all of it, embraced it, working his ass up against his Master, thrusting into Robert's hand, telling him he could give as good as he got. Fucking treasure.

When Robert finally stopped them, both winded, Ange laid his cheek down on the manger. Robert had covered the hand that held onto the corner, and their fingers were intertwined, their other set of hands still tangled against Ange's chest. Robert laid his jaw on Ange's back, against the remaining feathers and his flesh. "Thank you," he said quietly.

He might have been thanking Ange, or the angel over the manger, or whatever Power watched over them all. That Presence always seemed even closer at Christmas, like the orbit of the moon at certain times of the year, but the thanks were a prayer, offered to all of it.

When he at last had the energy to lift up, he brought Ange with him. Pulling the blanket out of the manger, he shook it out, laid it over the straw, and brought his sub down to the floor with him, curling up behind him, holding his hip and nesting his own cock in between the oiled buttocks, a promise that he'd be expecting more...soon.

Robert was going to take Ange home, fix him breakfast. Fall asleep in his bed, curled around that pale, lean body, after he gave him another workout that would leave Ange exhausted, throbbing with pain and pleasure both.

"I want you to dance for me again," he said, stroking the sweaty blond hair off Ange's neck. "In my home."

"I will," Ange mumbled. Robert smiled. He'd tired him out, his angel who said he didn't sleep much. He'd relish holding him in his arms when dreams took him, and he'd damn well make sure they stayed good dreams, the kind Ange would want to embrace.

"I'll make your heart dance, Master. Now and forever."

Since it was dancing now, Robert believed him. With all the hope of Christmas itself.

PART TWO

CHAPTER FOUR

*A*fter they recovered enough from what had happened at the manger, Robert took Ange into the back bathroom. He had him straddle a folding chair while he filled up a bucket with hot soapy water. Though Robert still planned for them to have a good soak in his cast iron tub, Ange could hardly get dressed with feathers and wax stuck to flesh also sticky from hot cider.

Robert applied a soaked and steaming washcloth to Ange's back, softening the wax and removing it, along with any lingering feathers. Ange shivered at the contact with the heat, and Robert watched the water drops roll down his glistening skin, to his buttocks and the seam between. Robert let his hands follow those same intimate tracks. Exploring without demand, but the promise of sexual intent was there.

The light in Ange's eyes, the drifting grasp of his hand on Robert's forearm, his waist, said he was floating in a true euphoria.

Robert loved seeing him in that state, enough that once the clean-up was done, he didn't push Ange to pack a bag or do anything practical, other than don clothes. The kid pulled on a pair of faded blue jeans, worn to thinness, and Robert's sleeveless tank again. Then he headed for the door.

"Whoa, there." Robert snagged his belt loop, hauling him back. "Socks. Shoes. Coat. I swear, if I didn't tell you to get dressed, you'd just prance out there bare-assed."

Ange's fair cheeks flushed, but he sent Robert a sheepish smile. "I'm not feeling the cold," he said.

More of that lingering subspace talking. Which was good, because under different circumstances, it might have concerned Robert. Ange's tendency to disconnect from reality always left Robert feeling a little uneasy. More protective.

But that was the thing. Ange was officially his sub now. They were going to Robert's home. At least for the rest of the night, he'd be safe in Robert's care. He plucked Ange's coat off the rack by the door, helping him into it after his sub struggled into his socks and shoes. Robert set the alarm, and they stepped out into the wintry night.

As they walked through the ankle-deep snow of the side street route to his place, Ange scuffed through it, kicking up powdery drifts. He twirled around Robert, doing short leaps and spins, coming back to him to link arms, hug up to him, then spinning away again.

It amused Robert, pleased him. Even managed to distract him for a while, so that he didn't notice exactly when that comfortable Dom-space feeling became harder to maintain. But he should have expected it. Some things refused to be put aside.

The closer they came to Robert's home, the more reality accelerated, overtaking and leaving bliss behind.

Ange had never been inside Robert's place, a forty-year old brick townhome in Charlotte's gentrified Fourth Ward area. The store was their shared world, where Robert went in order to absorb and experience all things Ange. Keeping Ange away from the other side of his life had been Robert's choice, one he hadn't examined too closely. Maybe because it wasn't that hard to figure out.

Robert had gone to the store to immerse himself in light, life, difference. His home was filled wall to wall with the murk of memories. Every step they took away from the store and toward Robert's place felt as if they were moving from light back to dark.

Articulating his feelings for Ange as he'd done tonight had been unexpected, no matter how wonderfully inevitable it now seemed. The whole world had changed in one evening. Yet suddenly Robert had a strange fear, that if he took Ange inside his home, the magic they'd found in the store would vanish. It couldn't survive what was behind his front door.

Robert came to a halt in his driveway and turned to look at Ange. The blond damp lashes, frosty breath billowing from sensual lips. The tousled hair over his fair forehead. They were going to a hotel, Robert decided. Or back to the store. They'd layer blankets on the floor, since there was no way he could fit on Ange's narrow cot in the back room. Even though he didn't mind the mental image of them trying to do so, limbs tightly intertwined.

Before he could say what was in his head, Ange closed the distance between them, put his mouth on Robert's. A sweet, almost shy kiss, fingers kneading at Robert's waist. He was nervous, too, Robert realized.

Maybe he was interpreting Robert's hesitation differently. Maybe he thought, in Robert's home, outside the whimsical surroundings of the store, Robert would find him wanting.

Just like that, Robert's concerns didn't seem as important. "Pull out my keys," he told Ange, because he had his hands on Ange's face, the side of his neck, holding him for the kiss, controlling the depth of it. He wasn't letting go.

Ange's long fingers slipped into the pocket of Robert's jeans, offering an intimate caress of the upper thigh, reaching for the hint of testicles until Robert growled at him. Ange produced the keys with an impish smile.

"Going to end up on the naughty list," Robert muttered.

As he let Ange go in order to unlock the door, Ange touched the antique doorknocker, a little girl with a wreath on her head, sitting on a swing. Grasping her feet and pulling her up to "swing," made the knocker work. Ange did it once, smiling. Answering the expression with a tight one of his own, Robert pushed open the portal.

The small, garage-level foyer contained an umbrella stand and a side table bearing a green carnival glass fruit bowl. He dropped his keys there with a quiet clanking noise. A wide polished wooden staircase led upstairs, while a door to the left led to the two-bay garage. On the right was a narrow elevator to carry a person or groceries to the upper three floors.

Ange hung his coat on a row of hooks beside the garage door, touching a black tweed fedora with a red and black spotted feather. "You'd look good in that," he said.

As he lifted it, obviously intending to playfully sit it on Robert's head, Robert grasped his wrist, stopping him. Took it from him with the other hand, set it back on the hook.

"It was my father's," he said.

Uncertainty flitted over Ange's face at the decisive gesture. "Oh," he said. "Sorry."

"It's okay." Trying to shrug off the unexpected reaction, Robert gestured Ange to precede him up the steps. Ange brushed past him, his hand briefly touching Robert's side. He had a feeling his sub might have let the gesture linger, if Robert hadn't introduced the stiff note to things.

He watched the shift of Ange's backside, the crease of his shirt over his back, then followed him up. When he reached the first level with him, Robert stood just behind his shoulder, watching Ange examine the space that held the kitchen and an open living space.

The townhome had almost four thousand square feet of heated space, each level accordingly expansive. However, this one was so overstuffed with furniture it could have been the display floor of a secondhand store. An old sectional sofa set, coffee and end tables were crammed in with a couple wingbacks and another sofa. The sectional and tables had been brought from his parents' home. The wingbacks and sofa were Robert's. Long, heavy drapes with blue and green stripes covered the bank of windows, making the room seem even smaller. His sofa was pressed against the folds of fabric, flattening them.

He couldn't remember the last time he'd opened the curtains. He'd moved some of the furniture back into a better viewing position for the flatscreen over the gas log fireplace, but it was the only change he'd made. As such, he could still see how all of it had been adjusted to accommodate his mother's hospital bed.

When Robert bought the townhome, he'd intended to tailor the interior to his tastes, make a home for himself. In his head, he'd planned out changes to create a welcome place for hosting dinners and entertaining friends. His plan was to get on that after trade show season was over. Then his father's health started to decline, and a decision on care had to be made.

His parents wouldn't use paid healthcare services. His mother, not in good health herself, would kill herself trying to care for his father on her own. Because he was running a business, Robert couldn't shut things down and care for them in their Virginia home. His guilt over that, along with a genuine desire to lessen the pain of their transition, meant he moved as much of their world into his place as he could. His mother had been reluctant to part with any of her possessions.

Around that time Freddie had bailed on him as well. Though all break-ups sucked, if someone was going to rip his heart out, Robert supposed he should be glad it had happened when he was in the midst of another emotional crisis. In hindsight, it was like dropping an anvil on his foot to forget he'd just slammed his hand in a car door.

The end result was probably the same, though. They'd passed the two-year anniversary of his father's death, and his mother had been gone a year and a half. His parents' rooms on the second level were unchanged, clothes still in the closet. To save trips to the store, he'd gone searching in their bathroom for extra toothpaste or toilet paper until that was gone, but everything else had remained untouched.

Why hadn't he taken the lift to his bedroom, where Ange wouldn't see all this? Though still appallingly generic, the third floor wasn't smothered beneath the heavy weight of the past. It held his bedroom, another living space, and led to the rooftop deck. Except for using the kitchen to prepare his meals, that was where he spent most of his time. He'd been acting as if he were living in a loft apartment, a convenient way to avoid doing anything with the lower floors.

Ange had left the stairs to take several steps into the first level living space. He faced the curtains, gazing at the lengths of striped fabric. Robert stood at the threshold between the kitchen and living room, watching him. Despite his conflicting thoughts, he said nothing. Maybe he was waiting to see what Ange would do, while he struggled to figure out his own best move to care for his sub properly in an environment that threatened to choke him.

Ange moved to Robert's sofa, bent and grasped the wooden trim at the bottom. When he pulled the sofa away from the windows, the curtains rippled, as if taking a breath from the release of pressure. Ange slid his slim form into the space he'd created, lifting his arms out to either side to pull back the curtains.

The track lights in the kitchen had been left on, but they mostly provided illumination to that area. Now the living room was flooded with the natural brightness of a moonlit, snowy night. It created a new canvas of shadows and shapes over the copious amounts of furniture.

Ange emerged from behind the sofa and extended a hand. As Robert came to him, his sub had a light smile on his face, but it was a serious expression, his eyes full of emotion. His grip held strength and firmness. His angel was such a mix of boy and man, the broken and the resilient. Reminders of the man, and the stronger-than-expected will, were always a pleasurable surprise.

"Each day when you came to the store," Ange said, "you'd have shadows in your eyes. A gloom. After about an hour, they'd disappear. Once you touched your favorite toys on the shelves. Once the customers came in. I could tell that every night when you went home, it was to grief and memories. So every day, I'd vow to do what I could to inspire you to smile, to ease your sadness. I wish I had known, Master. I wish I had really understood. I thought I did, but I didn't."

Those earnest green eyes, the set of his jaw, humbled and overcame Robert. It took him a moment to reply, but the answer itself wasn't hard to find.

"You made it better. Every day." Robert moved closer, his body brushing Ange's as he lifted a hand to his face, touched it with his knuckles. "Be easy on that."

Every night he'd leave the toy store with more energy than he'd brought to it in the morning. Ange was right about that. But by the time Robert set his keys downstairs and reached the kitchen, the energy to change anything here was gone. The oppressiveness was too much to alter on his own.

With Ange here, he could feel that energy shifting. Then Ange gave it an additional push. A corner of his distracting mouth curved. "You really would rock that hat."

"Nope." Robert considered him. "Not me. Stay here."

He turned and left the room, jogged down the stairs and retrieved it. His fingers slid along the interior band. His dad was the person who'd taught him not only to care for things well, but to appreciate how those things shaped themselves to a person, the longer they remained in his care. The hat was clean, but it had accommodated his father's head over time, the inside satin band discolored and faded from contact with his flesh.

Robert returned to the living room. As he crowned Ange with the hat, his boy's smile deepened, and he put both hands on it, his fingers brushing Robert's. He removed it, twirled it in his hand, put it back on his head, and did a low spin, one arm and leg out, a graceful move like a sundial. Then he nodded to the stairs.

"Can I see the rest?"

"Sure." Robert led the way. He dipped his head toward Ange when his sub's fingers hooked in Robert's waistband, the kid keeping pace with him. The stairs creaked, the sound their feet made echoing hollowly against the wall.

The next level held the bedroom and bath his parents had shared, on the other side of a smaller living space. He'd planned for that bedroom to be a home office. Just like the other two levels, this one had a fireplace. Closer to the stairs was a guest room and full bath. He kept them clean and ready in case he had a visitor, a habit his mother had always had in her own home.

He explained all that briefly, but continued on without leaving the stairs. Getting through the dense layer of memories on the first level had been difficult enough. Here they took up all the oxygen entirely. Having to step into his parents' bedroom, inhale the traces of their scents that he could still crazily detect in there? That would have made holding onto the light Ange had brought into the house—and not simply by opening the curtains —a far more precarious proposition.

He'd reached the third level. Imagining it through Ange's eyes, Robert could see his bedroom wasn't just generic. It was as colorless as bathwater in a white tub.

"Master."

Robert turned. Ange stood a couple steps below him on the stairs. Robert realized he seemed to be blocking the way, keeping Ange from coming up. A variety of expressions went through Ange's eyes. Robert glanced behind him, down toward the still visible opening to the second level guest room. Did Ange think Robert had altered his invitation, that Robert would share the space, but not his bed?

Not a chance in hell. Yeah, the second level guestroom was definitely the more cheerful of the two rooms, with pictures of sunflowers and a blue and yellow spread. He'd made an effort there, where he hadn't for the rest of the house. But that didn't matter. He didn't want Ange anywhere but with him. In his own king-sized bed, with room to stretch long male limbs, as well as spoon and tangle their bodies together.

When he extended his hand, confirming it, the worry left Ange's expression like the shedding of a coat.

Ange moved up to him, did a quick nuzzle of Robert's throat, then slid past him. Robert had intended this level to become a reading room. The built-in shelves were already crammed with Robert's favorite books. Ange's attention touched on those, but when he saw the open double doors revealing the master bedroom, he was on his way there.

Robert followed him, stopping at the threshold and leaning against it. His king-sized bed was tidily made with a solid beige spread. Brown and black pillows were arranged at the top. Mounted on the wall above the bed was a big vintage oil of a clipper ship from the 1970s, still in the original scarred frame.

At least the dresser had some items that personalized the space. There was the picture of his parents, flanking him in his uniform. Seeing him off for his second tour. His father's hand was on his shoulder, his mother pressed to Robert's side.

Next to the photo was a cast metal horse with a copper tone finish his grandfather had won at the county fair decades ago, when those kinds of toys had been offered as prizes.

His grandfather had had a barnful of cast iron toys, the kind of collection that would have given the *American Pickers* crew an orgasm. It was where Robert's interest in antique toys had started. Whenever he went to visit him, the older man would tell Robert about their history.

"Two things humans have always done," Grandpa once said, as he put a railway car into Robert's small hands. "Kill one another, and make toys for our kids. That's pretty much all there is to say about us."

While trying to decide what to do with himself after the

military, Robert had found himself holding that copper horse, turning it over in his hands.

"Make sure whatever you choose to do engages your passions," his father had said. "A man stays young with passion."

His grandfather had left Robert his collection. The value of it allowed Robert to sell a few pieces to fund the opening of his store, and the remainder formed his core start-up inventory. He'd built upon it, successfully enough he had this townhome and a life of comfort, but there were a couple pieces he'd never let go.

Like the first toy he'd bought as a collector. Ange had moved to the dresser and was looking at that piece now. Robert's lips quirked as Ange's sensitive fingers slid over it, his bent head evidence that it had captured his attention. And no wonder.

The Lehmann lithographed tin wind-up toy showed a baker peddling a tricycle. The tricycle bore a closed wagon for his wares. A chimney sweep had caught a ride, standing on the tailgate. There was a sweetness to the baker, with his bow-shaped mouth, round cheeks and curly hair. The chimney sweep wore a tightfitting black outfit head to toe, his hood close around his neck and framing his stern, unsmiling face.

He held what was intended to be a broom, but the long bristles and angle at which he held it, so it extended over the top of the closed wagon and rested on the baker's shoulder, gave the impression of a black hooded Dom with a flogger, teasing the nape of the baker as he furiously pedaled along.

Studying that clockwork toy, Robert had concluded its 1900s creator had nursed a few taboo fantasies.

Ange's chin tilted further right as he looked toward Robert, his hand still resting on the toy. Then his attention shifted past Robert to the solid dark wood bed frame. The tall spiral turned posts were sturdy enough to bind a sub against or between them. Not that he'd had the chance to explore that, since the bed had been a personal housewarming gift to celebrate the townhome purchase.

Ange had apparently registered the durability of the frame. His expression shifted to pure, provocative mischief.

"I haven't been in a bed this big in a long time."

Ange toed off his loose shoes in a blink, removed the hat. Taking a couple steps, he did a spin and a leap that tossed his body onto the bed like he was landing in a favorite swimming hole. He sprang up, put the hat back on at a rakish tilt and bounced on the mattress on the balls of his feet. Robert crossed his arms and shot him a stern look. But Ange had successfully dispelled his worries about the room. The only change it needed, at least for tonight, was the addition of Ange.

"Don't make me tan your hide, boy," he scolded gently.

Ange fell to a cross-legged position with a smile that went instantly from playful to wistful. The windows had blinds, pulled up and staying that way most of the time. As a result, the city lights added to that moon-and-snow brightness. Robert didn't need to turn on the electric lights.

Ange's teasing, the challenge in it, had changed the nature of Robert's thoughts, and his sub saw it, even before Robert did. Ange slid off the bed, gazing at his Master for just the right length of time before he lowered his eyes and knelt, lacing his fingers behind his head, lifting his chest and spreading his knees.

"What can I do for you, Master? How can I serve you?"

Ange hadn't indicated he'd ever belonged to a Dom, or been part of the BDSM club scene, but he offered and presented himself like he'd been born to it. And in so many ways, Robert had been Ange's undeclared Dom all these months.

"Take off the clothes. All of them."

Ange rose and complied, handing the hat to Robert first. Robert let his fingers run along the interior band as Ange's upper body did that graceful twist when he removed the tank. His hips shifted as he took off the jeans and socks. He hadn't worn underwear.

The light streaming through the window kissed pale marble

skin. He hadn't rushed, undressing slowly. Robert put the hat aside and his hand on the door frame, gripping hard.

There was a small sitting area near the bed, a sofa and chair grouping. Robert gestured to the sofa.

"Go there," he ordered. "Put your knees on the seat, hold onto the back."

After being steeped in the limitless pleasures offered by a dancer's body, how did anyone ever settle for anything different? As Ange complied, the divinely created choreography of muscle, flesh and bone made Robert's breath shorten and his cock harden. It also roused other feelings.

As he circled the sofa, he was conscious of Ange's attention on him, even when he went behind him, out of view. Laying his palm on the small of Ange's back, Robert felt flesh heat on both sides. He stood close, his leg against the back of Ange's thigh. He didn't say anything immediately, just absorbing the pleasure of the handsome, naked man waiting on his Master's desires. But as he thought of what Ange had said to him on the first floor, Robert's heart was too full not to say what he was thinking.

"There were days I thought, I just can't figure it out. And when I went to the store, my thought was... I'll go to Ange. Be with Ange. See Ange."

Ange's head tilted further down to show Robert his profile. His lips pressed together. "Master," he murmured.

Bending forward, Robert kissed Ange's brow, mouth lingering, teased by the strands of soft hair before he moved to Ange's temple, inhaled his scent. He detected the faint smell of sweat from earlier in the evening, first from when Ange had danced for Robert in the snow, and then when he'd given his body to him fully. Robert also smelled the store's Christmastime aromas— pine, cinnamon and sugar cookies. Plus the hint of clean snow and winter cold.

Robert was thankful he'd pocketed the small tube of lubricant from the store. He didn't want to step away from Ange to go rummage in the bathroom. He also stayed full dressed, merely unfastening his jeans and adjusting the boxers beneath to let him take care of things.

Then he put a knee on the sofa behind Ange, fitted himself to that welcoming, tight channel, and drilled in, slow but relentless, until he'd filled him to the hilt.

His sub. His Ange. In his house.

He deliberately chose not to indulge in foreplay. This was a full claiming, driving back the shadows trying to interfere with the glory of the change in their relationship. Ange registered it with a groan of need. His long fingers tightened on the sofa, a breath escaping him, followed by another more intent note as Robert pressed up tight behind him.

He wrapped his fingers around Ange's throat, let him feel that he had him, *had* him in all the ways that mattered. He gripped his hip with the other hand, but with Ange's strong arms bracing himself, Robert could shift that hold, reach around and grip his boy's cock.

Long and hard in his hand, he enjoyed stroking it, feeling the tremor that went through Ange, head to toe.

"Master...I'm afraid I'll make a mess...on your sofa."

Christ, he'd forgotten. His Duncan Phyfe rolled arm sofa with wooden trim. Yeah, probably not a good idea to risk that, though if anything was worth it, Ange was.

He found the condom in his pocket he thankfully didn't have to use on himself, and rolled it onto Ange. Then he started thrusting, enjoying every leisurely back and forth movement, the flex of Ange's shoulders and back, the working of his buttocks against Robert's pelvis. As the pulse beneath Robert's clamp on Ange's throat became more insistent, Ange's head dropped, his body rippling.

"Let go," Robert said, an unmistakable command, and his deepest wish. "I want to see you lose control."

Ange had no choice but to oblige, and Robert closed his eyes in bliss as those muscles clamped down, Ange's body rocking against him. The snow outside swirled against the windows from a sudden burst of wind. It disturbed the layer covering the roof deck, the tin roof over the outdoor bar. The moonlight found a clear spot in the metal to strike a reflection, as if a star had appeared right outside the window.

A soft cry broke from Ange's throat, and Robert pressed forward even as he pulled Ange's head back. Shifting his grip to the unruly hair, he tugged on it, brushed his open mouth over the stretched lips, teased them with his tongue. He collected all those sounds, the vibration, into himself, and let himself release as well, thrusting deeper, pushing Ange even harder against the side of the couch.

Ange lost his grip, his palm landing against the pane of the window behind the sofa. It left a steam-created outline when he grabbed the top again.

Slowly, they finished, bodies moving in an easy, rolling dance. Robert hadn't expected that resurgence of intensity so soon after the store. He should be bone-tired, and maybe he was.

But perhaps that was something else he'd associated with his home. Tiredness. Oldness. He'd shrugged on their mantle every time he crossed the threshold.

Ange was proving both of those things were self-mind-fuck bullshit. Robert was thirty-seven years old, damn it. Not eighty. He was more than capable and strong enough, not only to keep up with his sub's needs, but to keep that sub hopping to fulfill his Master's.

It was a grizzly bear roar kind of revelation, one that had his hands tightening on Ange's flesh. He bent, set his teeth to the top of a shoulder blade, giving Ange a sharp nip that held a promising threat, resulting in a satisfying shiver through Ange's flexible body.

Then Robert recalled a more practical issue. "Hell. Hold still."

He managed to shed his shirt and get it between their bodies, making sure when he pulled out, he had something to prevent the spill of his own seed from endangering the sofa or area rug. He used the pressure of his arm around Ange's waist to move them a shaky step back, then another. As he sat on the coffee table, he pulled Ange's fine ass down onto his lap. When he pressed his face to the center of Ange's back, Ange's fingers came up, covered Robert's, now on his chest. Ange's feet were braced between his spread ones.

"I didn't plan this too well," Robert said. "Now I have a couple wet things pressed to the table."

"And not a coaster to be seen," Ange said.

Robert started laughing. A good, from-the-gut sound. Second time tonight, and it seemed to please Ange just as much this time, because he turned his head fully to glance back at Robert with luminous eyes.

Robert tilted his head toward the glass doors that led to his rooftop deck. Next to them was the window where he could still see the faint smudge of Ange's handprint. "I haven't been out there since it started snowing. A perfectly pristine stage. You can dance again for me. The neighbors will get to watch."

Ange had followed his gaze, resting his face against Robert's jaw. But at Robert's words, his green eyes became more pensive, his relaxed mouth slightly more tense. Robert might not have noticed it, except the body in his arms also felt less post-coital relaxed.

"I like dancing for you," Ange said.

"But just for me," Robert guessed.

"Yes, sir."

Robert nuzzled the thick hair. He used the time to consider his next question, the obvious one. But just like examining the question of why he'd allowed time to come to a dismal halt in three-quarters of his house, he concluded it could be left alone, for now.

He'd also save the cast iron tub soak for later. He wanted to be in bed with his submissive. He gestured toward the bathroom. "Go clean yourself up. I'll do the same in a minute."

He got Ange started, lifting him up, letting his hands slide over the trim hips and firm ass, the upper thighs, but then he exercised a Master's prerogative, lingering. Ange responded as a good submissive would, picking up the cue, holding off on obeying his order until Robert was done touching him.

If Robert's cock had superpowers, it would stay hard all the time around the kid. But he could still enjoy the hell out of touching him while he was recharging. And doing more than that.

Robert turned Ange toward him. Ange's hand dug into his bare shoulder when Robert carefully stripped the condom from him. He dropped it into the nest of his balled-up shirt on the coffee table. Then he leaned forward, putting his mouth over the still semi-erect organ to suck on it slow, tasting the remnants of Ange's climax.

A half-moan came from Ange's lips, and his hand moved from Robert's shoulder to his short hair. It felt good, but so did other things.

Robert lifted his head, met Ange's eyes with a stern Master look. "Hands behind your back."

Ange performed the task with pleasurable reluctance, and Robert noted his command inspired a little kick in his sub's temporarily depleted cock. Some subs enjoyed and craved the dominance mainly in the framework of the sex, the foreplay. Others needed and desired reinforcement of it, whether sex was happening or not.

Robert already knew Ange was the latter kind of sub, which worked well, since he was that kind of Master. He wanted a sub with a limitless hunger for evidence of Robert's control.

Robert returned to a leisurely sucking and licking, exploring the area beneath the ridge. He curved his hand around the base, squeezing hard enough to make Ange's toes curl into the floor, and then he backed off and gave it a slap that had Ange's breath whistling through his teeth as he held his position.

"*Now* go clean yourself up. Then get into my bed."

Joy flashed through Ange's face. No matter the earlier cues, he still hadn't assumed sharing Robert's bed was a given. On one hand, Robert liked that Ange was the type of sub who would never take any reward as a given. On the other, sometimes he reminded Robert of the neglected and abused pet who couldn't quite trust he'd found himself a loving Master.

After Ange disappeared into the bathroom, Robert rose, tucking himself back into his boxers but leaving the jeans open as he went to his dresser. He studied the toy Ange had liked, ran his fingers over it. Stood there thinking a few minutes. Then he dug out two pairs of pajama bottoms, one with a drawstring that had half a chance of holding onto Ange's lean waist. He put the garment on the foot of the bed.

"Do you want me to wear those?" Ange asked. He was back, the shadows and light etching curves of muscle.

"No," Robert said. "Not right now. They'll keep you warm when we get up for breakfast."

He moved across the room, cupped Ange's face, running a thumb along the sculpted jaw, the sharp cheekbone. "I'll be right back."

Robert dropped a hand to his waist, squeezed, then stepped into the bath. He pushed the door to the jamb but didn't completely close it, giving himself enough privacy to do things that weren't all that fabulous to do in front of a lover. A smile touched his lips as Robert heard Ange winding the baker toy. From the sounds that followed, Robert guessed he was letting it roll across the area rug and then clack across the wood floor, until it bumped against the wall.

"Wow, it still works," he heard Ange say.

"Yeah. Someone took good care of it, didn't let the original clockwork get corroded." He paused, glancing at himself in the mirror. He saw a man with sharp brown eyes, a body in good shape, posture straight and strong, hands half curled, wanting to take. He liked what he saw. "It was the first valuable collectible I bought."

Robert had taken the other pair of pajama bottoms into the bath with him, so when he emerged, he wore only those. Ange had picked up the toy and was putting it back on the dresser. As he faced Robert, Robert's gaze coursed over all the bare flesh and graceful male beauty. Ange was standing in profile to him, so that moonlight gleam on his flank and the round of his shoulder, his dirty-blond hair, the smooth pelt of it over his dangling cock, made a picture.

"Here's my most recent valuable acquisition," he said quietly. Ange's sensuous lips pressed into a line. He was looking at Robert, too, his green eyes coursing over Robert's chest and arms and flashing with a hunger that went beyond sex.

They were likely both done with that for a while, but this was a different kind of hunger, one that had an answer in Robert's heartbeat against the wall of his chest.

He glanced toward the toy. "You like it."

Ange nodded. "It's like the secret code to a kids' clubhouse. Something that says we're here, and we know about each other."

"Way I've always thought about it, too. Probably a big part of why I hang onto it rather than selling it."

At Ange's chuckle, Robert's smile left his face. Ange cocked his head. "What, Master?" he asked.

"I know you're a grown man, Ange, but there are two times in particular when I know it. First, when you laugh. It's there, rich and deep." Robert crossed the room to him, and his gaze dipped. "Second, when I see you naked."

Ange's lips curved, the gesture sensual and yearning at once. "I feel like both man and boy with you. Because it feels like you need both. And I want that."

"That's another way you prove your age. You've seen enough, experienced enough, to know the things we learn as adults."

Robert's gaze touched on the toys on the dresser. "Even though we never fully leave behind the kid inside us."

Two things humans have always done...Kill one another, and make toys for our kids. That's pretty much all there is to say about us.

But a whole hell of a lot of things existed between those two points of a human's existence. Robert slid his hands to Ange's waist, thumbs caressing as he tightened his fingers over it. He moved them to the back, cupped his ass, and brought him up full against him, uttering a growling moan against Ange's lips as their cocks rubbed. Ange opened to him, let him take over. They swayed together, and Robert immersed himself in the kiss, tongues playing while he nipped at Ange's lips. His demand was urgent enough to get the kid going, his cock trying hard to come back to life. Robert took his time, savoring, but eventually he drew back and shot him a hard look.

"Didn't I tell you to put your ass in my bed? What are you still doing out of it?"

A flash of rueful amusement crossed Ange's face, but he obediently turned toward the bed. Robert followed close, his hand on Ange's lower back, caressing his ass, guiding him there.

They worked together to pull down the cover, blanket and sheet. As Ange got in, he shivered. Robert had a warming pad for the sheets. With all the windows in this room, it could get drafty in winter. Before he went into the bathroom, he should have thought to turn on the feature, warm the linens. He bent and clicked it on, but he had a more instant fix. Himself.

He slid in. "Come here."

The boy-versus-man duality was there in how eagerly Ange responded, snuggling closer, putting his head down on Robert's chest, even as the arms that circled Robert were strong. His semi-turgid cock pressed against Robert's thigh as his other leg crossed over it.

Hell. Robert wanted to fuck him again. Ange wouldn't refuse him. He'd let his Master have him as often as he wanted.

Robert curbed the desire, though. He was good with letting

the wanting simmer. There was a pleasure in that. And Ange accepted it, his cock settling back down as he also sank deeper into Robert's embrace, his body slackening.

It had been a long day for them both. Even so, Robert found it miraculous, the way Ange slid into sleep within a matter of minutes. In Robert's arms.

Was there any greater gift in the whole damn world than that? His lover asleep in his embrace, curved into Robert's body like they were made to be twined together like this, from now until the grave. Maybe even in the grave.

Ange's hand was tucked under his cheek, folded, the eyes lowered so his lashes fanned his cheeks. Robert remembered how snowflakes had caught on them when he'd danced.

Robert stayed up a little longer, gazing out the window, his hands trailing up and down Ange's back. The gunshot scars on his stomach didn't go all the way through, which meant they'd likely been hollow points, fragmenting to prevent a dangerous exit beyond the target. The downside was they wreaked havoc inside the body, and they'd hit an area that could have made that damage lethal. The kid should be dead.

He didn't like that thought one damn bit, and the way it speared through him must have reached Ange. His sub shifted, his brow creasing in sleep, an uncertain sound coming from his lips. Robert crooned to him soothingly, pushed the disturbing thoughts out of his head. Remembering how Ange had reacted to him touching those scars at the store, Robert had consciously avoided making anything more than incidental contact with them ever since.

When offered a miracle, people had a tendency not to let themselves get lost in the joy of it for too long. Pretty soon after, they started to worry when it would end. He was no less susceptible to that weakness than anyone else. However, he was a proactive and extremely capable man. He'd figure out what threats to head off, anticipate, diffuse. He already saw the flags, most of them having to do with what he didn't know about Ange.

But those gunshot wounds, as well as his own shrapnel scars, proved there were things he couldn't see coming. Or couldn't in good conscience step out of the way to avoid, because of what he was protecting.

He made a vow to keep that in mind with Ange. Protecting his own self wasn't an issue. Protecting Ange, helping him... loving him? That was everything.

CHAPTER FIVE

*R*obert woke about an hour past his normal time, greeted by the smell of coffee and the sound of a crash downstairs, like the clang of metal pots. It didn't sound ominous, and since Ange wasn't in the bed with him, the source was obvious. It did make him curious.

He slid out of bed, shrugged into his robe. The pajama bottoms at the foot of the bed were gone. He could hope Ange had grabbed one of Robert's sweatshirts, but doubted it. While he'd bounce on his bed, Ange would have been hesitant to go through somewhere as private as Robert's closet or dresser drawers without his explicit permission. Robert should have put another robe or sweatshirt on the end of the bed with the pants. He was out of practice for looking three or four steps ahead to cover all domestic bases for a sub in his care. He'd work on that.

Pulling a flannel shirt off a rack to take with him, he headed downstairs. He didn't find Ange in the kitchen, but thank the gods, he found the coffee.

When Robert arrived at the store in the mornings, he was alert and ready to work. But he didn't function as a human being until he had his first cup of coffee at home. Since Ange didn't sound in any danger, he stayed in the kitchen long enough to pour himself a cup, add French Vanilla creamer and a sugar substitute. While he did that and took a bracing sip, he listened to the intriguing mix of thumps, clatters and mutterings coming up the stairwell.

Robert descended the creaking wood steps and peered into the open door of the garage. One half of it sheltered Robert's classic 1985 M6 BMW. The rest of the space was over-crammed storage.

Seeing Ange's hindquarters in the air as he bent over a box wasn't a bad way to start the day. Since he was collecting a variety of items from the floor and putting them carefully back in the box, Robert deduced he'd been correct. Ange had likely tipped forward a box marked "non-fragile" on the upper shelves and brought half the overloaded contents down on his head.

There was nothing on those top shelves of specific significance. The contents had meaning more as a whole, in their continued presence in the garage, within touching distance. This particular box had been filled with pots, tools and garden supplies his mother had used at her Virginia home. Nothing fragile; just too loved to be left behind. Leaving things behind, or giving them away, was an acknowledgment the person would never use them again.

She'd nursed a thought she might do some pot gardens at Robert's place. She hadn't. There were so many little deaths on the way to the actual thing, he now understood the saying "one foot in the grave." And hated it.

"What are you doing?"

Ange straightened and spun, guilt on his face. "I saw how you felt about the way the house looked last night, and it got me thinking. You decorated the store so beautifully, and I started looking around in here..."

While Robert digested the run of nervous words, he noticed the pajama bottoms barely hung onto Ange's hips. As he'd suspected, Ange hadn't grabbed a warmer shirt, but he'd donned the sleeveless tank from last night. It drew Robert's interested eyes to the curves of his exposed biceps and shoulders. Since Ange was cold, his nipples pressed against the thin fabric.

Robert closed the distance between them, setting the coffee aside to reach out, grip the drawstring and loosen it. The pants fell even lower, down to Ange's pubic area, exposing the intriguing triangle of muscle and hint of darker blond hair there.

The move effectively halted Ange's flow of words, but if it hadn't, Robert's mouth would have. Robert brought him closer, hooking his arm around his neck and taking those lips with his own. While he did that, he dropped his coffee-warmed hand to cup Ange under the thin cloth, stroke the organ that sprang to instant, mouthwatering hardness under his touch. Ready for his command.

Ange made a quiet noise, and his hands were on Robert inside his open robe, on his bare waist and upper back. Robert raised his head after a good long satisfying kiss, and ran a fond hand through Ange's thick hair. Realizing he still had the flannel shirt tossed over his shoulder, he pulled it off, draping it around Ange's shoulders.

"Now put that on, settle down, and tell me what you're up to. And pull those pants back up to your waist. Stop tempting me."

With Ange's lean waist, Robert knew the pants were a delightfully lost cause, but he enjoyed watching him make the attempt. With a Master's satisfaction, he also marked how Ange had to fight through the haze of lust to find sleeves and then his words again. He left the shirt pleasantly open. "I was looking at the living room last night, and thinking we should bring some Christmas to it. A garage usually doesn't have things in it that are so private, so I figured it would be okay to come in here and get some ideas."

"Did you?"

Ange's uncertain look bloomed into a tentative smile as he registered the teasing warmth in Robert's voice. "Yeah. We could rearrange the furniture, clear out some space and set up a Christmas tree on that first level. There's one down here, and we have those blue and green lights left over from decorating the store. They'd pick up the colors on the curtains, and there's some other cool stuff in here we could turn into tie-backs, keep them open and let the light in."

It was his parents' tree, but Robert could already imagine it decorated in more of a Robert-Ange fashion, just as Ange had described.

"Oh, and this would really tie in the colors. Not just for Christmas." Ange shimmied through the clutter to the far back corner, disappearing behind stacks of boxes he'd obviously shifted to access the area. Some thumping ensued as he retrieved what he wanted to show Robert, then those stacks of boxes were swaying, telegraphing Ange's return. It reminded Robert of a gopher tunneling his way across the yard. The thought gave him a smile that greeted Ange's expectant look as he emerged.

He was carrying a wooden carousel horse. Robert had picked it up from a roadside vintage store on one of his trips, and had forgotten he'd had it. On the horse's saddle was a painting of a dragon and a knight having tea together, done in predominant colors of blue and green.

"Since this is beat up enough it's not really collectible quality, we could screw a piece of glass to the top of the saddle. Get rid of the sectional, use this as a side table between your two wing-backs. Add some throw pillows that pick up the colors."

Maybe someone else would find his actions presumptuous, but over the months since he'd hired him, Robert had given Ange his head on this kind of thing at the store. It had started as a desire to build his confidence, like taking him on errands. But Ange paid close attention. The store's décor reflected Robert's abiding interest in antique and vintage toys, and his preference for a classy upscale collector vibe, well-integrated with whimsy.

Ange's suggestions and changes had always respected that, while his childlike nature and artistic flair had given it an appealing twist. The result was an atmosphere that integrated the past and the future, showing how what mattered most never really changed.

When he'd found Ange in the alley with the broken toy Robert had tossed, he'd explained he couldn't sell a collectible that was broken or damaged. Ange had repaired it well, though, and one of his earliest suggestions had been to offer such toys for sale to those who couldn't afford collectible prices. They might be willing to pay half price to have toys that in all other respects looked just as good as those the collectors wanted. And their kids could play with them, just as the original manufacturer had intended.

The first day they'd set up Ange's "Recycled Piece of Yesterday" section, Robert had dedicated a portion of their window display to it. Not only had people come in to buy those pieces, overall traffic had increased. On that launch day, two separate young professional couples had made impulse buys of antique Victorian rocking horses and other pieces to decorate their babies' nurseries.

"Oh." Ange was continuing, spilling over with ideas. "I also found a frame and some corkboard, and put those together with some old pictures. I found them in a container on one of the lower shelves. I thought it would go great on the wall headed up the stairs, right there at the end of the banister before you turn into the kitchen."

He went to another corner of the garage, where the frame was leaning face forward against a shelf. When he brought it over for Robert's inspection, Robert set his coffee aside and took it in both hands.

Ange had found the memorabilia box that belonged to Robert's father. He'd fished out the postcards from his dad's travels, back when he'd been in the military and later, after Vietnam, when he was working for a computer company and traveling to meet clients. Ange had turned one of the postcards over and fixed it in the middle, a centerpiece for all the others.

Robert read his father's broad script, the message he'd written to his mother.

I never knew there was so much to see in the world.

Robert backed up to the steps, sat down, still holding the frame. After a long moment, he bent forward, placed it carefully against the set of metal shelves to his right so he could keep looking at it.

"It's a great idea, Ange," he said, his voice thick. "I like it a lot."

Ange's expression moved from careful observation into relief. Beneath it was an expectant, hopeful longing, left over from Robert touching him. He wanted to be touched some more. Wanted Robert to need things from him. Who was Robert to deny him?

Well, only in the ways that they both liked.

"Bring me my coffee," he told him, and when Ange complied, he ran a hand up Ange's thigh. He tugged at the pajama pants, pulling them down enough that he could enjoy running a thumb over Ange's hipbone. Ange squirmed involuntarily as he hit the ticklish spot, but Robert liked watching him fight it, try to stay still for his Master.

"We have a lot to do today," Robert said. Thinking about it conjured anticipation, a little uncertainty, but he wasn't nervous. He was looking forward to the things he wanted to show Ange, parts of his daily, outside-the-store life he hadn't shared with him except in hints of conversation.

And then there was Ange's Christmas gift, which he planned to give to him tonight.

"So." Robert took a sip of his coffee. "We'll grab some breakfast and then I need to make a cake to take by a friend's group home." He lifted his gaze. "Maybe while we're out we should hit the barber's, cut that mop."

Ange ducked away when Robert grabbed playfully at the thick blond strands. "You don't mean that. You like my hair."

Yeah, he did. He'd like to seize a handful of it and hold Ange still while he bit his neck, tasted him. Add to the two hickeys he'd given him last night, the faint reddish-blue bruising provocatively visible, above and below the collar.

He rose. Standing on the bottom step made him a head taller than Ange. Robert rested a hand on his shoulder. "After the group home, we'll grab the store truck. Load up that sectional and a couple other pieces from the living room. Take all of it over to the Salvation Army. Somebody will like getting that for Christmas. That'll give us room to put the tree in the living room, open up some space in there."

He glanced up the stairway. "That should cover half of any workout I need today. Getting that sectional up there was a son of a bitch. The pieces were too wide for the lift."

"So cake first. For energy."

Robert shot his sub a mock stern look. "You and your sweet tooth. We're making you a proper breakfast first."

"I saw frosted Pop-Tarts in your pantry."

"Christ." But thinking of Ange rummaging through the pantry like a squirrel brought a smile back to Robert's face.

He led the way back into the kitchen, directing Ange to pull out the eggs. As he did, Robert mentally sifted through the day's to-dos. There should be time for all of it. He'd known when he woke up this morning that Ange's Christmas gift was a time commitment of its own, commanding most of their evening.

He couldn't wait to see how Ange reacted to it.

When he'd gone to the store last night, Robert had intended to drop broad hints about the gift, get Ange excited and thinking about it. Ange liked the gift giving and receiving process. He'd really gotten into picking out gifts for their regular customers. Small things, but with special meaning, like the German ornament of a dog in a purse for Mrs. Fitzgerald. Or the miniature hand-painted train that ran on a track, so small it could sit on Mr. Dixon's desk. The eighty-year-old was still on the board of the company he'd started. He showed up regularly to his permanent office there.

Many of those customers, who considered themselves Ange's friend as much as Robert's, had dropped off similarly chosen small gifts. Ange had treated each one as if he'd been given gold, frankincense and myrrh by the three wise men.

As such, when Robert had started thinking about the best Christmas gift for Ange, the answer had been pretty obvious. Maybe Robert's subconscious had known even then he was going to take their relationship to a different level. The gift, while bigger than a small ornament or toy train, had been chosen with the same eye to its special significance to the recipient.

He wanted to start teasing him about it now, get him excited over it the way Robert was, but he would put some thought into how best to drop the hints. In his opinion, that was as important as the care taken to wrap a physical gift.

While Robert considered that, he whipped them up some quick scrambled eggs and bacon, made sure Ange ate a proper amount, then they got to work on the cake.

Ange's talent for seasonings and cooking didn't extend to baking. He showed surprisingly little knowledge of that process. However, like everything else, he absorbed everything Robert told him, retrieving ingredients and helping to mix them. The soul warming smells of sugar, vanilla and butter for the old-fashioned layer cake soon filled the kitchen.

Robert was an okay cook, but this was a recipe of his father's he'd done enough to excel at it. When he let Ange taste the batter off the mixers, Robert cherished the sparkle in his eyes. It was like he'd never tasted cake batter. It made Robert want to taste him, an urge strong enough he knew he wasn't going to deny himself, no matter what was on their schedule.

There was time for indulgence.

"Come here." He put Ange in front of the bowl of batter, Robert behind him, hands resting on Ange's hips.

"Do you want me to stir?"

"No. Keep still." Robert applied pressure to bend Ange over

the bowl. "Draw in a deep breath. It smells like all the good parts of wanting, doesn't it?"

"Yes," Ange said, his breath shortening as Robert stepped closer, pressed against his backside.

"Hands on the counter on either side of you. Lift that gorgeous ass that belongs to me."

Lust flashed in Ange's eyes as he complied. Lean muscle rippled along his long arms as Robert ran callused hands up under the tank to caress and stroke his abs, the light down of hair that led beneath the drawstring. Then up, to his chest, over the nipples. Ange's torso stretched in appreciation, his backside lifting even further.

"That's it. When I touch you, I like the way your body speaks to me. Asking me to be fucked. But never telling me. You're a good boy, respectful of your Master."

"Yes, sir." A quiver went through his ass, now under Robert's hand. He pushed the pajama bottoms down to Ange's ankles so he could see the bare beauty of it.

Where to start? He had a million perfect choices. He went for a handful of the confectioner's sugar he'd be dusting on the top of the cake when he was done. He pushed the flannel shirt and tank up to Ange's shoulder blades and smoothed the sugar onto the flesh below, letting the rest sprinkle over his ass and to the floor. Then Robert followed the sugar with his mouth, tasting the hint of sweetness on Ange's back, taking his time, sucking and licking down the valley of his spine, over his ribs, to the small of his back and the rise of his ass.

As he pushed his hands between Ange's thighs to cup and squeeze his balls, Robert nipped at those delectable cheeks, the upper thighs.

Ange's head dropped back, that guttural moan coming from him. From his body language, Robert knew he was absorbing how he was being touched the same way Robert was experiencing it. Full sensory input.

Robert rose to his feet, a possessive hand on Ange's hip

again. He reached over him, to the pottery container for cooking implements. The metal spatula with a dozen nice holes cut into it was in easy reach. He saw Ange watch his hand close over it, felt the erratic breath bellow his chest, then escape those distracting parted lips. The quick look Ange shot him told him he wanted what Robert intended, even as his eyes held that titillating apprehension that a Master liked to see.

"Lift up on your toes. Spread your legs as much as the pajama bottoms will let you."

It tightened all those muscles in a beautiful display of male power, all at Robert's command. When he landed the first swat, Ange jumped, let out a muffled yelp.

Yeah, he'd made it a little hard, because he'd wanted just that reaction.

"What do you say?" Robert growled in his ear.

"More, Master. Please." The desperation in Ange's voice spread inside Robert's chest like Christmas cheer.

He gave him several more swats to increase the feeling, and to reinforce the lesson of who was who in their relationship. They could be playful, Ange could redecorate, but when his Master gave him an order, he'd follow it. And be rewarded with punishment.

He inhaled the vanilla and sugar flavored ingredients, so evocative, the smell became the anticipated taste on the tongue. It wasn't the only thing in the room that had that capability. He thought of how often he'd absorbed Ange through one sense, like sight, and it had translated to the others, even before he was close enough to touch him.

Robert had intended to keep this to foreplay, but the Crisco was too damn convenient, the top already popped off. He scooped some up on his fingers and rubbed it on Ange's rim. As his knuckles pressed into that warm crease, he registered the jump in Ange's shoulder and arm muscles.

He had his head bent over the bowl, so he was getting an even more heady dose of that tempting scent. He also looked as if he was riding the same overwhelming wave of sensations Robert was feeling, only his were coming from the teasing touch of Robert's tongue on the back of his neck and shoulder blades, the firm pressure of his lips, his hands on his long, graceful body. The probing touch of his greased-up fingers, promising that his ass was going to be plundered by Robert's thick cock in a matter of seconds.

Robert fitted the head of his cock to the slickened opening, and sunk in. Growled at the pleasure of it. Pulled back, did a slow return. He cupped his hand over the boy's throat, drew his chin to the side to let him feel the pressure. His fingers rested on Ange's pulse as he brushed his lips over the sandpaper jaw. His boy—his man—hadn't shaved yet this morning.

"You have the sweetest, tightest ass," he said, and Ange expelled a shaky breath.

"Thank you, Master. It's yours."

"I know." Robert reached between Ange's body and the counter and gripped his dick. "What about this?"

"Yours, too."

"You going to touch it without my permission? Ever? Even when I'm not around?"

"No, sir. Thank you, sir."

That add-on, the fervency of it, told Robert his response wasn't just in the moment. Ange wanted that control. He gobbled up any rules Robert offered like a gift. The stricter, the better.

Robert was certain Ange had been a professional dancer, or had been striving to achieve that goal. That took discipline, total commitment, no shortcuts. Was it chicken or egg? Had the boundaries of submission made the structure of dance even more appealing, or vice versa?

Maybe it didn't matter. Perhaps it was like the relationship of arteries and veins, giving and taking to keep the heart pumping.

"Put some batter on your finger and let me taste it."

Ange complied, bringing his hand back to Robert's mouth.

Robert tasted, sucked deep on the finger as he stroked. Gripped, and felt Ange's cock convulse in his grasp. Ange let out another little moan, a grunt of need.

"You're thinking of my mouth on your cock," Robert said. "I'm thinking about it, too. But right now, I just want to fuck you into total oblivion. Push the bowl away, put your cheek down on the counter. Cross your hands over the middle of your back."

When Ange obeyed, Robert adjusting with him for the change in stance, Robert put one hand over his crossed wrists, a firm hold that told Ange where his hands should stay. Robert used that hold to increase the power of his thrusts, driving into the welcoming channel that gripped him so blissfully tight. It shoved Ange's thighs against the wooden cabinet below the sink, making the doors rattle.

"God..." Ange muttered it in a near whisper, biting his bottom lip, eyes half closed. His fingers curved tight over Robert's knuckles, seeking contact. His thighs quivered, his ass lifting so they were perfectly fitted each time they came together.

"You hold out," Robert warned.

"Always, Master. Never...without your permission."

He might never let an hour pass without Ange bent over or on his knees to take his cock. Or dancing for him, sleeping beside him. Robert's balls drew up. It was those provocative images as much as the physical sensations that had him spilling himself.

"Come, Ange," he snarled.

Ange's hips jerked, cock pulling in Robert's grip as his warm release flooded over Robert's fingers. Ange pressed his cheek hard to the counter as he ground back into Robert, taking him deep, using his body to beg Robert to stay that way within him.

Maybe neither of them would ever stop wanting, feeding each other with that spiraling desire, a meal that always satisfied but never relieved the hunger.

Robert moved with him, making sure Ange got the full measure of his squeezing grip. He made it a bit rougher at the end so Ange's mouth flattened and breath whistled, body bucking. Not to fight Robert's demands, but to dance with it, like the push-pull of a tango.

Did the kid ballroom dance? If he didn't, Robert was sure he'd pick it up quick. He'd never been so glad his mother had made him take those lessons with her as a teen. There was a gay club in Charlotte that had a ballroom night. They could dress up, tango, lambada, waltz...he loved thinking of doing that with Ange. Maybe Ange could dance in front of others if they were dancing as a couple.

They'd both finished, and he was having those thoughts while leaning against his boy's curved back, Ange's skin slightly damp from their exertions. As Robert nuzzled between his shoulder blades, he released Ange's cock to rub his come into his hard abs and higher up. He did a teasing, slick circle around the nipple that had Ange's ass flexing against him.

"Didn't put a condom on you," Robert murmured. "You made a mess. Take off all your clothes and use those to clean it up. The clothes need a wash and I want you naked."

He slowly withdrew from Ange, trailing his hands down his sides, the caress a balance to the stern words. He brought Ange up but then gripped his shoulder, pushing him down to his knees. Ange's gaze lingered on his cock as Robert tucked it back into his pajama bottoms.

Retrieving a washcloth from under the sink, Robert wet it down and tossed it next to Ange's crumpled pajama bottoms and shirt. "Get to it," he said. "We have cake to finish and showers to take."

Ange's eyes contained that spark of challenge that wasn't really a challenge, more a spirited response. He'd do as he was told, but he was aware of the teasing nature of it, Robert making him come, then accusing Ange of making a mess.

After pouring the cake batter into the pans and putting them in the pre-heated oven, Robert poured himself a fresh cup of coffee and leaned against the counter.

"Good thing we pushed the bowl out of reach," he observed, watching the flex of Ange's ass and thighs, the vulnerable soles of his feet, as his sub cleaned the floor and cabinets. "Else the recipients might have gotten a little something extra in that cake."

From what he knew of the group home's unusual members, they might very well appreciate that.

Ange managed a laugh at the joke, but Robert's keen ears picked up an odd note to it. Ange had kept his head down these past few minutes. As he straightened to sit back on his heels, clean-up done, his back was to Robert. A tremor went through the arm holding the washcloth.

"Hey." Robert immediately set aside his coffee and dropped to a squat in front of Ange. Taking the cloth and clothes from Ange's tense hands, he tossed them toward the laundry room and touched Ange's jaw. "Look at me," he said. "That's not a request."

Ange flicked a desperate look at him. He wasn't crying, but his eyes were glassy, and he swallowed as if the lump in his throat could choke him. Robert sat down against the cabinets and brought Ange down between his bent knees, leaning him back against him. Robert made sure the skirt of his robe was spread on the floor beneath him, between his spread thighs. It cushioned Ange's ass from the cold tile. Cupping his hand over Ange's forehead, he pushed it so his head rested on Robert's shoulder.

Ange tentatively gripped Robert's other hand, lying against his chest. When Robert didn't object, he brought it up so he could kiss Robert's rough knuckles.

"That's my boy," Robert said. "All good. Talk to me. Tell me what's going on."

A breath lifted Ange's shoulders, and he relaxed further. "I haven't felt this safe in a long time," he said. "It's...I didn't expect the way that would make me feel."

Robert's brow creased. "Explain that."

Ange's temple rested against Robert's jaw as he spoke. "I don't mean like safe from being mugged. More like a safety net, under my heart and soul. Keeping them from hurting so much. Feeling so lost."

The hollowness to Ange's voice suggested he was in that lost place. Robert closed both arms around him, crossing them over Ange's chest. When his hands curved over his sub's biceps, he had him fully banded against Robert's solid body.

"That has to do with the shit that you won't talk to me about," he said, not unkindly. When Ange tensed, he sharpened his tone, a reminder and reproof. "I'm not going to make you talk about it. I never have, have I? I haven't pushed it, but we're getting close to the time that needs to change, Ange. You're smart enough to know why. When you get lost like that—so bad you end up homeless and bleeding in an alley—withdrawing and closing yourself down isn't going to help anyone find you. Is it?"

Ange remained silent. Adjusting his head, Robert saw his brow was creased, the lowered green eyes troubled. He could feel all of it struggling inside of Ange.

Two years of grief had made Robert act in inexplicably self-destructive ways. Since whatever gripped Ange was at least as bad as that, Robert got how hard it was to do what seemed healthy and logical to someone not in that dark place. And hammering him with it might just increase the depth of that blackness.

So he quelled the automatic reaction to say more. Instead, he just held him, giving him that safety net, the reassurance that he was here. Only moments before, Robert had taken him thoroughly, at every level. He was going to teach Ange that was something he could count on, not just during sex.

The current surroundings had to help. The two of them were

cocooned by the smell of cake batter, the angles and gleam of stainless-steel appliances, the ticking of the wall clock. The blast of warm air from the vent above them. They were home. Together.

Robert was just about to bring them back toward the idea of showers and more casual conversation when Ange surprised him by giving him more.

"Sometimes it's like one of those stories where you're in an alternate reality, one step off from everyone else. You've gotten knocked there, and you don't know how to get knocked back."

Robert brushed a kiss over his cheekbone. "Maybe it's like a rebirth. You have to come through a womb, so to speak, to get back into the world with everyone else. And birth is a pretty rough process."

"Yeah." Ange shivered.

"Hey. It's okay. Stay with me."

"I'm here." He gripped Robert's forearm with both hands, hard. Maybe he meant it as a reinforcement of the words, but there was desperation in the clasp. The shiver rocked Ange again, his muscles getting as rigid as if he was being hit, not held.

Robert uttered a quiet noise of reassurance. As he did, he adjusted his hold, his palm brushing one of the gunshot scars on Ange's abdomen. It hadn't been intentional, but Ange jerked, a noise of pain coming from him. Robert didn't react to that, instead keeping the hand moving. His palm slid over his pectoral, along the bump of the nipple, and up to caress the base of his throat. He made Ange tip his head back to Robert's shoulder again, so he had to uncoil the tense curve of his back, lean into him.

"Easy," he said. "Stay with me right here. Still safe. We have errands to do today. Cake to deliver. No time for that nonsense. Right?"

Ange dropped his head against Robert's, a supplication. When Robert stroked his hair, tugged it, Ange sighed.

"Sorry," he said. "Don't know why I... Everything was feeling so good."

Robert knew why. Grief, loss and trauma had a lot of overlap in the ways humans dealt with them. Strong emotions could stay buried as long as you were vigilant. But when all the walls came down—like during a powerful coupling that was as much emotional as physical—they could break loose. Robert needed to help Ange understand that letting that happen wouldn't be the end of the world. Not even close. It could be the beginning of better things.

He'd been around Ange long enough to know how to help him handle this kind of episode. Only today, Robert had the right, and the opening, to respond to it a different way.

"Turn your head toward my shoulder."

When Ange complied, Robert put his mouth on his exposed throat and began to tease the flesh he'd marked with tongue and teeth, over and above the collar. He imposed demand and offered tenderness, a devastating combination to a man who craved a collar the way Ange did.

Ange's neck fascinated Robert more than any other man's had. With Ange's entire body trained for dance, the turn of his head, the way he dropped it back when in the throes of passion or pleasure, the dip of his chin as he was focused on something, highlighted the strength and grace of it, the flexibility.

When Robert tugged on the collar with his teeth, Ange's groan said he loved Robert's reminder of ownership. "You're here with me," Robert said against his flesh. "No matter what thoughts or memories come for you, you're never any farther from me than this collar is from your flesh. That's part of the message it sends. I'm the shelter in the storm."

"You're also the storm itself. It carries me away." Ange dug his fingers deeper into Robert's forearm. "Like a tornado. I've dreamt about dancing in one. Spinning and flying. When you're inside me, thrusting, demanding, pulling everything from me, it's like that. I feel like that. I don't want it to end. Even as you make me need to come so bad I can't think straight."

Robert liked hearing that, a lot, so he kept working on his throat, dropping his hand down between Ange's spread legs to grip his cock, already trying to rise again. "I want to keep you wanting like that. I like knowing my sub is ready for me whenever I want his ass. His throat. His mouth. Every part of him."

Hell. He wasn't ready to go again, in theory, though it felt like every other part of him was.

"But..." He transitioned the neck devouring back to dragging, easy kisses, nuzzles of the pounding pulse, "This is *not* getting my to-do list done. Go take a shower while I finish up with the cake. Put your clothes in the wash on quick cycle and I'll throw them in the dryer. You can grab a warmer shirt from my closet." He briefly touched Ange's throat. "This is leather, so you're allowed to take it off for the shower and put it back on right afterward."

"I wish I didn't have to take it off at all."

With an act of will, Robert got them back up on their feet and gave Ange a push. His sub wasn't helping, gazing at him as if he wanted Robert's mouth back on him. Robert retrieved the spatula, waved it at him. "Go. Or else."

Ange grinned, but turned away. Spun back, dashed in close to lay both hands on Robert's face, plunder his mouth for a heated, wet kiss, his body pressed fully against Robert's. Then he slipped away, headed for the stairs in a flurry of rippling muscle and twitching ass motion.

"You will pay for that," Robert promised.

"I hope so," Ange called back, his feet fast and sure, pounding up the stairs.

Robert shook his head, smiling. While he waited for the cake to finish baking, he turned his attention to the large gift basket he had stowed in the pantry. He'd been loading it up with small packages, nesting them in red and green paper straw. He had a plastic bag of ribbon and silk greenery, holly branches with bright red berries, and he laid them out next to the basket. He intended to festoon the handle with them as a finishing touch, and adjust the straw to accommodate the cake tin he'd use for the finished and cooled layer cake.

As he did all that, he kept an ear on the sounds of showering above. He sipped his coffee and let his mind drift, relaxed. Eventually, he remembered he hadn't told Ange he had a couple unopened toothbrushes in the bath cabinet, and to use whatever toiletries he needed, so he headed up the stairs. Robert had shown nothing but approval of the kid going through the garage and redecorating the living room. However, he knew it wouldn't change Ange's hesitancy about rummaging in more personal places unless directly invited. It was one of the interesting mix of things about his submissive.

His collared submissive. Best Christmas gift ever, really.

There was a cheap monthly rate gym within walking distance of the store, and Ange used their shower facilities, since there wasn't a full bathroom at the store. As such, Robert had expected him to linger in the indulgence of a private shower, but he hadn't.

Steam was still drifting out of the bathroom, but the door to his walk-in closet was open. As he stepped across the bedroom threshold and gained a view of the closet's interior, he came up short. Ange was standing right up against the wall of Robert's shirts. He had two full handfuls of them, the fabric against his face as he inhaled their scent, brushed the cloth against his jaw.

Robert braced a hand against the bedroom doorframe. Yeah, it was cliché, smelling a lover's clothes. But seeing someone actually do it, versus seeing it in a movie or reading about it in a book, hit him low in the gut.

Ange lifted his head. Whatever he saw in Robert's face kept him still, quiet, his expression open, not hiding from Robert exactly why he was doing what he was doing. Ange wanted to be close to him, even when he wasn't in the same room with him. He wanted and needed him.

"I'm finally here," he said at last, his voice low.

"You're finally here," Robert said. "I've never been so grateful for a gift from God in my entire life."

He came into the closet, wrapped his arms around his sub. Ange's hands slid under them to clasp Robert's back and waist. Robert kissed his hair, his mouth, and indulged another deep draught of his lips as Ange held onto him. They swayed against the bank of clothes. When at long last Robert raised his head, stared into Ange's gratifyingly dazed-looking eyes, he nodded, once. Slow. A confirmation for them both.

"There's a basket of sample toiletries under the sink, including unopened toothbrushes. Whatever you need here is yours."

Robert left to tend the cake, and Ange rejoined him in no time. After he examined the gift basket and Robert explained the contents, he hefted himself onto the counter to watch Robert handle the transfer of the four layers of cake onto cooling racks. The cake tin he had waiting was printed with a Dickensian Christmas scene on the lid and sides. Ange's glance swept over that and the counter, where Robert had efficiently arranged everything he'd needed to prepare the cake.

"No icing?" Ange asked.

Robert shook his head. "The cake is so good on its own, icing isn't needed."

He could say the same of the man listening to him. Seeing Ange in his now clean clothes didn't cool Robert's ardor. Ange had retrieved another long-sleeved flannel shirt from the closet, a green and black stripe pattern that brought out the colors of his eyes. He'd buttoned it over the tank he'd also laundered. Which meant Robert couldn't see the fine lines of his shoulders, the curves of biceps that would be highlighted by Ange's pose now, hands braced on the edge of the counter, body leaned forward.

But Robert could imagine all of it. And he could see the long lengths of his thighs in faded denim, the sensitive bare feet curled over the kitchen tile.

"I dust each layer with confectioner's sugar as I stack them, separating them with wax paper," Robert explained. He tapped the top of the confectioner's sugar box. "I think you recognize this."

Ange's cheeks tinged with color under Robert's heated regard, bringing back the memory of Ange's taste on his tongue, mixed with the sweet powder.

As Robert finished his coffee and Ange leaned over to pour himself one, the two of them watched one another, heat in their eyes as they waited for the cake to cool. It was a companionable, good feeling.

"How come you know how to cook great meals, but you don't know how to bake?" Robert asked.

"I started training to be a dancer when I was five." Ange gave him a wry smile. "Under my grandmother's regimen, white carbs were the ultimate evil. Particularly baked goods. She'd rather me club a baby seal than eat a Twinkie."

Ange had never volunteered information about his past so casually. Not wanting to spook him, Robert merely nodded, even as he pushed his luck with a follow up. "So she was the one who got you into dancing."

Ange folded his knee up, calf crossing the opposite thigh, heel to his hip bone, a flexibility that pretzels would envy. The spread of his thighs stretched the jeans' inseams, hinting at the curve of his testicles.

"She was a classically trained professional dancer," Ange confirmed. "Then she became a dance teacher. I think she was hoping my parents would have a girl, because she wanted to recreate herself, only better. Take her protégé further. When I was four, my mom would leave me at the studio while she was at work. I started emulating my grandmother's movements. She began teaching me, I showed promise, and it went from there."

A touch of wistfulness entered Ange's expression. "I think she never stopped wishing I was a girl. She didn't have much use or affection for me, except for teaching me to dance. But when I'd win a competition or get called back after an audition, she'd take me to this fancy tearoom she liked. Tiny sandwiches and cookies. That's as close as I was allowed to get to sweets and baked stuff."

"Explains your sweet tooth now."

"She'd be horrified. Say I'd let myself go. She said when you let yourself go, even a little bit, that was the gateway to the end. If I wanted to be the best dancer possible, I'd never open that gate. Never get anywhere close to it."

Robert pursed his lips. "Doesn't leave much room for life to be anything else."

Ange lifted a shoulder. "When you're fully in it, and really want it, love it? It doesn't feel like a limited world. Just the opposite."

Ange's intent gaze, caught between past and present, shifted from the cake to Robert's hands. He was spreading the sugar over the layers, the sifter making a pleasant clicking noise. "It's a whole universe of everything you could ever want, all inside those boundaries. Kind of like...being a Dom and sub."

His gaze flickered up to Robert. "Same theory."

"So the key is your passion for it," Robert said, clearing his throat. "It connects to the rest. You just can't have cake."

Ange grinned. "Yeah. But the good thing about the Dom/sub stuff is cake is included. If my Master will give me a piece."

Robert chuckled. "Nice try."

He was teasing, however. He'd fully intended to keep the fourth layer for them. After he cut a small piece of it, he came to Ange. Ange let his leg drop, opening up his knees so Robert could move between them and hold up the warm cake. "Open up."

When Ange took it from his fingers, Robert braced a hand outside his thigh. "So what do you think?"

Bliss took over the beautiful green gaze. Ange's eyes actually closed, making Robert grin. "Still with me? You look like you're having a religious experience."

"Oh yeah." Ange's eyes opened, locked on Robert's. "I know exactly what my grandmother meant about opening that gateway."

Robert tapped his thigh, a warning. "Stop being so you or I'll stripe your ass with another kitchen utensil. Believe me, I will make it hurt."

Ange's amused, slightly puzzled look only made the temptation worse. With an internal chuckle, Robert put the cake layers, separated by wax paper, into the tin. He rested the lid loosely on top to keep the lingering heat from creating condensation. "Get those few dishes washed up while I shower. Use the trimmings I've laid out to finish decorating the basket."

In addition to the ribbon and holly, there were some little dime store toys, like long-limbed rubber reindeer he'd intended to twine around the handle. He expected Ange would pick up on the same idea.

"It's nice of you to do this for a group home," Ange said. "Are they customers?"

"No," Robert said. "The person who runs it is an old friend. I think you'll enjoy him, and the residents. After we drop this off, we have another stop to make. We're getting you a proper suit."

He'd tossed that out as the first big hint. Ange's head came up. "What suit? What for?"

"I'm taking you somewhere tonight that's more formal. It's your Christmas gift, and you have to dress for it."

Ange's joy for gifts swept his expression, but then it was replaced by a more sober reaction, a set to his chin. "You gave me my gift. You came to me last night."

Robert's heart swelled at the simple, fervent sincerity. He crooked a finger at Ange, brought him close enough to run a hand over the firm butt, the lower part of his elegant back.

"You are such a treasure, I want to punish you for it. That's what I meant about you being you."

Submissive and willing was the *doing* part. Utterly irresistible was the *being* side of things. Ange was going to have to get used to punishment, not only for doing exactly what his Master demanded, but for what he couldn't help being.

Exercising such irrational logic upon a sub's tender parts was part of the perks of being a Dom, after all.

When Ange had to clear his throat to speak, it only increased the cock-teasing adorableness of his response.

"I could find a good suit at the Salvation Army. When we drop off the sofa."

"No doubt, but this is different. I'm taking you to a men's clothing store. The tailor said he'd do a same-day alteration for me."

"This close to Christmas?" Ange's fair brows rose.

Originally, a suit hadn't been part of it, but since last night, Robert had decided he wanted to expand the specialness of Ange's Christmas gift. So he'd texted Sully with a strong caveat that he didn't have to work them in if he was too busy. But Sully had come through.

"He's a friend. He also collects iron die cast toy cars. If I let him buy one from me at cost, he'll consider it an even trade. We'll get some lunch after the fitting, swing back to pick up the suit."

"Okay. But I have money saved up. I can help pay."

"Not this time." Robert shook his head. "The clothes are part of the gift. That's the end of it."

Ange's mouth set in a mulish line, but he dropped his attention to the floor, his head down as he thought it through. Robert put his hand on the back of his neck, ran a thumb over the bump of bone at the top of his spine. "What's happening? Tell me."

"I…" Ange shook his head. "Nothing. I just…I really do feel like last night was the gift, Master. It was beyond anything I ever expected or imagined." A faint smile touched his mouth. "And I imagined a lot. Nothing more is needed. Really. I promise."

The sudden slight note of desperation puzzled Robert. He tightened his hand on his nape. "I know sometimes you get worried, when we're going to unfamiliar places," he said. "But I'm with you. I'll take care of you. Right? You trust me?"

"Always." One shoulder lifted under Robert's hold before Ange met Robert's gaze again. This time there was a different look there, a different concern. "I know there are things that aren't quite right about me. But I don't need you to take care of me." He twitched. "I mean, I know sometimes I do need help… with things. And you care. I love how you care about me. I just want you to know I can take care of you, too. And more than that, I *want* to take care of you. It's a pleasure, it's an honor…it's all I want to do. You can count on me for that."

His jaw set, his eyes flashed. "I'm not Freddie. Not now, not ever."

On certain things, Ange didn't budge, even if he did it by creatively working around other people thinking they could tell him to do something he didn't want to do. While a Master like Robert would routinely bust his ass for it, he'd be glad of Ange's healthy self-determination. Every sub needed that core, to protect themselves from the assholes.

"I know. You've been taking care of me, looking out for me, for a while now. There's absolutely no doubt of it in my mind." He let Ange see the truth of it in his expression. "But I also like taking care of you. I like you wanting that from me, needing it, but in the right way. And so far I've never seen you do it the wrong way."

Ange smiled, obviously relieved. "Okay, then. Can I have a swallowtail coat? Like in the Jane Austen movies?"

Robert laughed. "That might be a little too formal, but we'll see what we can figure out." He caressed Ange's hip. "You've been a gift to me, in more ways than I can count. I really want to give you this. Surprise you with it. Try not to stress over it. All right?"

Robert saw that little flicker of uncertainty again, of tension, but then it was gone, and his sub's shoulders squared. "Okay, yes. Thank you."

"Good. I'll grab my shower and then we'll head out."

CHAPTER SIX

They took Robert's BMW to deliver the basket. He could walk to the store and most places in his neighborhood, like the local grocery and the bank. The light rail or bus were useful to go to city events where traffic could become even worse than the usual Charlotte gridlock. However, for some things, the car was the best way to go.

The group home was a private residence in the venerated older Myers Park neighborhood, off of Queens Road. While Robert had plenty of wealthy clients who routinely purchased four-figure collectibles, Ange's experience with them was usually in the store. Robert saw his eyes widen as they pulled up to the nine thousand square feet two-story with parchment-colored siding and black shutters. A glossy black Mercedes van was parked in the driveway that curved around the side of the house. *Old Queens* was written in floral gold script along the side panel. As they parked next to it, they could see the carport in back. A white Mercedes convertible and a pair of Harley Davidsons with lots of sparkling chrome were parked under it.

"Ever heard of Mad Donna?" Robert asked, putting the car in park. "She was a very successful drag queen, who passed about a decade ago. This was her place. She and her husband lived here until she died, and she left it to him."

Ange turned to study the features of the house as Robert continued his explanation. "Per her wishes, as the years passed, he turned it into a retirement home for about a dozen of her close friends. Those she knew would need a place to go, when the time came. They're in varying stages of health, so they have nursing care available and equipment on premises. The more able-bodied residents help and support the less-so. Like a community, which was what she wanted."

"She preferred 'she' all the time?"

"Yeah." Robert sent him a smile. "Whether in or out of drag, but truth, I never saw her out of drag. Even her lounging pajamas paid homage to 1940s screen starlets. Once she became successful, I bet her husband was the only one who ever saw her out of drag."

Robert paused, gazing at a line of hydrangeas that had been cut back for winter. Their mulch had been generously supplemented by the winter leaves of the trio of towering maples that shaded the rear of the house in summer. "She died before gay marriage was legal in this state, but during her last months they had a minister perform the wedding. In 2015, after it was legalized nationally, Charlie had a graveside wedding, a celebration so outrageous the police were called. 'Maddie says it's the most fun the laid-to-rest here have seen in a century.' That was his quote for the papers."

Ange offered a serious smile. "Did you ever see her perform?"

"Yeah, I did. Several times. I was there the night she performed Etta James's 'At Last,' just for Charlie, and it was indescribable. Well, here. You don't have to take my word for it. This was recorded later, but she said it would always be her song for him, so you can still hear everything she felt the first time she sang it, with him in her mind."

He keyed it up on his player, transferred the sound to his speakers. Robert settled back and let the music and Maddie's remarkable voice fill the car, all the spaces between him and Ange. When the throaty yearning and joy of the words, the way she offered them, had penetrated to the center of his heart, Robert wasn't surprised to feel Ange's hand curl around his wrist. Their fingers twined, clasped and held.

After the last note died away, they were silent for a few seconds. Ange looked at him with awe. "It makes you want to hold someone in your arms and dance. Not like I dance. That slow sway, holding someone tight to you."

"It sure does. Be sure and tell Charlie that. He'll like hearing it." Love and sorrow gripped Robert as he thought of Charlie and Maddie, the love he'd seen them show one another. On the night he'd told Ange about, it didn't matter that Maddie had been on stage, Charlie in the audience. She sang as if it was just the two of them, and when she was done, there wasn't a dry eye in the place. All the pain and loneliness of her life's journey, the joy when she'd found Charlie's love, had suffused every note. Everyone knew what those emotions felt like.

"He called her his Madonna, while the rest of us called her Maddie."

Ange's hand tightened on his. "How did you meet them?"

Robert let the sadness dissipate, freeing his hand to stroke Ange's hair back. "Charlie was my high school history teacher. Hell of an educator. He demanded a lot out of his students. That's the kind of Dom he is, too, but of course I didn't know that about him until later. I stayed in touch with him, the way a student stays connected to a favorite teacher. But then, when I was at a New York trade show, I went to a drag performance at a popular club. He was in the front row. He and Maddie were already involved, and he'd joined her for a weekend gig. Later that night, they had plans to hit the same club I was planning to visit. Our friendship went from teacher and student to fellow Doms at that point."

"So Maddie was a sub."

"She sure was, not that anyone would ever have guessed it.

She was as strong-willed as they came. She had to be. The submission, the need for a strict Master, gave her a sanctuary she'd never had before."

"Sanctuary." Ange's eyes were thoughtful as they met Robert's. "Yeah. It's like that."

"When done right, it is. For both Master and sub." Robert squeezed Ange's shoulder, grinned. "But he had to earn it. Charlie told me she was a real brat at first. On their third date, for a fancy restaurant, she wore a schoolgirl uniform to tease him. Come on. I want you to meet him."

As they exited the car, Ange retrieved the basket from the back, but Robert took it from him. He tossed Ange a wink. "You'll need both hands free. The residents here are a good group, but impulse control is an afterthought for them. They'll grab your ass and won't even have the decency to claim dementia made them do it."

Ange chuckled. "I have faith you'll defend my virtue, Master."

"The National Guard couldn't defend the Pope's virtue from this group."

On the spacious front stoop, they heard Ella Fitzgerald's version of "O Come All Ye Faithful" filtering from behind the door. Robert didn't bother to ring the bell, instead opening the portal, which chimed to alert those within of his entrance. "Hello, the house," he called out, wiping his feet on the mat. The pattern showed a handful of reindeer toasting one another with wine glasses as they sat on a tied up and thoroughly annoyed Santa. "I have cake."

He saw Ange staring. The foyer was impressive, with a shiny black and white checkerboard tile floor, curving staircase and chandelier. However, what had caught Ange's eye was what captured every guest's attention. A nine-foot tall oil portrait of Mad Donna herself, mounted on the wall over the curved staircase.

She wore the silk lounging wear Robert had mentioned, while

reclined on a divan. Her striking red hair poured over the rolled arm upholstered in blue silk brocade. Her black stilettos were tied onto her feet with blue rope looped around the soles and her ankles, bound to the leg of the divan. Her wrists, wrapped in the same rope, were clasped under her chin as she gazed at the viewer.

Maddie had often done performances playing up a Domme angle to tease her audience, but in private she'd been wholly Charlie's sub. Charlie's Mastery allowed her to let go in that vital way a powerful personality with a rocky past often needed.

Mad Donna's eyes had been her sucker punch. They were full of everything—a submissive's devotion, a Dominant's power, a woman's mystery and something indescribable. It kept a person looking, trying to understand what it was, and why it felt like a call straight to the soul.

Humanity. That was what Robert had decided it was. Everything complicated, blessed, profane, lost and found about the human race was in those astonishing blue eyes.

Much like what he'd seen in Ange's eyes, so many times.

"*Robert.*" The crisp-voiced crow of delight came from his left, so he moved to that archway, which led into a spacious and comfortable sitting room. As Ella's melodious voice flowed into "Silent Night," Robert saw a gaunt man on the couch. Dressed warmly in sweatshirt and flannel pajama bottoms, he was draped over a body pillow with a dove gray cotton case over it. An IV was attached to one thin arm.

The greeting hadn't come from him. It belonged to the man crossing the room toward them with energetic strides. He'd emerged from the deeper recesses of the house. Despite being in his sixties, Charlie wore snug jeans and a T-shirt that displayed well-developed biceps and broad shoulders. His reddish-blond hair was cropped military short and he had a bristling moustache with hints of gray.

"Charlie, Merry Christmas." Setting the basket on the glass coffee table, Robert clasped the extended hand. Charlie pulled him into a warm hug which Robert returned with equal strength. He drew back to meet Charlie's gaze, already moving with great interest toward Ange. "We can't stay long, I'm sorry to say. We just wanted to drop by some holiday cheer."

"We'll forgive it, as long as you're coming to the New Year's Party." Charlie's bright dark eyes came back to Robert. "And bringing this beautiful thing with you. Robert, you dog. Where have you been keeping him? Oh, don't tell me." That piercing regard flicked back to Ange, lingered on the collar the flannel shirt didn't completely hide. "This is your assistant, the one whose fine ass you've wanted to call yours since the moment he came into your store."

Ange flushed, even as his attention immediately went to Robert for confirmation. Robert gave him a "don't let it go to your head or I'll kick your ass" Master's look that had Ange tucking a smile away into pressed lips.

"This is Ange Fournier." Robert introduced him formally. Then he took it further. Charlie was a good friend, and understood. "And yes, he's mine. Officially, now."

Charlie squeezed his arm as the man on the couch stirred, his next words showing he hadn't been asleep at all.

"About time. Thought I'd have to hear about you finally making a move on the kid once I was up there doing the Electric Slide with the angels."

Charlie chuckled and looked toward Ange. "We were taking bets on it, you see," he said in a conspiratorial tone.

"Do not spoil him," Robert said severely. "He needs to be able to sit down before New Year's, if only for when you play musical chairs."

Robert moved around the coffee table to help the man on the couch push up to a sitting position. He was concerned to find Amos thinner and more fragile than last time he'd seen him, and that hadn't been too long ago. As Robert sat down on the couch, sliding an arm around him and accepting the kiss on the lips with easy amiability, he gripped his hand. "How goes it, Amos?"

No surprise, Amos didn't care a thing about being coddled. "I'm holding out for that New Year's party," he rasped calmly. "Then I can be done with this mortal coil, Robert. But I won't leave until I can lead the dance one more time."

"Amos was a DJ at the height of the disco era," Charlie told Ange, transferring the basket from the coffee table to a cushioned runner on top of a baby grand piano. "He'd get the tunes going, then jump down to the floor and lead the line dancing. He was also a couples dance competitor."

When Amos reached out toward him, Ange moved forward and dropped to a knee by the man. Amos put his hand on Ange's face, stroked his hair. "So young," he observed. "Do you dance, pretty thing?"

Ange's lips curved as Robert chuckled. "A little."

"Not this ridiculous hip grinding they do now. Real dancing, like we did to dissssccooo." Amos drew the word out with a sibilant reverence.

"I do a mean Hustle," Ange said, without a blink, and Robert loved him more, if that was possible.

"Then you'll come back at New Year's and prove it," Amos said stoutly. "And dance with me."

Ange looked at Robert, waited for his nod, then came back to Amos. "I promise," he said. "As long as you promise not to stand me up."

"Only one Thing in the universe can keep me from it, and that's with the capital T," Amos said solemnly. "But God enjoys dancing, too. I expect I'll still be here."

A sound like an approaching flock of manic cackling birds filtered into the room, drowning out Ella's crooning melody. Charlie's expression shifted to fond exasperation. "Oh, God help us, Robert. They know you're here."

A blink later, the room was filled with a handful of exuberant residents, festively dressed in reds and greens, with accents of gold and silver. Jingle bells chimed, dangling from ears or on bracelets and necklaces. Everything from dresses to jeans and T-shirts were represented in the fashion mix.

With the exception of Charlie and Amos, the current inhabitants were all drag queens—hence the name playfully detailed on the back of the van. It was also there because a few members of the group still did performances, using the van for gigs.

Robert had been here on routine days, when the residents were pursuing normal tasks and interests, like reading, paying bills, gardening, doing home repairs. Bradford looked like he'd been engaged in that last one, in clay-dusted jeans, work shoes and a green Duluth Trading shirt. An angry beaver wearing a Santa hat was printed on the pocket. Despite the masculine garb, Bradford wore lipstick in a cheerful glossy red. Probably in anticipation of holiday drop-in visitors like Robert.

Guests activated the residents' performance genes, which ran blood-and-bone deep. In a group, in this scenario, their mannerisms were uniformly feminine and flamboyant. They'd spent their lives on stage—even when they weren't formally performing. There was no "practicing their feminine wiles." Every one of them had mastered the art and could exercise them effortlessly and effectively.

Seeing Ange only heightened the response. Tenfold.

Robert was inundated with Christmas wishes, but almost immediately after, they swarmed upon his sub like bees. Robert tolerated it until Theopolis tried a crotch grab, and then Robert stepped in, swatting him away and putting Ange behind him.

"Show a little self-restraint," he scolded.

Theopolis wore full geisha face makeup, a contrast with his jeans and close-fitting thermal shirt. Since it was dusted with the same clay, it suggested he'd been helping Bradford. He shot Robert an unrepentant look from under thickly mascara'ed lashes and held out his wrists.

"I'd much rather you do it, darling."

That set off a wave of raucous, full-throated laughter, but a meaningful glare from Robert, reinforced by a few admonitions from Charlie, set the boundaries. Everyone settled into slightly more decorous behavior. They shifted their attention to the basket, crowed over it, and then the cake was broken out. A couple residents dashed into the kitchen and returned with a tea tray, plates and forks.

Robert pushed Ange down onto a love seat with him and kept him close to his hip, his hand high on Ange's thigh. He ignored Charlie's amused look.

Whenever he came to visit, the queens flirted outrageously with *him*. Trying to dampen their enthusiasm with someone young and beautiful like Ange was a challenge that would drive God to despair.

And probably resigned laughter.

So Robert tolerated Trixie Bell perching on the arm of the couch so he could play with Ange's hair and pet him. The black queen was outfitted in a crimson tunic top with sparkling green trim, draped over casual black slacks. His ginger wig had shining thick curls that fell to his elbows and tumbled against Ange's arm and shoulder.

Robert had shifted his hand to Ange's lower back, a way to gauge any tensions. He found he didn't need to worry. Despite Ange's occasional social awkwardness and shy nature, in this situation he rose to the occasion. Ange unfailingly offered his sweet smile, charmed them all with the constant blush on his fair cheeks, and laughed at even the most blatantly sexual teases. He knew he was in the deep end of the pool, but his glances toward Robert said he could tread water as long as Robert had his back.

Robert did. Plus, despite his warnings, he was confident the residents themselves wouldn't take it too far. The queens were well practiced in being sexually aggressive on stage when the environment called for it, but they were also generous in heart and possessed shrewd instincts and intuition about their audience.

His mother had accompanied him to this haven several

times, when he hadn't felt comfortable leaving her at the town-house on her own. She'd found a second home here, because Charlie and the others had encouraged Robert to drop her off on days when she wasn't doing as well. It had allowed him to keep the store operating on at least a limited schedule. They'd even given her a stage name purely for fun—Yasmine, since she liked the Aladdin Disney character. They'd dressed her up in a Hollywood-worthy costume for her last Halloween.

As such, Robert guessed he should have anticipated Charlie's toast when the tea was poured.

"To your mother," Charlie said, raising his cup. "She'd be so glad to see you with someone."

"Amen to that," Theopolis added. Dallas, a slim queen delicate as a fairy and in her nineties, who dressed and looked a lot like Jessica Tandy, turned a serious eye to Robert. She leaned toward him from her chair.

"Yasmine loved you so much. That's all she wanted for you. Your happiness, and for your heart to be held in the right hands. Are they the right hands? Is he treating you right?" She—because she preferred the feminine pronoun, just like Maddie, whether on stage or off—tilted her head toward Ange.

Well, hell. Maybe it was because she reminded him of his mother, the wizened frailty of her body and lined face. Or how she gazed at him with such familiar maternal concern. That, coupled with the emotional surfeit of Christmas itself, its peculiar way of underscoring loss, rose up, making Robert's chest tight. Words couldn't get past his closed throat.

Ange shifted so his thigh pressed closer to Robert's, his shoulder brushing him as he slipped his arm under Robert's. His palm pressed to Robert's lower back, his thumb hooking under the belt of Robert's black slacks. For their visit to the Queens home, he'd matched those with a white dress shirt and casual sports jacket. The queens appreciated a man who took extra time to look good for them.

When Robert turned his face toward Ange, their noses almost brushed.

"Okay?" Ange asked softly, just like that. As if none of them were here. He wasn't being unfriendly. Just...focused. It choked Robert up even more.

He could say he wasn't used to having someone have his back intimately like that, but that wouldn't be true. He just hadn't acknowledged how many ways Ange had watched after him these past few months. But his sub had stated it straight out, less than a day ago.

I'd vow to do what I could to inspire you to smile, to ease your sadness, every day.

This place's significance to his mother in her last days made it impossible not to open the door to how much her absence had affected him. He was a grown man, fully in charge of his life, enough so he'd been able to reverse the roles and serve as his own parents' caregiver. However, there wasn't a day he didn't miss the maternal qualities his mother had possessed in full measure, and how she'd reinforced their steadying touch upon him with her physical presence.

"I'm okay," Robert confirmed, clearing his throat. He needed to get back on top of this. The alpha and Master in him pretty much demanded it.

Ange's look held a partial apology, an acknowledgement that this was putting Robert on the spot, but the other part said he wasn't sorry for championing him. He slid his hand from Robert's back to rest on his thigh, a reminder of their connection. That he was there, at his side.

"This baby's a keeper," Amos said abruptly, before Robert could say anything else. Dallas nodded firmly in agreement, her eyes warm.

"Definitely bring him back for New Year's," she said. She directed her next comment to Ange. "We have karaoke and candy bingo early in the evening. If the singing doesn't make you poke your eardrums out with a pencil, it's good fun."

That produced an outraged wave of protest and a burst of song from several skilled throats. Amos screwed up his face in mock pain, holding his hands over his ears as they deliberately hit high notes with a shrill tag.

But as they took a pause to eat more cake, he shook a finger at Robert, his dark eyes glinting. "You hold onto him. He has the nicest butt I've seen since yours. I'm at ass-level most of the time these days. Gives me an optimal view."

"Good God," Robert said, rolling his eyes. Ange nodded.

"You do have a great butt, Master."

"People of a certain age have no decorum," Robert informed him reprovingly. "You don't have that excuse."

"Oh honey, that's because at our age, the grave's too close." Herman, stage name Hermione, shot him and Ange a wink. His natural hair, curled under at his shoulders in a sleek bob, was dyed green to go with the glittering red eye shadow and matching lips. A sparkling snowman was face-painted on his cheek. "Exercise diplomacy or beat around the bush, and you might drop dead before you make your point."

"Fucking hell, the bitches are starting to talk about death. We need something that isn't Christmas music," Bradford announced. He was up and headed to the music player. Over the cacophony of suggestions, he chose "Doncha" by the Pussycat Dolls and Busta Rhymes. When it blared from the sound system, it was met with various groans and squeals of delight. Then Bradford was back to pull Ange up off the couch. Theopolis gave him an encouraging swat on the ass and then shook his palm, shooting Robert a teasing look. "Buttocks of steel, that one, you lucky dog. Amos is right."

Robert sighed, exchanging a mock look of commiseration with a grinning Charlie. Then he settled back to watch the show, his ankle on his knee, his arm stretched over the back of the sofa.

He watched carefully, but things were okay. Ange had tossed him a reassuring look. This was obviously a radically different scenario than whatever made Ange uptight about dancing in front of others.

Ange and Bradford took the space by the baby grand, an impromptu dance floor. Though Bradford's hands did some wandering, this time they stayed mostly above the waist. Bradford shot Robert a wink that said he was aware of Robert's hawk-like regard.

As the lead singer of the Pussycat Dolls asked if you wished your girlfriend was a freak like her, Ange copycatted Bradford's bump and grind. Yet in the graceful undulations, dips of the knees and close footwork, Ange's innate talent was clear. When it came to dancing, he was as sure of himself as a cloven-hoofed Pan in the forest.

His audience's focus shifted from mischief to professional absorption and critical approval of how he and Bradford moved together. Even at seventy-six, Bradford, stage name Hot Pants, could still easily command a dance floor, and Ange complemented those skills impressively.

The tender grief of the past few moments melted away before a wave of laughter and fun. When he was tugged to his feet, Robert joined the dancing. Though they didn't let him have Ange back, that was okay. When his sub's eyes met his on the turns, in the forward and back motion of the dance, Robert felt as if they were dancing heart to overflowing heart.

They took their leave about a half hour later—the Southern version of the "we can't stay long" visit. As they headed for the door to a warm chorus of holiday wishes, Robert was pretty sure Ange knew he had a second home if he ever needed one.

His looks didn't hurt with earning that invitation, but for all their irrepressibility, most of the residents had spent a good chunk of their lives fighting to be who they were. Robert had yet to meet the queen who didn't have a raw and vulnerable soul, battered by wounds that didn't always heal. Stage performance and solidarity helped them armor themselves. As he'd seen them recognize Ange's subtly similar vulnerabilities, love for all of them had swelled in his heart.

Good. The more ports in the storm Ange had, the better. But Robert wanted to be Ange's first stop, always. For that reason, after the dancing, when his sub was allowed back within touching distance, Robert made sure his hand was on him.

For his part, Ange hadn't stopped glancing his way for cues, and the reminder of that bond between them. Maybe also to confirm Robert was doing okay, same as he was checking for Ange. But as a card-carrying Master who'd already exercised his one grudgingly allowed and mortifying vulnerable moment in front of others with his sub, Robert would ignore that. Even as he knew it only fueled the strength of the feelings between them.

Charlie had noticed everything. When Robert made his reluctant but firm explanations for departure and they were headed to the door, Charlie drew him to the side for an additional word. Amos, surprisingly, had risen to escort Ange, though it seemed the reverse was true, since the former DJ was gripping Ange's arm and leaning on him heavily for support. Since he was saying something earnestly to Ange, it ensured Charlie and Robert's conversation was not being overheard.

"Bring him to Patriarch on Christmas Eve," Charlie said, fixing his gaze on Robert. "We're having the usual small holiday party and gift exchange, followed by scene play. You've been gone a long time, Robert. We'd love to have you back."

"We'll see."

In the past, the suggestion had caused a nervous, almost sick twist in Robert's gut. Since Freddie, since his parents, the idea of coming back into a club environment, particularly by himself, had been met with a hard *no*. He'd been a well-respected and sought-after Master, and he'd known there would be overtures from unattached submissives, seeking his Dominance. But that inclination had gone fully dormant under the weight of grief and loss.

Until Ange had woken it like a sleeping dragon.

He was glad to find that sick feeling was no longer there. But he had a concern about Ange himself. Though Ange was a natural submissive, and evidence suggested he had some familiarity with BDSM protocols, there were things in Ange's personality Robert needed to understand better, to avoid triggers.

Even as he acknowledged that sensible caution, another sly mental voice reminded him that Dom/sub play, done right, could be useful in opening up parts of a person that needed to heal, in healthy ways.

"Good. You're thinking about it." Charlie nudged him. "Your collar looks damn good on him, Robert. I'm glad you never put it on Freddie. It was never for him."

Charlie shook his head before Robert could answer that. "You know I won't push. Do whatever you know is right for you and Ange, but no excuses for missing the New Year's party here. And you know what I'm thinking? If you do show up at Patriarch, you should wear your full leathers. You'd knock that boy on his ass."

Robert chuckled, but shook his head. "I don't know."

Yet the idea made him think about how Ange responded to his strict side. Turning out for the club Christmas party in full leathers, maybe dressing Ange in just the collar and jeans... He'd put him in a borrowed leather jacket of Robert's for warmth, until Robert peeled it off those pale shoulders and warmed him up other ways, binding him, showing his claim by marking his fair skin...

He scowled at Charlie. "You're terrible."

Charlie grinned. "I'll wear mine if you'll wear yours. Stern daddy bears like us keep the young'uns' dicks in line. And at full attention."

Robert had said they were leaving, but he'd stopped to have a final word with Charlie. It gave Ange a few extra moments with Amos. He was sure his Master wouldn't want him to cut Amos short, regardless. The older man had dropped down onto a gold-cushioned chair at the base of the curving staircase, beneath Mad Donna's grand picture. The walk from the living room was as much energy as he had to give.

Ange obligingly dropped to a knee beside him again. Amos touched his hair, seemingly fascinated with the thick strands.

"To be young again," he said. "You don't know...it's inside me. Just ready to leap out and happen. I can feel it close, and it's a good thing." His gaze slid away to the past. "I've lived a lot, seen a lot. A lot of pain. The eighties...there was nothing like it, losing so many friends, so fast."

Shadows crossed his face. "I was a young buck, hooked up with a man who'd served in Vietnam. He'd wake up screaming and needing to be held, but afraid to be touched, afraid he'd hurt me. Afraid he'd tainted his soul. It's that way when the hard things of life take hold of you. I'll be glad to see him again. He taught me to love music, got me DJ'ing."

He dropped his hand to Ange's shoulder, gripped. "Closer you get to death, the clearer you see. Sometimes in life you can't handle what you see. Gets unbearable."

He held Ange's gaze, even when Ange's faltered. Amos touched his knuckles to his face, a surprisingly gentle but firm contact.

"Yeah. Sometimes it gets so bad you have to go to ground for a while, like a hibernating animal. Least until you realize you can't love or live that way. You've helped him remember that, same as he's helping you figure that out, I'll bet. Robert is a good Master, a strong one. He'll give you the steady hand you need, young man."

Amos's gaze turned inward again. He didn't seem to need a response, just Ange's attention. "Back in those days, there were times the pain would just overwhelm me. How do we keep going when things are so difficult, when no one seemed to care except others going through it, drowning just like you? But we did. We held together and we did, and discovered just how strong we really are."

His look upon Ange sharpened. "There's a difference between having a weak moment and being weak. It's okay to look to others to take care of you in the weak moments. That has its place, but we shouldn't forget our caregivers. The ones so strong they don't seem like they need care until it's too late. Charlie's like that. So's Robert. But they need someone strong for them. He looks happy, Robert does. He hasn't, for a long time."

Ange turned his gaze to Robert. He stood, solid as a rooted tree, paying attention to Charlie with those steady brown eyes. "I'm trying to learn and give him everything he needs," Ange said. "I want to do that, more than anything."

Amos studied him. "Good. Hopefully far better than that last piece of trash. We all hated him."

"I like you," Ange said, with a smile that made Amos smile back, despite the weakness of the gesture.

"Charlie says teaching history taught him hard times come and go. So do good times. Some things will test you in ways you can't even imagine. But there will be other glorious moments. Worth all of it. And every one of them has to do with love, with the people you connect with. In the end, young man, that's all that matters. Truly."

Those dark eyes searched Ange's, probed deep, all the way to his shadows and scars. "The rest of it? It's just history."

CHAPTER SEVEN

*A*s he drove toward their next destination, Robert noticed Ange was quiet. Not a bad quiet. Just thinking. As they pulled up to Sully's store, his sub reached out, brushed Robert's leg with a questing fingertip.

"Will we go back to the New Year's Eve party?"

"If you want."

"I do," Ange said simply. "I'd like to do the Hustle with Amos."

"I'd like to see that." Robert closed his hand over his, rubbed a thumb over his knuckles. He expanded on the image Charlie had planted in his head, Ange on his knees, taking a paddle. The sharp slap of it against his denim-covered ass, then Robert reaching under him to pop the button, push the zipper down and pull the jeans off those sweet buttocks.

Robert moved Ange's hand to curve over Robert's cock beneath the tailored slacks he wore. He used Ange's fingers, molding them with his own to straighten the swelling shaft. "I haven't had your ass or your mouth in a couple hours. I need to fix that."

Ange's eyes sparked, and his strong fingers stroked. "I serve you, Master. Whenever, however you want."

A rattling drew Robert's attention up. Through the windshield, he saw Sully unlocking the store for them. His desire to fuck Ange senseless wasn't going to be fulfilled right now, but he was okay keeping it on simmer. He tilted his head down, studying Ange's hand, then shot him a meaningful hard glance.

"I put your hand on my cock for my own purposes. I didn't give you permission to play with it."

Ange's fingers immediately stilled, and Robert nodded his approval. "Keep in mind what I'll be demanding from you later. When and where will be up to me."

"Always, Master."

No snarkiness in Ange's response. Just pure obedience and desire to serve. The kid created want with nothing but words and a look.

Robert covered that craving with a short nod and exited the car, joining Ange at the curb.

In Robert's opinion, Jack Suleiman was the best men's tailor in Charlotte. He was a third-generation craftsman, having trained with his grandfather and father at their shop in Turkey. Sully had eventually migrated to the States and set up a place here. Since tailoring alone wasn't much of a living these days—not in a modern-day world that bought most its clothes off the rack and tossed them when they no longer fit—his shop had evolved into a high-end men's clothing store. Robert bought most of his dress shirts, slacks and more formal needs there. If cared for properly, the quality garments lasted decades.

Robert also appreciated Sully's shrewd professionalism, which meant he wouldn't show any curiosity as to why, in the crisp cold winter air, Robert had decided to shed his jacket and carry it folded over his arm, concealing his erection until it subsided. He put his other hand on Ange, guiding him over the threshold into the warmer recesses of the store.

"Appreciate you doing this so close to the holiday," he told Sully. "This is Ange."

The tailor was a good-looking man approaching fifty, with a

gray pepper beard, dark curling hair and deep-set eyes. His brows had a rakish crook to them.

"You ask so little of me, Robert, and give so much. My customers know I close the week of Christmas, so they request their alterations and clothing well in advance. All of which means I had only a couple last minute things like this."

"But I'm still taking you away from your family."

"Pfft." Sully waved his hand. "I was underfoot. My wife and daughters are in a flurry of activity at home, so I was quite enthusiastically banished."

"I thought you were the master of your household, the lord in your castle."

Sully shot Robert a droll look. "Such things mean nothing when a woman has an invading army of relatives. My dearest love is a hundred percent general today, my daughters her battalion of colonels. I'm grateful to be the lowly courier picking up the few items she is having catered."

He winked and glanced at Ange. "Ange. It is a pleasure. I expect you are the reason my friend Robert has an easier smile than I have seen on his face in a long time."

Seemed to be a common observation today, but unlike the queens, Sully didn't dwell in the emotional territory. His gaze was already sliding over Ange critically. "Such a beautiful young man needs a suit in a tan or caramel color. Perhaps a tie with a touch of pink, like a sunrise hitting glass and turning it gold. All of it to make the most of that lion's mane of hair he has. Yes."

Pivoting on his well-shined brogues, he moved to the several racks of suits on his showroom floor. His casual and inviting gesture drew them along with him. He pulled a coat off the rack and held it up to Ange, touching his shoulder to turn him toward Robert, let him see. "The caramel coat, the pink tie. The right clothes bring out what is truly within. Makes it impossible for your significant other to look away."

Sully's dark eyes twinkled at Robert. "Not that I expect you have any desire to do so. You have love in your face, my friend."

"Sully," Robert said, eyes narrowing.

Sully elbowed Ange. "I am giving myself license to tease. He has been alone too long. Though not as long as I had thought. This is the young man you've mentioned so often, who works in your store."

"Yes. Now shut up and focus on the suit."

Sully laughed, a deep, rich sound that would have competed with Santa Claus. "So you like the choice."

"Yes."

"Good. Come over here and we will do some measuring." Sully guided Ange to the counter and picked up his tailor's tape. "You have a crease in your brow, my young friend. But..." He stopped short and studied Ange's face, reaching out to cup his chin. "Look at me."

Surprised by the direct order, Ange obeyed, tightening things in Robert's lower belly. Sully's gaze sharpened. "I was an idiot to miss that," he murmured. "The hair distracts. No pink tie for you. Nor this jacket."

He whisked it away, keeping them there with an upheld hand as he returned to the rack, rehung the jacket and came back with another style, though in the same color. He also held a dress shirt from another nearby display.

"No tie. Instead, this green shirt, a shade slightly lighter than his eyes. Sea foam, they call it, though sea foam is usually a dirty ivory color, so I have no idea why they call a bluish green that. But see the jacket? It is Western style cut, treated fabric to give it the sheen of leather. The slacks that go with it are a remarkable cross between khakis and dress slacks."

Sully dipped his head toward Robert. "An interesting fashion decision from our Dolce and Gabbana designer friends. I thought it was misguided when I saw it on the runway, but I think this young man of yours invaded their dreams and inspired them. There is a rogue Billy the Kid look in those intense green eyes."

Ange blinked as Sully's attention returned to him. "Now,

what was the furrowed brow about a moment ago? You have a question? Or you don't like the suit."

"No, it's not that. If my Mas—if Robert likes it, then that's all I need. I was wondering... You said, the clothes bring out what's truly within. What does that mean?"

"The inner beauty. Truth of the soul, and who you are to the one looking at you with such hunger and pleasure."

"For some there's no containing it inside," Robert remarked. Ange's words pleased him. *If my Master likes it, then that's all I need.* "He'd look good after rolling in manure."

Sully laughed. "That is youth. Irrepressible. But if I may say, your companion is exceptionally beautiful in body. Like a dancer."

"He is a dancer."

"So as usual my wisdom is without compare." While he mused, Sulieman had begun to measure, positioning Ange efficiently with a tap here, a gesture there. "For the shoes, I have a pair of ankle boots that look like a cowboy's. It does not disrupt the line of the pants and makes them easy to take off, because I always allow for the unexpected moment."

He flicked a glance at the two of them. "Like driving to a beach after a special event, to walk along the shore. The man's tie loosened, his lover's hand drifting along the silk line of it, up to caress the early morning shadow on his face..."

Suleiman's eyes went dreamy. As Robert met Ange's gaze, he could well imagine the scene, the sunrise touching his boy's hair just as Sully had described it.

"Sounds like we're invading one of your memories, Sully," Robert observed.

"Not invading," Sully said, eyes clearing and smile deepening. "Invoking. My wife and I, walking on the beach after our wedding. She is my angel, my demon, my conqueror and my slave. The definitions are so many."

He tipped his head forward, putting his hand on Ange's neck, an intimacy that seemed so natural to his disposition, Ange didn't appear startled. Sully also twitched aside the collar of the flannel shirt, eyes touching on the braided band it partially concealed. Robert was sure he'd noted it the second Ange had stepped through Sully's doorway.

"If Master is what he is to you," the tailor said in a confidential tone, "you may feel free to call him that in this shop, just the three of us here. My wife is to me as you are to him, and Robert and I first met over a spanking bench, as it were."

Sully's gaze sparkled and he withdrew, returned to his measuring. "This one still blushes," he noted.

"Don't take advantage," Robert said.

Sully had been well aware of Robert's attention to the intimate touch on Ange's nape. Another man touching what was his. It was Sully's nature to touch, and Sully loved his wife, so it was all good, but even so, Robert couldn't help tossing out the reminder.

From the string of Dom and sub intimates they'd encountered in only one morning, Robert suspected Ange was starting to realize how much of his private life had once been about the BDSM scene. Many Doms found a newbie sub's behavior irresistible to play with.

Sully shot him a droll look as he scribbled measurements down on a pad. "There are apps I can use to do this now," he told Ange. "But I don't trust the numbers, and always measure myself, so why do two steps? Go into the dressing room now, and take the coat and shirt, plus these slacks."

He plucked the pants off another rack after examining the sizes. "Put everything on so we can do the next step. Robert, I have coffee and a tray of Turkish delight. A mixed variety, some with nuts and a hint of Bergamot orange, which I remember is your favorite."

As Ange went behind the curtain of Sully's dressing area, Robert agreed to the coffee and considered his choices on the tray of sweets. Sully's wife prepared them weekly for his customer's consumption.

At Sully's insistence, he took a seat on a cushioned bench. As he settled, Robert realized why the proprietor had deliberately pointed him to it. It offered a direct view through the side crack of the curtain, which Robert fully exploited while talking with Sully and drinking his strong Turkish coffee.

His submissive had stripped off the flannel shirt, tank and jeans. Knowing Ange might be trying on different pairs of pants, Robert had loaned him a pair of boxer briefs, the elastic making them only a little loose in the waist. As Ange straightened and reached for the slacks, he discovered Robert watching him. Robert let his attention deliberately slide over every inch of Ange's skin, and Ange shivered, as if his Master's regard was a breeze lifting the tiny hairs on his arms.

Without words, he understood what Robert wanted. He straightened and stood still, so Robert could look his fill. While Ange didn't lower his eyes, since the interaction was non-verbal, he kept his gaze politely fixed on Robert's shoulder, so he'd see when Robert gestured to him to continue dressing.

Robert took his time doing so, intrigued by how Ange's cock stirred, testing the stretch fabric of the boxers. He knew their seemingly insatiable desire was probably due to the newness of it, of consummating what had been between them for so long. Even so, desperate amusement and a soul deep contentment filled Robert, at how marvelously overwhelming it could be.

Sully was still talking to him, Robert decently managing his end of the conversation. He sent Ange a slight nod, though, giving him permission to get dressed. While Ange obeyed, his gaze kept flicking Robert's way. The rakish angle to the look made Robert think of what Sully had said, and smile. Billy the Kid.

The pale green shirt had silver outlined pearl snaps. As Ange tucked the shirt into the pants that hugged his hips and thighs, Robert saw what Sully meant. The slacks were dressier than khakis, but had that khaki casual look to them, creasing in the right places. Sully had paired the pants with a wide brown belt.

When Ange slid it through the loops, his head dipped, hair falling over his brow to focus on the task. Robert easily imagined stripping the belt back out and applying it to his drum-tight backside.

The dull gleam finish of the jacket did make it look leather-like, though it had the give and shaping of fabric. Robert wouldn't have picked the suit out for Ange, but even without the planned alterations, he could tell the ensemble would offer a mouthwatering presentation of Ange's attributes. Sully's judgment was as infallible as always.

His savvy tailor had also known it was best for him to see Ange in it before talking about price. Dolce and Gabbana meant at least four figures.

Robert could cover it. He'd haggle it down, negotiating with the iron die-cast toys Sully wanted.

As Ange emerged, shrugging into the coat, Sully's white teeth gleamed from the frame of his black beard, making him look like a pirate. "Yes. I am a genius."

Robert chuckled. "Your talents are exceeded only by your modesty."

"Why be modest about one's talents? I have a wife to detail my faults." Sully flashed him the same smile and closed back in on Ange. "Mm-hm. As I expected. A slight lengthening of the sleeves, a taking in of the side seams so the trim shape of the man beneath is more obvious. A suit fit correctly highlights the parts that delight the interested lover's eye. Not from being too tight or, God forbid, too loose. Accentuating, framing the positive, brings forth the best features. What makeup is to women, a suit is to a man."

"Sully's philosophy of life comes out in his tailoring," Robert told Ange.

"Putting in the work to achieve one's passion is rarely a moderate pursuit." Sully shot Ange a considering look. "You are a dancer. Robert's store is not just a store. I do not simply sell suits. Serving what we love with our whole selves means we give something of value—perhaps even unforgettable—to others."

Sully dropped to a knee to check the fit of the pants, measure some more, add some markers as he'd just done to the coat. "The work is never done, because life is always throwing new challenges at us that must be added to the scales. Good and bad."

Sully's phone resting on the counter began to buzz. The tailor shot Robert a glance. "My apologies, my friend. It is my love, and I dare not leave it unanswered. When she calls instead of sending a text, she is requesting my voice and opinion right away."

"Or your instant obedience to the general's further commands," Robert noted, and won another of those rich laughs from Sully.

"Today you are correct. I will exact my punishment on her in the future. When I am more likely to survive the attempt. Maybe even receive a warm thank you for it."

Sully winked and picked up the phone, disappearing into the back. Robert rose, and approached Ange. His submissive's lips parted, as if to speak, but Robert shook his head.

"Not a word," he said, sliding a hand to Ange's waist. "Think about dancing. Hold my gaze, but turn your mind inward. Think of dancing."

He saw a puzzled flash in the green eyes, but then Ange displayed that perfect trust that was so miraculous and addictive to a Master. For so long, Robert hadn't dared a soul-deep appreciation of it. He'd feared dependence on it would make his whole world realign to that axis. If ever he lost it, his world would spin off into chaos.

A stupid fear. As if fear of loss could ever nourish one like the gift of love, however temporary. Now more than ever he understood one of his mother's stout adages, *Not dying is not—and never will be—the same thing as living.*

"Master?"

"Think of dancing," he reminded Ange, coming back to him with the soft command.

"Can I put my hand on you?"

"Yes."

Ange settled his palm on Robert's chest, and an easier look crossed his face. His eyes, holding Robert's as he'd ordered, lost focus, but only externally. Robert saw the emotions drift, felt tiny twitches go through Ange's body. He wasn't wearing the boots yet, so a glance down saw him flexing his toes in his socks. Those small movements were the mind translating Ange's thoughts, sending signals to the physical body to obey his Master's commands.

"Now," Robert said, a quiet push, "Inside your head, dance in your favorite place."

"Should it be outdoor or indoor?"

"Doesn't matter. It's the air. You love being in the air. I see it every time you leap or spin. Every time your feet leave the ground."

Unexpectedly, tension rippled through the body under his hands. Shadows clustered in Ange's eyes, his mouth tightening. His hand on Robert's chest curled, dug in, and his head dipped.

Looking too deeply into his sub's soul could bring storms. Robert stroked back the thick strand of hair that fell forward, tugged. "Hey. Come back to me."

He wondered what demons had interfered with the thought of soaring, in ways they didn't when Ange was talking about dancing in a tornado, or actually leaping into the air. But to pull Ange out of that dark place, Robert changed direction, drawing on his earlier musings. "Can you ballroom dance?"

"I can do any kind of dancing," Ange responded, relief evident in his voice.

"Good. There's a place I'll take you after the holidays. Gay men's dance club, specializing in 1940s décor and ballroom dancing. It's a satellite club from its original sister club in New York. It's been doing really well in Charlotte."

Moving closer, he tipped up Ange's face, capturing his mouth with his own. Not gently either. Aggression surged, his thumb hooking the collar around Ange's throat as he clamped his free hand on one buttock. He pressed Ange's semi-turgid cock against his leg as he plundered the heated inside of Ange's mouth.

Come back to me. Don't you dare cut yourself adrift. You keep your ass right here. Mentally. Physically.

A Master's kiss, his touch, could convey all of that, and Robert made sure it did. He knew when the message had been received, because his sub was gripping his sides, his waist. When Robert pulled back to gaze into the fevered eyes, he felt the sheer pleasure of a conqueror. "Watching you dance with Bradford made me want to fuck you, right then and there."

The clutch of Ange's hands increased, reminding Robert of the man's strength. "Anytime, anywhere, Master. I'm all yours. Doesn't matter who else puts their hands on me."

"No, it doesn't," Robert agreed. "But you have the right to tell them to keep their hands to themselves, too. No matter what I do or don't say about it. You get that, right?"

"Yeah." Ange offered a sheepish smile. "There was no harm to it, and you didn't seem upset, so I figured it was okay."

"Yeah, it was, and you were a good sport about it."

It took Robert back to that very first meeting in the alley. Ange had made it clear he would fight someone who would try to take what wasn't theirs. Whatever broken parts he had, his will on that issue wasn't one of them, thank God.

Returning things to a less intense bent, Robert lifted a brow. "Doesn't mean I won't strap your ass later for allowing it, though. Just as a reminder."

Ange's quick grin, the heat in his gaze, told him he was okay with that, too.

~

After Sully returned, he completed the pinning and markups on the suit and shirt, and told them he'd have all of it ready later in the afternoon. Robert and Ange headed off to the shop to pick up the truck. At his direction, Ange packed up his few sets of clothes in his Army surplus duffle bag. The kid looked pleased at the confirmation that Robert wanted him at the house for a prolonged period, not just for last night.

While Robert couldn't imagine how Ange would doubt it, it reminded him once again how Ange didn't take anything for granted. As a strict Master, Robert appreciated that caution about anticipating the wrong things. But he also wanted Ange to understand down to his heart and soul how much he meant to Robert. That kind of confidence took time, though.

After they returned to the house, Robert changed into jeans and T-shirt. Then he and Ange set themselves to the task of moving the sectional sofa and other superfluous pieces of furniture out of the living room and down into the panel van.

When Robert drew in those Master's reins, Ange could be docile, spirited, passionate, offering a breathtaking desire to serve. But when they worked side by side at the store or on something as simple as moving furniture, that was when the truth formed a complete vessel, and filled it to overflowing.

Sex was sex, and a Master/sub relationship was limitlessly complex and satisfying. But finding they worked well together and enjoyed one another's company, never tiring of it, no matter what they were doing? That was something he wasn't sure he'd ever experienced as easily as he did with Ange. He sure as hell hadn't had it with Freddie. Having Ange in his home drew a big circle around it, indicating this relationship had a balance and satisfaction to it Robert couldn't imagine doing without, ever again.

After they wrestled the pieces of the sectional into the truck, they sat on the tailgate. Ange brought them out a couple bottles of water. As they sipped on them, Robert had him put his coat back on. Ange wore the open flannel shirt over his tank, but Robert didn't want him to get a chill as the sweat dried on his flesh. Ange smiled at him. "You're such a dad," he said.

Robert chuckled, surprised, but then he lifted a shoulder. "I like watching after you. Let's get this to the Salvation Army, then we'll grab a late lunch and go pick up your suit."

"No hints on where we're going tonight?" Ange asked, his eyes bright with curiosity.

"Nope. It's going to be a full-on surprise. There may even be a blindfold involved until the unveiling moment."

Robert saw Ange sift the possibilities, most of them temptingly sexual. "A BDSM club?" Ange asked, confirming it.

"No. Not tonight." Robert nudged him. "If we do that, it will be with your eyes wide open, and we'll talk about it first. But just off the cuff, what would you think of that?"

"Did you used to go to them with Freddie? Or other people?" Ange's expression and voice were neutral, except for the natural distaste he didn't bother to hide while uttering Freddie's name.

"Yeah. I was a regular at one. When I was single, I'd pick up a willing sub for the evening. I haven't been for quite a while. Since Freddie and my parents." Robert took another swallow of water, considered. Decided. "They have a Christmas Eve party, an early evening thing. Charlie was suggesting we should drop in."

"Will we?"

"Yeah, maybe." Robert tapped the bottle against Ange's inner thigh. He had one leg braced, the other bent and swinging, curling and uncurling, under the tailgate. "Have you ever been to a BDSM club?"

"I think so." Ange's brow creased in a curious way as he thought about it, then he nodded more decisively. "With friends. One of them was into it, and had the membership, so we went with him as his guests, curious. I watched, mostly. There was a Dom...he invited me to do a rope tying thing, and I did that, but I didn't lose myself in it. My friends were watching, and we were all laughing, so it didn't get really intense. It was just play, checking it out."

He shifted so he was facing Robert more squarely. "But it took hold of my head. A lot. That night, after he untied me, the Dom answered my questions one on one, told me what it was all about. I guess he realized I had it in me and so he was patient. He pointed me toward the right information to look up on my own. Which helped me figure things out and learn how to stay safe, if I went that way again."

"Sounds like a good Dom." Robert was glad the man had been around for Ange, to help provide that guidance. He wondered why Ange had initially seemed confused over the memory. It was like watching a dim bulb behind his eyes grow brighter as the memory came more into focus.

A person who'd endured a severe trauma could lose pieces of their lives that way. With a cold trickle in his stomach, Robert wondered if those bullet wounds had happened near or even at a club, but then he discarded the thought. Even if it had happened in another state, the BDSM world was closely knit. He would have heard about it through the grapevine.

"Have you lived here all your life?" he asked.

Ange shook his head, shifted again. Talking about the past was starting to unsettle him. Robert weighed the pros and cons, determined he could probably squeeze in a couple more questions. "Where else have you been?"

"I was born here," Ange said. "But my parents moved into my grandmother's place in Atlanta when my dad lost his job and my mom's wasn't enough to pay rent. Once my dancing reached the right level, Sharon—my grandmother—relocated me and her to her second home in New York. After she died, I stayed, lived up there with other dancers."

Ange rose from the tailgate, crushed the bottle into a pancake and held out his hand for Robert's, which was also empty. "So, ready to go to the Salvation Army?"

All the usual signs. Jittery, eyes shifting, body tense. Robert rose, drew close. "Be still. Look at my eyes."

Ange obeyed the command, with effort. As Robert faced him, he could tell the direct confrontation of body language was making things worse. "Drop your gaze," he ordered, and Ange complied, relief lowering his shoulders a half inch.

"May I say more about that other Dom, Master?"

"Yes. Tell me."

"I recognized my sub side because of the type of men who attracted me." Ange's gaze remained on Robert's feet. "Alpha males who had Dom traits, but they never took the reins in the way I seemed to want. I wanted something like what I found through the structure of dance. Inside those boundaries, the possibilities are endless, because of the discipline and commitment it takes to create them. Stuff deeper than I knew how to explain. I couldn't tell them..."

His gaze flickered up, made it to Robert's knees and dropped again.

"That you needed a stronger, steadier hand," Robert said. "A very much stronger, steadier hand."

"Yes, sir."

"You found one."

Ange's lips quirked, but his response was a little breathy. "Yes, sir."

Robert curved a hand against Ange's neck, kneaded. "I know there are trouble spots," he said. "I know there are dark areas inside you, Ange. I want you to work on trusting me."

Ange's gaze came up fast. "I do."

"Eyes lowered," Robert reminded him, in a mild tone, and they snapped back down again. "Don't talk back. Listen to what I'm telling you. Giving yourself to me fully means unfolding every bit of yourself, even the parts that hurt or scare you. I won't push for that too hard or too fast, but when I ask a question, I expect it to be answered honestly, even if the only answer you have for me is, 'I can't talk about that right now, Master.'"

He closed the distance between them now, wrapping both arms around his sub. Ange was rigid in his arms for a second, then a little breath left him and he slid his arms around Robert. As Robert stroked his hair, Ange dropped his head onto his shoulder. Robert pressed his jaw against him. "There you are," he said quietly. "It was bad enough it took away blocks of your memory, didn't it?"

"It didn't take away enough of them," Ange mumbled. "Or the right ones."

"Yeah. I get that." Robert caressed the middle of his back, the tense shoulders, then eased back. "You can look at me now."

When Ange lifted his gaze, Robert cupped his jaw. "I'm here and I won't disappear. Try to do the same for me. Okay?"

Ange nodded, his expression troubled. "Today has been a really good day," he said abruptly. "I just want you to know that."

"For me, too." Robert tilted his head toward the truck. "Let's do this."

CHAPTER EIGHT

*I*t didn't leave Robert's mind as they drove to the Salvation Army. Though he'd suspected it throughout the past six months, the past couple days had confirmed it. His boy likely needed some formal PTSD therapy to safely get to the bottom of what had happened to him. If Robert could talk him into that after the holiday, Ange might be able to fully heal the wound still open and bleeding into other parts of his life.

They dropped off the furniture, then grabbed some Thai for a late lunch. When they made their final stop at Sully's, the tailor banished Robert from the fitting. "I want it to have the full effect." Sully tilted his head toward Ange. "In this, I overrule your Master. Get dressed on your own tonight, so he sees everything at once and is overwhelmed."

Robert lifted a brow. "I think you're forgetting who's paying the bill."

Sully snorted. "By the time you finish bartering with me over the collectibles I'm seeking, I will be the one paying. But I will recoup the loss. When people see him, they will be asking where he bought this wonderful suit, and I will sell ten of them."

Robert rolled his eyes but left them to it. He ran an errand at the bank, picked up some groceries, Then, thinking again of

Charlie's invitation and Ange's interest, he stopped at a Lebo's, which had a big selection of clothing for dance students. After that, estimating he had some time left, he ducked into an Adam and Eve store to browse. It was only one strip mall over, so it was convenient.

When he found something that ignited his imagination, he didn't let himself hesitate. He bought it, reasoning that even if they didn't go to Patriarch, he'd enjoy the hell out of using it on Ange.

Sully texted him when he was checking out. He'd finished the fitting session. Stowing his purchases in the trunk where Ange wouldn't see them, Robert headed that way.

Ange emerged from the store with a garment bag over his shoulder and a shoe box under his arm. As he crunched across the melting snow, the wind flapped open the coat and flannel shirt so the triskelions and angel-wing engraved buckle of the braided collar on Ange's throat bore a sheen from the winter sun.

Sully waved from the store window, including a serious look similar to Charlie's parting expression. One that said, *I am glad for your happiness.*

Robert had never forgotten he was blessed in friends, but at Christmastime in particular, it was nice to have the reminder.

Back at the house, they put away the groceries. Then, since they had some time, they ascended to the roof deck. Sitting side by side in warm coats, they studied the view while sipping hot toddies Robert had put together. They talked of easy things, hands brushing often. Sometimes they didn't talk at all, simply sitting, Ange's shoulder pressed to Robert's.

"If I could choose a day to repeat over and over, it would be this one," Ange said.

"Yeah. Me, too. But you know what? I'm looking forward to tomorrow. And the next day and the next. Thanks to you."

Real love never ends. It's not the flood of fickle rainstorms. It's the endless current of a river.

Theopolis had said that, at the funeral of Robert's mother. The queens had attended wearing elaborate feathered hats, mesh veils, long gloves, sturdy but fashionable high heels. His mom would have loved it. Dallas had sung, "I Come to the Garden Alone," the notes drifting out and lingering over the corner of the cemetery where his mother had wanted to be buried. Next to his father.

Robert's heart tightened. As good as things were, the days ahead could also bring the kind of change Robert didn't want. Sully had said it. Life had a way of throwing a lot on the scales of happiness, unbalancing them. But Robert knew what stagnation felt like. He'd allowed it to take over a significant part of his life these past couple years. Maybe that pause had served its purpose, when his heart had been too battered and bruised to handle the risk of anything new. But he was ready to move forward. A healing heart needed nourishment.

"Go grab your shower and get dressed in the second-floor guestroom. We can do our great reveal on the first floor, make Sully happy." Robert consulted his watch. "Will an hour be enough time to make yourself pretty?"

Ange's eyes narrowed. When Robert reached out to give his head an affection smack, he was blocked, and the wrestling match was on. Ange was quicker, but Robert was stronger and had him on bulk. He just had to be patient and wait for the right opportunity to put him in a lock and hold on, take Ange down.

A lot of laughter, good-natured cursing and scattering of fortunately sturdy deck furniture happened first. But when Robert seized his opportunity, they were conveniently behind the covered bar, a mostly dry space, and sheltered from the wind.

As he got him down on the ground, Robert changed his grip, shifting smoothly to stretch full out on Ange. That, and his sudden squeeze on Ange's throat, stilled his submissive. Told him that kind of playtime was over. Ange's lips were already parted and trembling when Robert claimed them. He reached between them, cupped Ange's cock and balls through the jeans, squeezed and stroked as Ange groaned against his mouth.

"Hands above your head. You don't have permission to touch. That liberty's all mine."

Ange complied, his eyes glittering with need. Robert unhooked the button of Ange's jeans, pushed his hand beneath the zipper and boxers to grab him in a cold hand, warming it against the convulsing rigid flesh. Ange's hips bucked against the sensation, his hands opening and closing above his head. Robert worked him until he could tell Ange was just about to spew, then he pushed himself up to his knees and stood, opening his jeans.

"Suck me off," he ordered. "Then you'll get to come."

Ange's eyes filled with deep pleasure at being ordered so brusquely to serve, particularly when he was trembling on the precipice of his own release. Just the kind of sub Robert cherished. He injected steel into his voice.

"Un-unh," he said as Ange reached for him. "Hands behind your back. Only your mouth."

He used his own hands to guide himself in, holding the base of his cock. He savored the bliss of his submissive's strong tongue and sucking lips, the urgent pull on his organ, the friction on the head. Fuck, Ange was good at giving head. The temptation of Robert getting this whenever he wanted it from his sub, stretching those beautiful, willing lips? Heaven on earth.

He considered himself a civilized man, but the pure fantasy of having a slave, someone he owned completely, was undeniable.

But that was the thing. Forcing Ange to be his slave, versus him seeking the position with eagerness, a desire to embrace Robert's full ownership...there was no comparison. Willing submission was the gateway to every level of submission worth having.

He pulled on Ange's hair as his climax rolled up through his cock, pumped into Ange's eager mouth. While his hips worked and vision grayed, Robert dropped his touch to Ange's throat to feel him swallow rapidly, taking everything Robert had to give.

His other hand braced him on the bar, keeping his knees from buckling. Christ, the kid might have an angel's name, but he had the tongue of a devil.

When the world steadied, Robert reluctantly drew out of that devil-blessed mouth to tuck himself in and refasten his jeans. Ange was staring at the movement of his hands, his lips still pressing together, wet and needy, his eyes glazed.

Robert touched his ear, caressed the shell and the tender skin behind it, drawing those green eyes up to his. "Take your cock in your hand and stroke yourself to release," he said roughly. "Don't look away, and when you're close, you ask my permission."

"Yes, Master." Ange dug into the stretched boxers to comply. As he began to stroke his cock, his eyes held Robert's. His mouth was rigid, then open, working as his hand moved faster, his shoulders twitching, knees splayed, his ass rocking on his heels.

"Oh...God..." The words whispered out of him, pleas and entreaties. Robert watched, keeping his expression stern, expectant. "Master, may I..."

"Eventually. Keep going."

Ange's eyes widened, but he continued, his desperation mounting as he kept jerking off, but also holding back.

"Stop."

Ange came to a complete halt, his body shuddering, trembling. Robert spoke low, menace in his tone. "I've changed my mind. You can't come. You have to just suffer, hold it in. What do you say to that?"

Ange's whole body was a vibrating cable. His voice was a rough rasp. "I would say... Thank you, Master. For giving me the chance to prove my devotion to you. To prove I value your desires far more than my own."

Ange had said he'd only been in a Dom/sub situation that once, and even that was more of a teaching thing. Now Robert believed it. Because if someone had discovered this side of Ange fully, they would have locked him up in their personal dungeon

147

and never let him go. They'd have kept him there with Pop-Tarts and the demand of full 24/7 service, all the things the boy obviously wanted.

"That's a good answer. One I'll likely test way more than you want. But for right now, I want to see you come. Do it. Now. No. No hands again. Put them behind you."

Ange's hand froze on his dick, then he took it away. As he locked his hands behind his back in a tight knot, it lifted his chest, made his back arch in a pleasing way. His exposed buttocks tilted within the loose circle of his jeans, his cock jutting out over his thighs. Robert bent eye-to-eye level with him, and hooked his fingers under the braided collar, caressing even as he tightened the hold of the buckled strap.

"It's not your hand making you come, but my will. My will is wrapping around your dick, rubbing it, flicking it, stroking it, teasing the head, lapping at your balls, sucking one in to roll it over my tongue. You feel it?"

Ange nodded, green eyes bright like fire, his breath coming faster, hips jerking. "I've got it held tight," Robert told him. "Just my will, but it's like a collar and lock on your cock, squeezing tight, reminding you with every move you make I own your orgasm. I own your dick. I own everything around it. You serve me and no other. Now, tomorrow and always."

"Yes, Master."

"I didn't ask for your words. I asked for your obedience. Your climax. I'm rubbing the skin off your dick with my will, and it's never going to stop stroking. You'll feel it when you're in the store, in my bed, walking down the street."

"Oh...*oh*." Ange's head dipped against Robert's hand, his jaw pressed hard against Robert's knuckles as his body undulated, jerked again. Translucent white fluid pumped from his slit, coating the head, teasing Robert with the desire to taste, to enjoy that salty, musky Ange flavor.

The power of the climax toppled Ange forward, but Robert had him, a hand on his shoulder as Ange's body humped air. A raw groan ripped from his throat. It became a short shout of desire when Robert reached down with his free hand and gripped the convulsing organ, made the spoken claim a physical one. Ange muffled his groans and cries against Robert's thigh, pressing his face and mouth hard against the column as the climax worked through him.

It wrung him out like a dish rag, leaving him twisted and limp against Robert.

Robert slid his arm around his back, bent over him and squeezed him close, uttering his fervent approval and visceral male satisfaction in Ange's ear.

"That's my boy. So good. Now you can get dressed. Once you can walk."

It hadn't taken Robert as long to get ready, so once he was dressed, he passed the closed door to the guest room and went down to the first floor living room. His anticipation for the evening was building. While it was a good feeling, he wanted to be steady for Ange, who was sometimes a little twitchy in public situations. So to even out his own nerves, Robert started the gas logs, poured himself a glass of wine and took a seat on the two-person couch they'd moved to a less cluttered arrangement in the room. They hadn't had time to decorate the pre-lit tree yet, but it was set up, throwing a nice holiday glow over the room with the multi-colored lights.

He clicked on the music player, found the smooth jazz Christmas album he wanted, and let the tune add to the room's tranquil ambiance. He imagined the changes Ange had suggested for the room, embellished with ideas Robert had himself, and was content with how it was shaping up. How it felt.

Then he heard the door on the second level open and Ange descending the steps. The hard soles of the cowboy boots tapped against the wooden stairs.

While he was sure he'd be pleased with the alteration results, Robert didn't expect to be knocked on his ass as Sully had predicted. After all, Robert had seen the suit on Ange in the store.

He should have known better than to doubt Sully's prophetic powers.

Ange had paused at the bottom step as Robert rose to face him. If anything proved his sub had been on stage, it was that subconscious pose, back straight, head tilted, all senses alert.

The caramel color picked up and enhanced the lighter strands of Ange's white-gold hair. The jacket was perfectly fitted to his upper body, outlining the handsome breadth of shoulders, narrowing along the waist, draping over the hips. As Sully had noted, the suit had a roguish cowboy outlaw look to it. The narrow and pointed lapels were edged with piping, the vest beneath held snugly with a row of wooden buttons over Ange's flat stomach.

The shirt with the pearl snap buttons was open at the throat, the sea foam color of the fabric bringing out the vividness of Ange's gaze. Robert could see the black braid of the collar on his strong, graceful throat, the hint of silver working with the silver outline of the pearl snaps of the shirt.

The whole outfit, including the leather braid of the collar, evoked the open range of romantic Westerns. Wide-open fields of golden wheat grass, dotted with green trees whose twisted branches had been sculpted by the elements. All of it overseen by endless, changing skies and rolling clouds.

As Ange descended the last couple steps, the wide brown belt with its pewter-colored buckle moved provocatively with his hips. It drew Robert's eye to the crotch of the pants, the fly creased and fitted over Ange's endowments. From there his attention moved and dwelled on the lengths of his long thighs. It took a while, but Robert finally made his way to the masculine pointed tips of the cowboy boots.

Ankle length for easy removal. For that walk on the beach with a lover.

As he returned his gaze to Ange's face, Robert noted his artfully tousled hair was still damp from his shower. He was clean-shaven.

So absorbed had Robert been in his reaction to his submissive, he only now registered Ange's reaction to *him*.

Ange's gaze clung to Robert, his lips parted in a distracting way. His stillness had increased, like a tuning fork where the vibrations couldn't be seen, only felt. That intensity raised a reaction on Robert's skin, flesh calling to flesh, even beneath the layers of clothes.

Those layers were simple, severe. Robert wore a charcoal gray suit, his black shirt open at the throat. Black polished shoes finished the look. The suit was one of Sully's offerings, more traditional than Ange's, but fitting Robert's personality and tastes. If Ange's nearly open mouth and avid gaze could be believed, it worked on the Dom level as well as for the evening's dress code.

"What?" Robert asked.

"You're beautiful, Master," Ange responded. Breathless. "Very authoritative. I want to do anything you desire." He sent his Master an impish look. "Very Christian Grey."

Robert laughed; he couldn't help it. The rich response earned an even deeper shine and fascination in those green eyes. "I don't know about that. But get over here."

When Ange complied, Robert gripped his nape and brought him close to enjoy his sweet mouth. He finished it up with a sharp nip at the sensitive lips before pinning him with a hard stare. "But it's good to know you feel that way. Comments like that make me want to stay here and put you through your paces."

"I'm down with that," Ange said, his fingers curling over Robert's wrist.

"Tempting, but no. Don't make me kick your ass. Your whole

look says topping from the bottom without you saying one word. Sully knew the suit would get you in trouble, call up that vibe."

Switching tracks from the teasing, Robert gave Ange's neck an extra squeeze. And offered his sub brutal honesty. "I want to give you this night. I started planning it back in October. Fantasized about it, backed away from it, let my own head fuck with me. Telling me I shouldn't make that step. That being your Master in every way wasn't what you needed from me. That what I was for you at the store was enough, and to leave it there."

Ange's eyes darkened, and his own grip tightened. "If you had made that decision, something important would have been missing for me. May I say something, Master? Please."

"I think you just did." Robert nudged him. "But yeah."

"Without giving me what you need, you're holding back the most important part of what I need. I want to be what you need, Master. I know I am, that I can be." Ange's earnest tone faltered. His other hand rested on Robert's abdomen, his fingers curling into the black shirt. "I get afraid...that I'll fall short of it, that I'm lacking something inside me. I had doubts about that, too. But I just had to offer everything of myself I could. I wanted you too much not to try."

They'd been in the same spot, just different sides of the Dom and sub coin. Robert figured the Fates routinely vacillated between laughter and tears at the stupid obstacles people threw in their own paths.

"You lack nothing, Ange." Robert touched his forehead to his, squeezed his nape once more, this time even harder. "Okay, stay still. I want to take a look at you from all sides."

Ange's eyes glowed, his lips parting in that unconsciously distracting way, but Robert had the reins firmly in hand now. On his own emotions, as well as on his submissive. As he circled Ange, taking his visual fill, he resolved to cherish every moment of this evening. He was also going to count down to the moment when he could pull that fitted coat to Ange's elbows, hold him pinned as he savaged the vulnerable column of his throat exposed by the shirt. He'd use teeth and tongue, sucking lips. The kid would never be without marks there again.

He moved close behind Ange, laid the lightest of kisses on one of the fading bruises from Robert's mouth, and felt him quiver. "I'm going to look forward to stripping you of that belt," Robert growled. "Binding your hands with it to my headboard and devouring you inch by inch. Taking that suit off a piece at a time. I'm going to leave you with so many marks on your flesh you won't have any doubt who your Master is."

"Yes..." Ange barely breathed it. "Thank you, Master."

Robert put a hand on his shoulder. As he did, he let the blindfold he'd slipped out of his pocket dangle down so Ange noticed it. "Do you get car sick if you can't see?"

"Not that I know of," Ange said. His voice had gotten intriguingly rough.

"Let me know if you do." Robert fitted the blindfold over his eyes, caressing the fair brow, the bridge of his nose, then tied the blindfold in back. "Can you see anything?"

Ange shook his head. "No, sir."

"Let's go, then."

Robert guided Ange down the steps carefully and into the car. Before they'd come home, he'd run the classic BMW through a touchless car wash, having the crew wipe it down with soft cloths afterward. He kept the inside pristine, so with the wash it was ready for the formal and festive nature of their outing.

Ange's lips were curved beneath the blindfold, his hand relaxed in the guiding hold of Robert's. Robert couldn't wait to get to their destination, but he savored this as well, this trust his submissive was offering him. It made him imagine plenty other versions of it. Like in their bedroom tonight. Or at Patriarch on

Christmas Eve. The likelihood of that happening was getting way stronger.

As they drove through town, Robert kept an eye on Ange in case he showed any signs of being nauseous, but any tension in Ange appeared to be the right kind. Expectant, eager, wondering what Robert had planned. Robert clasped Ange's hand, enjoying the grip, the caress of his sub's fingers on his palm. He was also a serious fan of the way Ange's long legs looked, one of them stretched out in the slacks, the other knee bent to brace the cowboy boot against the floorboard, a ridiculously sexy look.

Robert's gaze also lingered on Ange's slim fingers, resting on the car door armrest, the tilt of his head, the way the blindfold drew attention to his mouth, his jaw. A couple times he released Ange's fingers to brush his knuckles along his throat, the edge of the collar, before recapturing his hand. The kid had used his aftershave, because Robert could smell it. He liked knowing Ange bore one of his scents, another form of marking.

Yeah, this was kind of a honeymoon period, but he didn't see himself getting tired of looking at Ange. Nobody got tired of looking at an angel. Especially one endlessly eager to be commanded and fucked senseless by his Master.

When Robert reached their destination, he pulled around to the rear, parking at the door he'd been instructed to use. As he emerged, there were a few people coming and going, involved in the flurry of activity happening inside. They gave him quick, amused glances as he opened the door for his blindfolded passenger and guided him out of the car.

A man in black jeans and a coat embroidered with a yellow security badge stood by the door. When Robert put a finger to his lips, he smiled under heavy brows, blue eyes glinting as he checked their pass. Then he leaned closer to murmur to Robert.

"Know where you're going?" At Robert's nod, he continued in his smoker's rough voice, the habit evident in the scent of his clothes. "Hug the walls where you can. Lot of people and stuff moving around. On a show night, folks can get snappish if you're in the way, even if you're a VIP."

Robert led Ange through the door the man opened for them. The man's advice hadn't been exaggerated. A lot of props and equipment were being moved in the narrow pathways, groups of people rushing from one thing to the next, speaking in sharp bursts. Costumes in bright hues and sparkles contrasted with dark, nondescript clothing that could blend into the shadows.

Robert had detailed directions on where to bring Ange backstage, a place where VIPs not only had a unique view of the performance, but they could observe the preparations for the lifting of the curtain. Two chairs would be in that alcove. He and Ange would remain there until the conclusion of the first act, after which they'd be escorted to premium box seats overlooking the stage.

He kept a firm hand on Ange's lower back, Ange clasping his other hand, following Robert's lead as they moved forward or stopped to flatten against the wall to allow people to pass. The constant movement and close quarters meant there wasn't time to pause, keep moment-by-moment tabs on Ange's reaction, but Robert had been assured that the VIP section wasn't too far from the backstage door.

One of the reasons he'd wanted Ange to wear the blindfold on the way here was to determine how he'd handle the lack of sight. In the car, Ange had been relaxed and seemed excited, reassuring Robert he was okay trusting his Master's lead. Even at the door, a light, puzzled smile had stayed on his mouth as Robert conferred with door security.

But in the brief pause before they crossed the direct path to the stage, in order to get to the alcove and chairs Robert saw waiting for them, he realized Ange's tension level had shot up. His body was stiff, nostrils flared. The clasp on Robert's hand had become a death grip.

Robert pressed close, keeping his touch relaxed, easy. "I

know you're not big on being in larger groups of people you *can* see," he said in Ange's ear, brushing his lips over it. "Trust me. It's okay. I'm here. We're almost there."

"Robert," Ange said. It sounded like he was having trouble getting air. His hand remained in a tight clutch.

Shit. "Okay, come here." Though his Dom skills might be rusty, Robert had dealt with a sub in crisis plenty of times. He'd used that experience to handle some of Ange's bad moments over the past six months.

First, safe space. Robert took them across the pathway to the stage in several quick strides, no matter that he had to bring a couple stagehands up short. He kept his body and formidable shoulders between them and Ange, in case he had to take the brunt of the collision, but they pulled up in time, the only thing hitting him a pair of ferocious scowls Robert ignored.

He pressed Ange down into one of the two chairs, then moved behind him, resting his hands on the rigid line of shoulders. "Easy. That's it, we're here. Would you like me to remove the blindfold?"

The quick jerk of Ange's head wasn't a yes or no. Instead, he reached toward the blindfold himself, something he could pull off easily, but he didn't. His fingers curled against the fabric, paused. Robert saw a hard tremor go through them before Ange dropped the hand back into his lap.

"I know where we are. I can smell it, sense it...feel it, in here." He pressed a hand to his heart, then grabbed for Robert's on his shoulder, a lifeline. As Robert bent over him, he let his other palm slide down, cover Ange's hand on his chest. Alarm filled him. Even through that skin and bone buffer, he could feel the kid's accelerated heart rate.

Ange loved to dance. Loved it. How could coming here just as an observer be putting him in a bad way? Maybe taking him backstage had convinced him Robert was going to somehow put him in the spotlight.

Robert could fix that. He slipped in front of Ange and

dropped to his heels. He let Ange hold his hand until he got there, but then Robert let go so he could put his hands on the outside of Ange's thighs, close to his hips. Ange's jacket draped over his knuckles. The move turned their bodies into a circle, making him Ange's primary sensory focus, taking away the full impact of their surroundings.

"Breathe," Robert said steadily. Since Ange seemed to want to keep the blindfold on, he wouldn't remove it yet. "I know how much you love to dance," Robert said conversationally, stroking one strong thigh, reaching up briefly to touch the taut mouth. "I've loved watching you. Your immersion in it, your passion for it, was part of what brought passion and the desire to live back to me."

Ange's chin tilted down as he listened. Whatever had set him off shuddered through him, squeezing Robert's heart. Hell, he needed to see his eyes to get more information.

"I'm going to remove the blindfold. Close your eyes, and don't open them until I say. Tell me you understand."

"Yes." Ange swallowed.

Robert straightened to pull the blindfold off, then dropped to his heels again, pocketing the scrap of fabric. "Now open your eyes, but look straight at me. Only at me."

Ange did slowly, as if he feared what he would see. The effort to keep his gaze on Robert's face was visibly difficult, his features strained. "All right. You can look around when you're ready, but focus on individual details. Don't get overwhelmed by the whole thing."

The whole thing would be a feast for the senses. The stage was set with glittering props. Christmas trees, brightly colored packages, large velvet drapes in green and gold. There was synthetic snow, little flakes of it tracked all the way to where they were. As promised, he and Ange were positioned for a prime view of the stage, a spot specifically reserved for an audience of two.

"Can't be Christmas in Charlotte without a performance of

the Nutcracker ballet here," Robert said, giving Ange a serious smile, even as he continued to monitor his reactions closely. "I thought you'd enjoy being in the audience. It's a pretty highly rated troupe. The Markham Company out of New York."

"Helena Markham," Ange rasped.

Robert thought Ange was proving he knew the company. But his eyes had gone to the stage. As Robert turned on his heel, he saw a tiny woman with the majestic presence of a queen. Clad in flowing dark slacks and a green blouse, she had the lean body of a retired dancer and a braided tail of golden hair. She was headed in their direction, though her body was half turned as she issued last minute direction to various crew members scrambling to keep up. As soon as she waved her hand, they dispersed with swift efficiency to do her bidding.

Ange rose from the chair abruptly, as if jerked by strings. Robert came to his feet, shifting to his side, his hand on his back. The woman turned toward them at the same moment.

Her attention was caught by their movement, but her distracted gaze passed over them. Until it came back, as if she'd been jerked by the same kind of strings that had brought Ange to his feet.

She moved a couple steps forward. Robert saw her awareness of everything around her vanish, replaced by a million other things, every one of them connected to his companion.

"Ange," she said. Her voice held wonder, disbelief...pain.

In a blink, she'd closed the gap between them, had her hands out and was grasping Ange's upper arms as if she expected him to disappear right in front of her. When she touched him, she let out a little gasp, as if the reality of his flesh startled her. Robert still had his hand on Ange and felt another shudder go through him, so violent it was almost a convulsion.

Helena's gaze had reflected pain, but Ange's showed pure anguish. If his sub could live up to his name, Robert thought he would have let the wings tear through the new suit and shoot him away, far off into the dark skies.

Fuck. He'd screwed up. How badly, he didn't know. He was in unfamiliar waters. He had to wait for the cues, push aside the flood of worry and kneejerk desire to protect Ange, which he could do in the absolutely wrong way if he acted before he knew what was going on.

Even the best scene could go off track, especially when things got intense. The key was the Dom keeping calm and not overreacting. That way he could focus on what was happening, not miss the details that would bring things back to balance.

"Ange. My God." The director's gaze passed over him, and now she registered Robert. He could see her making the connection that he and Ange were here together, in the VIP area. She would have been informed that Mr. Robert Bauer and a guest would be here, witnessing their performance. She was professional enough to recall herself, offer a hand, though it wasn't steady, and her gaze kept darting back to Ange, dwelling on his pale face. "You must be Mr. Bauer. I didn't realize..."

"I need to go to the restroom," Ange said abruptly. He stepped back, further into the clasp of shadows that concealed too much of his face. But he gripped Robert's forearm, a hard squeeze, meeting his gaze with reasonable clarity before he pivoted and vanished behind another drape. Everything about the look and his body language said he needed a minute.

Robert struggled between the desire to follow him, figure out what was happening in his head, and respect that unspoken plea. The latter won out, primarily because the key to some of his questions about Ange's past might be standing right in front of him. That information might help him help Ange, and he had only limited access to it. Perhaps only a few minutes, before she'd recall all the responsibilities pressing around her.

Helena had reached out to Ange when he stepped back, and her hand was still in the air. Now she lowered it, but she was staring after Ange. "I can't believe it," she said. "To find him here, tonight of all nights."

"I'm sorry?" Robert touched her arm to draw her out of the well of her thoughts. She started at the contact.

"Forgive me," she said. "It's...I can't tell you what a shock it is to see him. We thought...I thought...well, to put it frankly, we didn't even know if Ange was still alive."

Now she'd startled Robert, but then it flashed through his mind, how he'd found Ange. Homeless, beat up, in an alley. Ange's behavior had suggested he'd been on the street for some time. Making some quick deductions, he pressed onward, hoping to give Helena the impression he knew more than he did, so he might fill in some empty pieces.

"He used to dance for you."

"Yes. More than that..." She looked at Robert now, fully. Her eyes registered a lot more than he would have expected. "You love him. You love him more than anything?"

A pretty personal question, but emotions were swirling from her like that synthetic snow in front of an industrial fan, so the usual formalities didn't apply.

"Yes. I do."

"He asked to come here tonight?"

"No. It was a surprise. He loves to dance. He works in my toy store, and I could tell he'd danced, maybe professionally..."

He trailed off as her expression morphed through various powerful emotions. "My God." She perched on one hip on one of the chairs, gripping the top of it with a white-knuckled hand. When one of the stage crew came her way, she shook him off with a sharp gesture that startled him. "I need a moment," she informed him. "Figure it out."

She brought her gaze back to Robert. "I'm the current owner and artistic director of the company started by my father, Mr. Bauer. Before that I was a professional dancer, and then a chore-ographer. I am tough and exacting, and can always find ways for a dancer to improve. It is the way our world works."

She put her hand on Robert's arm, the same place that Ange had gripped so strongly. Her nails dug through his jacket. "He was the type of danseur we expected to take his place alongside Baryshnikov and Bruhn in dance history. Maybe even Nureyev. There was something very special about him off stage as well. This is a brutally competitive business. But Ange...he was so open and caring. I'm not one for sentiment, but I have thought of him so often. To put it plainly, when he was on stage, he reminded anyone watching what our dreams are, undiluted by ego, fear or competition. He made us feel the most important parts of those dreams could all come true."

"Yeah." Robert was very familiar with that feeling when Ange looked at him. To hear it put into words, evoked in a world so different from his own? *Holy hell.*

"He was a quiet man, but ready to laugh and play, always. Forever a child, yet also a mysterious and sensual man. He never lacked for bed partners, but he never chose anyone specifically, permanently, though he and Leo were so close... And Clarissa... beautiful Clarissa."

She shook herself, snapped out of the memories as someone else called her name, urgently. The other crew member was still waiting, with a look of near desperation. "Shit. I can't talk about this now. Perhaps later, please bring him back." She fished out a card, handed it to him. "My cell is on there. We can set up a time and place before I leave town. Since you say he's still dancing, I'd love the chance to see him dance again. Find out what his plans are."

She rose, obviously trying to pull herself together. Though he was revealing his ignorance, Robert attempted one more question.

"I'll encourage him to do that. But please, Ms. Markham, what happened? He can't tell me. Not won't. *Can't.*"

She stared at him, her gaze an open wound. "I can't discuss that right now. Not before a performance." She swallowed, turned away, then paused, glanced back. "Look up Markham Company. The Nutcracker." Her lips tightened. "Fatal shooting."

As Robert's heart leaped into his throat, she nodded. "You

will get some of your answers. Those you don't, I will help as I can, when we meet." She looked toward the shadows, pointed. "But for now, I think you should go check on him. He didn't go to the restroom, Mr. Bauer. He headed for the back door."

∼

The spike of alarm gave wings to Robert's feet. Despite her certainty, he checked the backstage area fast, then he was out the rear door. It took two steps to confirm Ange was no longer in the building.

The caramel-colored suit jacket was on the ground.

Robert called Ange's name, shouted it. He checked the car, then searched the parking area. From there he worked outward, combing the well-tended grounds around the auditorium. The parking area started to fill with arrivals for the ballet.

He checked a nearby city park, then re-canvassed all the immediate surroundings before getting into the car and using it to cover more area. He stopped endless times to probe shadowed alleys between buildings. He rolled up next to pedestrians, asked them if they'd seen him, watched their expressions change from wariness to sympathy or curiosity before he continued onward.

Ange was out in thirty-degree weather and slushy, icy snow with no jacket. Robert kept his hand on the coat, folded in the passenger seat. In some crazy way, he thought the contact would help him find his way to Ange, like scent did a bloodhound.

By the time he stopped a couple hours later in a Krispy Kreme parking lot, he was bone-cold and his hands were shaking. As the light of the neon sign flooded into the BMW, he told himself he needed to calm down.

Ange was a grown man. Yet Robert kept being pummeled by the memory of that very first meeting six months ago, Ange on his ass in the alley by Robert's store, bleeding from the mouth, bruised from the beating he'd taken from a bunch of thugs, the green eyes lost as lost could be.

No. He was just wandering, getting a grip on the ghosts that had risen from his past tonight. That Robert had stupidly stirred up.

Guilt wasn't going to help anything. "Shit. Take a breath. You're just scaring yourself half to death, and you can't think straight that way. That won't help him."

He purchased a large coffee at the drive-through, then chose a parking spot. As he drank coffee, he called up his browser on his phone.

North Carolina was a long way from New York City, and a million tragedies were reported on the news. One that happened in the dance world wouldn't have registered in Robert's world. Not before he'd met Ange.

Bracing himself, he entered the key words Helena had suggested. The answer came at the very top of the search results: **Dancers shot onstage at Markham Company theater. Suspect kills himself...**

As Robert read the details, his heart twisted, torturing him with the reminder of how Fate, once it had you in its grip, could be a cruel son of a bitch.

Clarissa Wyndham, 21, was fatally shot by Angus Corwin, 27, while rehearsing for a performance of the Nutcracker. Wyndham had recently broken off a relationship with Corwin. The shooting occurred Tuesday afternoon at the Markham Company theater.

Corwin allegedly entered the theater and fired thirteen shots at the stage. Wyndham and another dancer, Leo Seichek, died on stage. Also critically wounded was Ange Fournier.

Wyndham and Fournier were leads for this weekend's upcoming Nutcracker performance. This is the second year Markham has offered a version of the popular holiday season ballet. Critics have put it at the top of the list of worthy competitors with the classic New York City Ballet's performance. Fournier was also recently cited as "a star whose rise could be as breathtakingly high as his grand jeté."

Robert clicked the phone off, put it in his pocket and laid his head back on the seat. Then he snarled, hit the steering wheel several times with the heels of his hands. "Stupid, stupid, *stupid.*"

Yeah, guilt-tripping himself was pointless, but fuck if he wasn't going to do it to himself anyway. The alternative was losing his mind over Ange's whereabouts and imagining worst-case scenarios.

He'd been so proud of himself, so excited about giving Ange this Christmas gift. Because Ange loved to dance so much, it had never occurred to Robert that the gunshot wounds had connected to the dancing itself. But Ange's reaction to his visualization about dancing in air had been a flag. Not a big one, but Robert should have pursued it more. Not let himself off the hook with a decision to hold off on a deeper exploration of Ange's issues until after Christmas.

Trauma didn't observe a holiday schedule, for fuck's sake.

He'd been so out of practice as a Master, so arrogant, he'd missed the signs. If he'd paid closer attention, he could have read the shadows in Ange's face more quickly, the shift in the type of tension he was experiencing, and headed this drastic reaction off. Instead he'd been so sure he was in charge, the Master bolstered by his sub's trust and devotion. He'd gotten sloppy.

If ever anything could be called a trigger, dropping Ange backstage at the ballet he'd been preparing to perform when he'd been shot would certainly fucking qualify. Of all the stupid, fucking mistakes he could have made...

As bad as the guilt was, the fear was worse. It was cruel and jagged, slicing into his lungs and making it hard to breathe. Robert pulled Ange's jacket closer, smoothing it with his palm, remembering the heat of Ange's body beneath it. The pump of his heart, the smile on his beautiful mouth. If Ange wasn't clearing his head, if he was lost in it, then he was wandering the city streets with no situational awareness, not even of the cold.

That possibility meant only one thing that mattered. Robert's ten seconds of self-flagellation and imagining terrifying what-if scenarios were over. His sub needed him. Robert had to find him. It wasn't just Ange's mind that was in danger—his very life could be as well.

~

He kept going, looking. The fear didn't abate, but it wasn't in control. He was focused and thorough. He gave police patrols a description of Ange, told them he was a past violent trauma victim who might be experiencing a PTSD episode. They listened, told him they'd keep a lookout, and Robert believed them, particularly those he could tell had run into that situation, personally as well as professionally.

"I love you," he said, more than once, to the silent inside of his car, to the spirit of Ange, out there somewhere. He said it with fierceness, with fear, as a plea to any force that would listen to what he considered a three-word prayer. If he'd had any doubt how much Ange mattered to him, not being able to find him when he might be in trouble drove it straight through his heart. In a situation like this, Cupid's arrow felt like a railroad spike.

He lost track of how many times he left his car to talk to street people, couples walking home from restaurants. He had to assume Ange had stayed on foot, but if he was wrong and he'd boarded a bus, Robert would have fuck-all idea of where he ended up. He had to stick to the idea he was still within range.

At four in the morning, he was back at the store for the third time, hoping against hope he'd find Ange there. He didn't. Robert laid his keys down on the store counter, and braced his hands there. He closed his eyes, dropped his head down between his sunken shoulders, giving himself the moment of weariness. He was going to lose his fucking mind.

He ticked off all the places he'd checked, some of them more than once. He'd gone to Charlie's, to Sully's, gone home. Hit the homeless shelters. Returned to the theater, banged on the back-stage entrance insistently enough to earn the ire of the security guard sitting just inside, but his desperation had gotten through. They hadn't seen Ange, but when he called Helena with the card she'd given him, he discovered she was still there, attending a cast party in the dressing rooms. When he explained the situation, his voice hoarse with cold and worry, she told him she'd come to the back entrance to talk to him face-to-face.

As she emerged, wearing an ivory wrap over her clothes, she said something to the security guard. He disappeared back into the building with a more sympathetic look toward Robert.

"Do you have any idea where he might go, things I might not know?" Robert asked.

"I wish I could help you." Worry lines creased her forehead, her eyes sad. "But you see, Ange disappeared on us, too. After he got out of the hospital, he left his apartment, paid his rent, vanished. We were his family. He was not in close contact with his parents, but we checked with them, nonetheless. They didn't know where he'd gone, either. None of us did. It never occurred to us that he left the city, but obviously he did."

The idea that Ange might be headed somewhere hours away, where Robert had no chance of ever finding him again... Hell, the kid hadn't seemed to know his last name for the first several months. When Robert insisted on having it, needing to put him on the payroll officially rather than continuing to hand him cash off the books, it seemed like Ange had to dig his surname out of some forgotten closet in his soul.

Robert had built up his business using a lot of networking, contacts in the hobby and collectibles world. He provided guidance to the marketing firm that handled his social media presence and advertising, but it wasn't second nature to him to go to the computer to search for anything except the toys he was tracking down. If he'd searched on Ange's name months ago... but how could he have suspected a homeless kid had been a famous NYC dancer who'd light up a bunch of search results?

He was on the guilt train again. Hell, on that note, what if

Ange had hit the Amtrak station? He could end up in DC, or back in NYC, brimming with millions of people...

No, he couldn't even consider it. It wasn't happening. He would find him. He would.

The security guard emerged with a steaming cup of coffee that Helena pressed into his hands. "You look frozen," she said. "Please drink this. He'll turn up. I know he will. Your love for him is so obvious. It will call him back to you."

Returning to the present and his store, illuminated by the six Christmas trees he'd switched on—maybe to add to that beacon Helena had mentioned—Robert stared down into the display case. He resisted the urge to hit it. Cutting open a major artery by accident wouldn't be useful.

He was exhausted. He'd have to go home and get some sleep. But he couldn't handle stepping into the space and reliving everything they'd done there together. Or seeing the small things that Ange had already done to change the space, make it more open to life and love, to living again. He couldn't. He'd sleep in Ange's cot in back.

Think, think, *think*...

Robert pushed aside everything he thought he knew, and focused just on Ange. He remembered last night, when he'd brought Ange to his bedroom. Ange's expression, his sensitive fingers moving over the Lehmann clockwork toy. The baker's cheerful face and sweet smile, the chimney sweep with his broom slash flogger. When Ange looked over his shoulder at Robert, his expression had reminded Robert of the night he'd met him, that openness.

Everything, good and bad, kept leading him back to that first fateful meeting. How he'd felt—

Well, fuck.

Robert bolted away from the counter. Of all the stupid places not to have checked...

He barely dared to hope, but his gut said it made so much

sense. In case he was right, as he passed the small office area, he grabbed the extra coat he kept hanging on a rack in there.

He shoved his way out the side door and into the alleyway. As his gaze coursed over the dumpster and a couple trash cans, Christmas past and present overlapped. He remembered Ange's long legs, clad in ratty jeans and even rattier sneakers, no socks despite the cold, sticking out from behind the dumpster.

Now he saw those same legs, only they wore Dolce Gabbana slacks, his feet in cowboy boots, though the boots were a lot more scuffed than when he'd last seen them.

Robert's heart seized up, because those expensively clad legs were limp as a rag doll, dropped on the ground and abandoned.

"Ange." He still wore his suit, so in his dress shoes he slipped on an icy patch and nearly fell, but he got there. As his gaze penetrated the darkness behind the trash receptacle, he made out the shape of Ange lying in a half-sitting up position, his head resting against the hard metal, eyes closed. But his lips were parted, and he was breathing.

"I'm here, Ange. I'm here. It's me. It's okay." Robert knelt next to him, already stripping off his jacket. He pulled him away from the wall to get Robert's still body-warmed coat around him, then double-layered it with the coat he'd grabbed. The green shirt was dirty, suggesting Ange had fallen or leaned against a lot of less-than-clean places tonight. But Robert didn't see any blood or sign of injury.

The vest was gone, the shirt's pearl snaps open to his waist, exposing the pale skin to the elements. That, and his lack of a jacket, explained why Ange felt like an ice cube. The kid was giving his heart a complete workout tonight.

When he lifted him away from the dumpster, Ange thankfully lifted his head. His expression was bleary, out of it, but he was conscious.

"Who am I?" Robert demanded, giving him a little shake. "Tell me, Ange. Answer me."

"R-Robert... Master. Help. Safe."

A little sigh, and Ange's eyes closed, his head tipping forward to rest on Robert's chest.

Shit. "Okay. Okay." Robert held him tight, rubbing his hands up and down the coats pulled around Ange, helping to warm him as much as to reassure himself. He was here. He was okay. "Come on. We need to get you where it's warm."

Robert hauled him up to his feet, keeping a secure arm around his waist, a palm flattened on Ange's chest. Ange stumbled the first step or two, but then regained enough awareness to use his legs, show Robert that he had feeling in them. He also had a cough. The temperature wasn't low enough to risk frostbite, but prolonged exposure to the cold without the right kind of outerwear wasn't good for anyone except penguins.

Robert took him straight to the car and folded him into the passenger seat. The house was less than a couple minute drive. He could get Ange into the cast iron tub, warm him up. Robert knew how to deal with cold. Once Robert got Ange out of his clothes, as long as he didn't discover any injuries he couldn't see now, home was a better place for Ange than a medical center.

He pumped up the BMW's heater as he turned over the engine. Ange lay against the seat, his head turned toward Robert. Robert glanced at him, then looked again, seeing the tears running down Ange's face. No words, just all the suffering of the world in those big green eyes.

Robert cursed softly, reached over and gathered him in, holding him tight once more as the warm air blew on them. "It's okay. I've got you. It's okay."

"I'm so sorry. So sorry." Ange shuddered once, that hard shake, and then he was weeping against Robert. He grabbed Robert's shirt, fingers clutching the muscle beneath, as if he was afraid Robert was going to let him go, let him spin away on the current of those feelings.

No worries of that. If Robert could figure out how to do it, he'd never take his hands off him again.

"No sorries needed, kid. You've done nothing wrong.

Nothing at all." Except scare the life out of him tonight. When Ange was in his right mind, Robert was going to take a permanent strip off his hide for it. But right now, he was just grateful to every god and guardian angel and Ange himself for not taking him beyond Robert's grasp.

His boy had come home to him. *Help. Safe.* Those thoughts, the unconscious knowledge of where he could find them, had been the lifelines that had brought Ange back to Robert. It told Robert exactly what his job was right now. To provide those things, in whatever ways Ange needed them.

CHAPTER NINE

hen Ange's sobs had died down some, leaving him even more exhausted—and he was pretty close to comatose now—Robert drove back to the townhouse. He did it one-handed, keeping his other arm around his passenger. Ange leaned against his side, over the console, his forehead pressed to Robert's shoulder. There seemed to be no strength left to him, so Robert was glad for his own strength. It helped him get Ange into the house. They took the lift up to the master bedroom floor. Once there, he guided Ange into the bathroom, made him sit on a folded towel on the commode seat as Robert ran the bath.

He'd imagined sharing this tub with Ange under far different circumstances, but Robert wasn't complaining. Ange was here, watching Robert with empty, red-rimmed eyes. When he dozed off once or twice, Robert adjusted him so he was propped against the adjacent bath counter until the water was ready.

He undressed him, pulling off the boots. Where the vest had gone was a pointless question. He removed the shirt, unfastened the slacks, got him out of everything but the collar, which was still securely buckled on his throat.

A thorough body check confirmed nothing but a handful of

scrapes and marks likely to turn into bruises. Probably from where Ange had run into things, or slipped and fallen on icy patches of ground.

Nothing dire, but the marks reminded Robert of what could have happened. His hands briefly tightened on Ange, a reproving squeeze he didn't follow up with any scolding. This wasn't the time for that.

When he began to take off the collar, Ange surged out of his half-doze, his hands closing over Robert's with near-violent intent. His green eyes were wild, his gaze wheeling around the bathroom.

"Ange." Robert spoke sharply, bringing his sub's focus to him. "You're here. I'm not taking it away. I'm taking it off for your bath."

Ange blinked at him, his rapid breaths settling. Robert saw a spurt of shame, but he touched his face, shook his head at him. Telling him it was all right. Slowly, Ange nodded, relaxing by increments. Robert set the collar aside then guided Ange into the tub, holding onto him until he was fully seated. Robert had added eucalyptus, Epsom salts, even some lavender bubbles. Anything he'd found in his mother's bath supply basket he thought might soothe and restore. He was glad he hadn't pitched them, despite how rarely he took a bath himself.

He pulled a stool over by the tub and leaned in, his arm around Ange's shoulders. He brushed his lips across his forehead, held there, his eyes squeezing closed for a brief, powerful moment. Knowing he was holding Ange, and everything was okay, after hours of imagining just the opposite, was going to require quite a few of these tactile reality checks. "Be easy now," he said, to both of them. "You're home."

The water rippled as Ange put out a hand, gripped Robert's shirt collar, dampening it. His fingers brushed Robert's throat, the curls of hair below on his chest. "Would you...can you be in here with me?"

"You haven't earned that. Gave me a scare tonight. But yeah,

I will." Robert backed off enough to strip off his clothes. Ange rested his head against the high double slipper lip of the tub, his eyes closed. He'd dropped his hands limply against his thighs under the drifting bubbles. Robert nudged him enough to get behind him, settle Ange against his chest, his bent knees on either side of the kid.

Any further thoughts of giving Ange hell went away as a deep sigh deflated his sub. Ange melted against Robert. He didn't seem to have any energy left for conversation, so Robert lay there with him, holding him, both of them dozing off and on.

He used his foot to turn the tap on a couple times, add more hot water and let out some of the lukewarm. They were turning into prunes, but it was okay. Robert didn't want to move from the cocoon of heat and steam until Ange gave signs that he was ready to do so.

Then, unexpectedly, Ange spoke. Robert didn't know if he'd deduced that Robert had figured out the missing pieces, or Ange was so deep in his head it didn't matter. The picture his slow, painful words created was stark. Desolate.

"I was holding her in my arms, looking into her eyes, and she just went away. But she was holding onto me tight, so desperate. Like maybe, if she held on, she wouldn't go away. But she did."

Robert put his hand over Ange's forehead, pressed his lips to his temple. A reminder that he was here, in the present, even as he kept talking about the past.

"I didn't even know I was shot," Ange said. "I tried to get up, holding her, and I couldn't. I'd lifted her, so many times, so easily, and then, I couldn't. Fell on my ass like a baby leaning to walk, who isn't sure what balance is."

Ange paused. "Then I thought I couldn't breathe. I hadn't realized I'd been holding my breath as she died. It all happened in seconds, they told me. But...it was like when I leaped in the air, and it seemed like time stopped, like I could stop time, for myself and my audience, when I danced. To find that's the way death works, too... Everything after that, everything reminded me of it, and it drove me mad."

"Helena said you left. She didn't know where you'd gone."

"I remember going back to my apartment," Ange said, after another long pause. "But I couldn't stay there. Leo and I...we were roommates. Best friends." His voice got thick, choked, and Robert kissed away the tear that slid along Ange's cheekbone. "I paid the last month's rent, left the check on the table for his parents, and a note under the landlord's door, took a bag of stuff. I don't know what. I lost it along the way. I couldn't stay anywhere. I fled my life, any sense of stopping."

He curled his hand around Robert's wrist, ran a fingertip over it, back and forth. "I ended up here, and I was able to fix that toy. I fixed something. And I looked into your eyes and saw pain and sadness become something else, when you looked at me, and thought...I might help fix him, too. And then I didn't need to think about anything else."

Robert closed his eyes. He didn't know how to hold Ange any tighter without cutting off his air, but he could keep kissing his cheek, his jaw, tilting it away with a hand on his chin, drop more kisses on his throat, his shoulder. Ange held onto him, shaking, smaller, quieter sobs working their way through him.

"I'm here," Robert kept repeating between kisses, caresses. No, he wasn't going to bust Ange's balls too much tonight about anything, but Ange had given him the opening to lay something else down. Because they had to do with that help and safety which had called Ange back to him.

"Ange, I love you," he said, his voice rough. "You hear me?"

Ange nodded, slowly. His gaze was on the water, but his hand was back to making those circles on Robert's hand, clasped over his chest. Robert put his mouth to Ange's throat, registered the thud of his pulse through it. "Though I came out of my military service okay, I saw what violence can do, on both sides. It tears into the soul the way it tears into the flesh. Once you see the horror of what we can do to one another, it becomes a truth that never leaves you. And that truth, if you can't figure out how to make sense of it, can become an infected wound that never heals."

Ange quivered. Robert could almost feel the memories rising up to claw at him, but he tightened his grip on Ange once more, the kind of grip that said his Master was demanding he stay fully in the present. When Ange stilled, steadied, Robert knew his soul had heard that message, too.

"Because I love you, and I'm your Master, I'm putting it to you plain. This shit that happened tonight is *not* going to happen again. Ever. You need help. More help than I can give, but I know where to take you to get it. No more running from this. You could have ended up dead tonight, and that would have ended me. You understand that?"

When Ange ducked his head, his shoulders shaking anew, Robert toughened his heart, took him by the jaw and throat and pulled his head back to his shoulder to pin him with a hard gaze. "I want to hear it. And you know exactly how I expect to hear it."

Ange's gaze was filled with so much troubled emotion, but Robert showed him in his own answering expression that he was the port. Ange just had to be willing to bring himself into it. "Yes, sir," Ange managed. "I'm sorry, Master."

"I don't want you to say you're sorry. This isn't about that. What'd you say to me earlier? That me needing you, that's the best gift I can give you. Well, there are things that go along with being needed. You taking care of yourself, resolving the things that might interfere with you being there for me, the way I intend to be there for you. Got it?"

He'd bet that taking the hard line, bringing down that struc-ture and strict discipline Ange craved, might penetrate. He won that bet. The maelstrom of emotions died back, leaving room for Ange to digest the words, see how much Robert meant them. It helped hold Ange in one fixed spot, where he could examine things a little better, not be swept away by those emotions.

When Ange at last nodded again, a slow movement that ended with him resting his forehead against the side of Robert's face, he cupped his hand over Ange's nape, massaging that favorite spot for both of them.

"I'll be with you, every step of the way. You won't do it alone. Soon as we get some sleep and it's a reasonable hour, I'm going to call a friend of mine in VA counseling. I'll see who in the civilian world is a good fit for what you're handling. Even if they can't get rolling with you before Christmas, we're putting things in motion. All right?"

∿

Ange heard everything his Master said to him. Always before, words like that had felt like weights piling upon him, crushing him, triggering a need to dodge, avoid, escape.

But something important had changed over the past few months. Such that, earlier tonight, when he'd bolted and he'd lost time and space, some part of himself had known where to go. Where help and home could be found.

Words could also be a blanket, surrounding, covering and warming him. In the end, Ange wrapped them around him, pulled them tight, the way he did Robert's arms now, his fingers holding onto his Master, securing and accepting the binding.

"Yes, sir."

∿

They woke in Robert's bed mid-morning. As they roused themselves enough to get up, shower, work their way to the kitchen to find some breakfast, Ange didn't say much. His Master didn't push. When Ange went into the bathroom and glanced in the mirror, he was fragile-looking and hollow-eyed, explaining the kid gloves. He felt more like himself, though.

Before going to sleep, Robert had texted Helena to say he'd

found Ange. So when Ange padded into the kitchen and saw Robert checking the phone, Robert laid it down on the counter and showed him her response. She'd expressed relief and a strong desire to see him before she headed back to New York.

"Can we go see her today?" he asked Robert.

His Master raised a surprised brow, giving him an assessing look. "You up for it?"

"Yeah. I'd like to see her. At the theater." Where there was a stage. That was important, because it was the only way he could show her...what she would need to see.

Robert frowned. "I don't want to set off the wrong things for you again."

He wanted to say it wouldn't, but Ange made himself consider it before he ventured a truthful response. "I think...it will be okay. It'll be empty, just her there, not the company and everyone getting ready for the performance. That makes the biggest difference. I really want to meet her there, if that's okay with you. But..." He took a breath. "Can you go with me?"

"After last night, you really think I won't be sticking to your ass like glue for the next century?"

"Only if you're establishing enough distance to beat it black and blue."

"Smart kid. Okay." Robert shot him a look but texted her. As he did, he added, "I called my VA buddy. He put me in touch with a trauma counselor, Dr. Friar. I spoke to him about an hour ago. He's traveling for the holidays, but he's already set you up as his first appointment two days after Christmas. Okay?"

Robert followed that up with another no-nonsense Master look. While Ange's habitual aversion to the subject wanted to kick in, last night had been a wake-up call he couldn't ignore. Robert had said it straight out, in a way Ange couldn't deny.

There are things that go along with being needed.

"Yes, sir," he said.

Robert dipped his head toward the pantry. "Think you've earned a Pop-Tart."

His smile was warm, and helped settle Ange. He was pulling the Pop-Tart out of the toaster when the phone buzzed and Robert glanced at it. "Ms. Markham says she'll be at the theater in an hour and a half. That gives us time to finish breakfast, head that way."

Ange looked down at the frosted Pop Tart, something simple, innocent, cheerful. Then back up at his Master's dark gaze. "I'm sorry. It was a really nice Christmas gift. I feel bad that I messed it up that way."

Robert left his bowl of cereal and came to him, putting his hand over Ange's tense one. He cupped Ange's face with the other, conveying the sincerity of his words through his firm touch. "You've got nothing to feel bad about. I mean that. I learned things about you I didn't know, and ways that I can love and care for you even better. Help you heal from things that hurt you. That matters more to me."

Ange gazed at him. If he told Robert he'd become his Christmas miracle, his forthright Master would laugh, but the truth was the truth, even if unspoken. So Ange settled for a simple nod and two words that came straight from his soul.

"Thank you," he said.

This time, when Helena saw him, Ange moved into her arms, wrapped his own around her, and held her tight. A little sigh left her and her fingers tangled in his hair. She tugged it the way she'd used to do, though more forcefully then, when she was correcting something during practice. It brought back so much, and had him holding her even longer.

Memories of Clarissa and Leo swamped him. He might have lost himself in that quagmire, but he'd promised Robert he'd be okay. He called to mind everything they'd talked about in the tub, focusing on details, holding himself in the present. With

Robert's hand rubbing his back gently, it worked. He was okay. He could do this.

Helena snuffled a sob against his shoulder. Then she shrugged her shoulders irritably at herself and pushed at him. She gave Ange a wet-eyed but slightly amused look, covering him from head to toe.

"You got fat, I see."

He found a weak chuckle. "By our standards, yeah. And I just learned what cake tastes like. There's no going back."

"It's the devil for sure. And cookies are its minions." She smiled. "You have always been a beautiful boy, but love has made you a breathtaking man. But if you tell anyone I said something so ridiculously romantic, I'll beat you with my cane."

He swept a pointed look around them. They were standing in the open space between the front row of seats, the stage at his back. "I was shocked to see you without it. I thought it was surgically attached to your palm."

She dipped her head toward the stage. "It's up there, behind the curtain. I was glad you wanted to meet here. One of my last appointments before I catch my plane is with a children's group. Aspiring dancers from a prominent dance studio here. They are due in a few moments." She quirked a smooth brow, her lips pressing together. "Mr. Bauer says you still dance. Would you be willing to show them the possibilities with a small demonstration?"

He'd fully intended to dance for her, since it was the best way he could express to her the things that were far too difficult for him to say. However, being asked directly to do so, and in front of a group, sparked instant tension. His Master stepped to his side, putting a hand on his hip. Ange was certain Robert was about to issue a decisive though polite *hell no* on his behalf.

But Helena was equally trained, if for different reasons, in detecting changes in body language. She lifted both hands, chagrin crossing her face. "Forgive me, Ange. It was a selfish desire, wanting to see you dance again."

She smiled, a painful gesture. "My fondest memories of watching you dance weren't when you were in front of an audience; did you know that? It was after practice. My office door would be open, so I'd see you come back out onto the studio floor and dance the steps again, or whatever combination you wished. No music other than what was in your head."

"Like you do in the store," Robert noted.

Ange glanced at him, and Robert gave him a bracingly warm look. That look reminded Ange of how he'd danced for him in the snow, ribbons trailing his wrists and ankles.

"I had the privilege of being your silent audience," Helena said softly.

Before Ange could respond, they heard the backstage door open, the sound echoing across the stage and through the silent theater. Youthful chatter, tones charged with barely suppressed excitement, said the class had arrived.

Helena sent Ange an amused look. He knew she was remembering the times her company had hosted similar visits up in New York, and how he and others of the troupe had helped her simultaneously terrify and thrill the students with the tough reality of pursuing a dance career.

For him, the toughness had only fed his passion for it. Until that day.

Though shadows cloaked his heart at the thought, Ange turned to see the couple dozen kids of varying ages emerge onto the stage. They were shepherded by two instructors, who were hushing them to keep the noise to a decorous level.

When the dancers saw Helena, the admonition was no longer necessary. As she'd said, these were serious students. They knew just how valuable even a few minutes of personal mentoring from a successful dancer, director or choreographer was. Helena was all three.

At the sight of the students, Ange's tension about dancing dissipated. He liked working with kids. When they came into the store, he often took over with them while their adults shopped. He kept a box of cheap toys to entertain the littler ones, while the interested adolescents and teenagers received a detailed tour. Ange showed them the more complex operations of toys that had to be handled with care.

"If you wish to stay, we can go have coffee afterward," Helena said. "There's a place within walking distance, and I'll have about an hour before I need to get to the airport."

While regret was in her dark gaze because of his reaction to dancing for her, she wasn't letting go of the subject itself. Her gaze swept him again, a professional appraisal. "We can talk to you about your plans, if you wish."

"Yes, Mistress." He looked at Robert a weighted moment before he brought his gaze back to Helena. "I actually don't have a problem giving them a short demo. Should I do what we did when we had similar groups in New York?"

Robert's hand tightened on his hip, but he kept his eyes on Helena an extra beat. The way she brightened like a light bulb shot some pain through him, but it was pain for the past. Not the present. He covered Robert's hand with his own as Helena responded.

"Whatever is in your head is fine. A mix of classical and contemporary styles?"

As he considered all the possibilities, he managed a smile. He knew it held so many memories, so many emotions. Robert turned him in his direction. "Look at me," he said.

Ange did, but he met Robert's gaze, clear-eyed. "I can do this, Master," he said. "With your permission."

"Promise me this won't take you to a bad place in your head," Robert said, his brow fierce in that way that could make Ange's heart skip an extra beat.

"I promise. It won't." Ange looked over his shoulder toward the stage. Since he was cognizant of Robert and Helena's concerns for him, he absorbed the students' enthusiasm, let it show in his expression, his additional response. "This is as different from that day...as I can imagine."

Helena made a small noise, and he felt her hand on him. He gripped it, even as he held his Master's clasp.

"All right, then," Robert said, but he shot him that look that added a toe curl to Ange's reaction, a little weakening in the knees. "If you're lying or mistaken, I really will beat your ass black and blue."

~

Ange's answering smile had that sweet, guileless look. When he nodded to Helena and moved toward the stage, Helena hung back to toss Robert a droll look.

"I always thought there was something particularly provocative about why he preferred calling me Mistress, and why I allowed it."

Robert chuckled as she headed for the class. She probably wasn't a Mistress—he figured her job would make that feel like a busman's holiday—but she was a seasoned New Yorker deep in the sensuality-saturated dance world. Dominant and submissive relationships weren't likely a new thing to her.

As Robert took a center seat in the third row, he noted there was a technician in the control pit, tinkering with the many panels of equipment. The man gave him an affable short wave.

Helena was saying something to Ange on the stage steps. Ange nodded, then headed toward the curtains at the far end. Helena began to address the students in a brusque tone that had them coming to attention like a military squad. She jumped right into a frank and stern discussion of what a professional dancing career involved.

Definitely a busman's holiday.

Ange's response had helped lessen his concerns, but Robert didn't like his sub disappearing behind the curtain. It was way too much déjà vu, though he reminded himself Ange seemed okay, which hadn't been the case at all last night before he vanished.

Plus Helena had a view into the wings, so when she nodded subtly, Robert knew she was communicating with Ange, acknowledging his readiness. He took a steadying breath, aware he'd been about to jump up and check for himself.

"I am telling you many hard things about our world," Helena said to the children. "But I also want to show you the possibilities that can come with true dedication. One of the best dancers who ever belonged to my company is here. He will perform a mix of styles in a quick program. Please form a single line against the rear curtain so he has the full stage."

As the kids obeyed, Helena descended the stairs and returned to sit at Robert's side. She gestured the tech in the control booth. "Spotlight, please, Cortez."

Cortez gave her a thumbs up. The lights came down, dousing the wings and audience in shadows. Then the spotlight brightened, creating a fan of light across the front of the stage and drawing all eyes there.

Making it seem like a performance worried Robert, but Helena hadn't cued any music. The only noise for the next held-breath moment was a light scrape of feet, and then a collective smothered gasp greeted Ange as he leaped onto stage. He came down lightly on one knee and the top of his other foot, rolling forward on a shoulder and a hip. Then he was up again, executing a fluid series of turns, kicks, dips. A full, up-in-the air split, a *grand jeté*.

The night he'd danced in the snow for Robert, he'd worn ribbon. Now he was the ribbon, carried, turned and twisted by the wind.

Music began to play through the speakers. Cortez, evaluating Ange's pacing, had taken some initiative. Since the poignant instrumental, using strings and winds alone, didn't seem to be affecting Ange's absorption, Robert's spike of alarm settled.

The song was a touching and inspired choice. *True Colors.* Robert could hear the lyrics in his head, Cyndi Lauper's distinctive voice expressing how unimaginable pain and darkness could become bearable with the bonds of love.

Ange had changed clothes, explaining where Helena had sent him. He wore flat soled ballet shoes and flesh-covered tights with a rolled waist band that exposed his hip bones as he stretched and leaped. Every miraculous movement of his body praised the beauty of it. Who needed to breathe or have a heartbeat? The dancer on the stage became breath and heart both.

Here on stage, it was obvious this was where God had intended Ange to be. Robert would have to be deaf, dumb, blind, soulless, not to see it. It made things in him ache in that painful way loving someone did. Especially while watching them do what they'd been born to do.

When Ange finished, he was on his knees, head bent toward his shoulder. He looked like a flower that had shared its glory with the world, reaching for the sun, dancing in the wind. Then, succumbing to the inevitability of winter, the bloom fading, closing, he'd bowed back down toward the earth that had nourished him.

That ache increased to the point of pain.

The children applauded, and Ange rose, gave them a little bow. But Robert noticed he first sent a long look toward Helena, a message of sorts. Punctuated with a faint smile that could have broken the heart of a stone.

The kids were crowding forward to talk to him, their excitement overcoming their discipline. The teachers shot a look toward Helena to make sure it was okay. Helena gave them a curt wave to say it was.

Perhaps she would have taken control first, given Ange more space to back away, but when Robert looked toward her, tears were running down her face. Her mouth was tight, showing the effort to restrain her emotions, but he saw the anguish in her face before she reined that back as well.

"It is to be expected, of course," she murmured.

"What's that?" Robert carried a pack of folded tissues inside his jacket, so he offered it to her now. She accepted one of the tissues, dabbed at her eyes.

"The damage to his body," she said with a sigh. "It is evident in his reach, his movement. He is exceptionally gifted, an innate talent. That will never change. But he will not headline again. Not on the stages he would have commanded if his career had progressed as it was intended."

Robert blinked. He didn't doubt her knowledge, because the sorrow in her eyes was real, but... "Do you think it matters? When people watch him dance, do you think they'd even notice?"

"Not a layperson. I do not mean that in a patronizing way." She sent him an apologetic look. "But in the dance world, yes. He knows it, too. It is why he agreed to dance for me. To show me, let me know. An answer to the question he knew I would ask."

Robert's gaze went back to the stage. The two lifetime dancers had a language they'd understood without words. Much as a Master and sub communicated.

It also explained why Ange had been reasonably certain this wouldn't cause him any bad flashbacks. He'd had a purpose that kept him focused and away from that dangerous edge.

Ange was laughing at something one of the kids had said to him. He showed them a couple steps, slowly, correcting the form of one little girl who emulated the movement with impressive skill. He adjusted the stance of a teenage boy doing the same.

Helena squeezed Robert's arm. Rising, she went to the front row, where she'd parked her rolling suitcase. A satchel was on top, a three-ring notebook resting in the zippered opening. She picked it up and returned to Robert, handing it to him.

"Look," she said.

It was a scrapbook, detailing Ange's accomplishments, the progression of his career. When Robert paged through a few sections, he saw there were notes written in the margins, some of it in Ange's handwriting, as well as various other people.

Teasing notes, playful insults. Friends who'd added to the contents like a yearbook.

He paused at a picture of someone even a non-dancer would recognize. Mikhael Baryshnikov, standing next to a younger, obviously awestruck Ange. The legendary danseur's signature was scribbled over the playbill the photo overlapped.

"He visited our rehearsal for that show," Helena said. "Came on stage afterward to shake Ange's hand and encourage him."

She raised her head to look at Robert. "This notebook was left in Ange's apartment. Leo's parents, when they came to pack up his things, said Ange had left a note that whatever they didn't want could be donated or thrown away. He wouldn't be back." Her lips tightened. "They brought this to me, and I have kept it. I carry it with me, a talisman of sorts. But it needs to come home to him. If he will not take it, I hope...you will?"

"Yes. Definitely."

"When he's ready to remember the good things, I want him to have it. I have the images in my head." She gazed back down at another page, where a promo postcard showed Ange holding a ballerina easily over his head, with steady, strong arms. Based on the info on the card, and remembering the picture in the news article he'd read, Robert knew it was Clarissa, a dark-haired slim beauty.

"He was an incredible classic ballet dancer," Helena said. "But contemporary dance, seeing what he would do with the freer forms, that was where it was a miracle to watch him."

"It still is."

A slight smile touched her mouth. "Yes. In my world, it is impossible to see the dance without judging the form. But you're right; his injuries didn't affect the spirit that inspires him. In some ways, it seems to have increased the potency of it. During his performances, I would see members of the audience reach for the hand of the one next to them. They'd hold onto one another, squeeze hard, because you simply had to share how watching him dance made you feel. He did not master the craft so much as he..."

She paused, seeking the right word, but Robert already knew it. "Submitted to it. Gave himself to it fully. Let it have him."

"Yes." She nodded. "Exactly so."

∽

Helena returned to the stage to address the students. As Ange stood at her side, he looked toward Robert. His expression didn't reflect Helena's pain. It suggested his grief over what he'd lost on the stage was about something different. Robert couldn't put his finger on what it was, but it helped alleviate the crazy fear that had risen in his chest, that Ange couldn't belong to anyone but the forces that had created the miracle of what he was.

Ange held Robert's gaze another long moment, then turned away as Helena touched his arm, brought him back into the conversation.

Robert digested what she'd told him. Yes, Ange had the spirit of an innocent child. From what Helena had revealed, that was something he'd always had. Ironically, his fragility came from his adult side. Parts of him had been badly broken, which meant those cracks would give way if they experienced too much pressure.

But those cracks could be healed, making the whole grow stronger. Ange had so much talent and passion to give. Maybe he couldn't headline, but Robert had no doubt Ange could still perform professionally.

As his Master, he would be possessive of Ange's heart and soul, would command and keep it as long as he knew his submissive wanted that possession, but he also needed to be sure Ange knew the gates were open.

Being a professional dancer again could take Ange from him physically—travel, commitment to practice. Even more disturbing, it could take him from Robert emotionally—into a world and with people whose company might eventually not include Robert.

He refused to let his heart falter over it, though. If he loved him, encouraging Ange to flourish in every way he desired was the right thing to do. There was no denying that Ange had a wealth of possibilities for his future.

The class visit was done, the students taking their leave. Helena and Ange had left the stage, Ange standing at the base of the stairs, Helena one step up. He held her hand, was speaking to her earnestly about something. Robert saw her eyes get misty. They embraced another long moment, then Ange stepped back, moved away. She held his hand until he had to release it. As Ange was walking toward him, Helena's eyes shifted to Robert. "Take care of him," she said, in a less-than-steady voice.

"I will."

They'd both answered her. With Ange's back to her, he'd interpreted the words as applying to Robert. With her gaze locked with Robert's, Robert knew it was directed to him. But their dual response gave her a pained smile. Turning, she mounted the stage steps. She disappeared behind the curtains, following the students out.

Exiting Ange's life, stage left. For the moment.

CHAPTER TEN

*S*ince Ange gripped Robert's arm when he reached him, gave him a look that said all was good, Robert didn't push him for more. At least not right away. In the car, he focused more on keeping tabs on his sub, making sure he was okay. Ange's expression remained pensive, his mouth serious, but his body was relaxed against the seat, his hand resting close enough to the center console Robert put his own on top of it and held it.

When they slowed down for a stoplight, Robert knew he should wait to ask the question. But if he didn't ask it, open that gate right now, he might not, and that would be selfish.

"Ange."

Ange's vivid green eyes shifted his way, through that unruly fall of white-gold hair. Pain blossomed in Robert's chest. If only Ange's beauty and youth were all that had attracted Robert. The man's soul had captured Robert's heart. If Ange left, it would tear right out of his chest and flop on the ground like a fish, gasping for air until it died.

Oh, hell and Christmas balls. Stop being melodramatic. And a chicken-shit coward.

"I know you have things to work out," Robert said, clearing his throat. "Like what we talked about earlier, needing to see a therapist. But as you work through that stuff, you should consider dancing professionally again."

A long silence filled the car before Ange spoke, cautiously. "Is that what you think I should do? Want me to do?"

The question was unexpected, but he could handle it, since there was only one acceptable response. "That's not one I can answer for you. I want you to be happy. Life doesn't seem short when you're young. But it is. Way too damn short for the things you really want to do." Robert managed a tight smile. "The good news is it's also long, if Fate is kind. Other experiences of value will work their way back into your life when it's time, if that's what's meant to happen."

Ange frowned, a puzzled gesture. Robert knew that second part didn't make sense to anyone in their twenties, so he probably shouldn't have muddied the waters with it. It was more directed to himself, anyway. Helena would have gotten it in a heartbeat, especially since one of those experiences had shown back up in her life today.

"Ange, it's not a question you have to answer right this second. I just want you to realize the possibility is there. I know you're going to say you're happy working with me in the store. But the way you dance, your love of it, there's got to be more you want to do with that."

Ange turned their hands over, his fingers knotting with Robert's as his grip tightened. The light had changed, so Robert had to keep his eyes on the road, but he kept that hold, intending it to be reassuring to Ange. It helped him, too.

"I don't want to dance professionally again."

Robert glanced at him. Ange met his gaze squarely. No tension, no avoidance. "But if you don't mind, Master, I'm not really ready to talk about why."

"Okay." All the problems of the world, let alone Ange's, didn't need to be solved today. Robert looked up ahead of them. "Want to hit the Panera drive-thru and get soup and a sandwich?"

Ange brightened immediately. It twisted Robert's heart, tempting him to believe his sub's statement. "They sometimes put in extra bread when you order takeout," Ange said.

"Yes, they do." Robert smiled; he couldn't help it. As they pulled into the drive behind a couple waiting cars, Robert lifted their clasped hands, pressing his mouth to Ange's knuckles. Ange stilled at the unexpected courtly gesture, and then his green eyes darkened as Robert took an extra moment, holding his lips to the warm skin that smelled like Ange. Ange's other hand touched his thigh.

"I love you, Master."

"Can I take your order?"

Robert had let off the brake to slide up to the menu board. The cheerful voice came in right on the tail end of Ange's quiet declaration. Robert met his gaze, the two of them grinning at one another.

"Yeah. Question. Just confirming. You get extra bread with a drive-thru order, right?"

~

After picking up the lunch, they took it to the store and ate it there. Then they did some housekeeping tasks to prepare for tomorrow. The store was closed Sundays and Mondays, but tomorrow and a half day on Christmas Eve they'd be open, as people stopped in for last minute impulse sales they couldn't get anywhere else. Then they'd be closed through Christmas and a couple days after that.

One of the tasks was having Ange replace the straw under the manger. Since it was impossible for that not to conjure how his sub had baptized it with his release, Robert gave him a hard squeeze on the ass and a nipping kiss before sending him to do that. Over the next hour as they handled that and other chores, they talked of easy things, but touched frequently in passing.

Letting that underlying heat set the tone was a deliberate

choice on Robert's part. It had been an intense twenty-four hours. They both needed some breathing time, some playfulness. Fortunately, this close to Christmas, others were willing to help with that. Robert was at the counter, working on his computer, Ange adjusting ornaments on one of the Christmas trees, when an insistent tap on the main store window drew their attention.

A mother and two children were standing on the sidewalk. She'd tried to stop the boy from knocking on the glass, but she'd been too late. Though she shot them an apologetic look and started to tug the children firmly forward, it was obvious the kids were going crazy for the giant toy carousel in the window. From the little girl's dramatic spin, and the boy's additional pantomime of a twirl with his fingers, they wanted to see it revolve.

Ange was already on his way, no surprise. As he waved at the mother, Robert suppressed a smile at the usual double take most females experienced at Ange's appearance. Ange bent and turned the switch, setting the carousel in motion. The kids got all excited, pointing out their favorite horses as the toy revolved. The little mirrors and sparkling pieces caught the Christmas lights that framed the window.

Ange made faces at the boy and waved at the little girl, who beamed at him. Her instant adoration was typical for a kid when someone pleased them, but when it came to Ange, Robert knew it was more than that. Ange connected to kids so easily.

Maybe because of his own appealing childlike traits, but Robert thought it was just a whole package kind of deal. Ange picked up on what they liked, talked to them as equals, and was sincerely interested in what they had to say. Yet he also projected an adult's protective kindness that made a kid feel safe, like the kid could trust him. And they could.

By the time the mother moved on, sending Ange a thankful look and warm smile, Robert had been struck by an idea. He decided to toss it out there, see how his sub might react.

"You know that Fifth Ward community center? My mom took a one-day pottery class there, when she was still doing pretty good. She knew a glazing technique the instructor didn't, and he talked her into a short demo. The center's director encourages volunteers with skills that can expand their programs."

Ange sent him a curious look. "That's cool."

"Yeah. I'm betting they'd do backflips if a classically trained danseur good with kids wanted to offer some instruction."

A mix of reactions went through Ange's face, hard to decipher. "It would take me away from helping at the store."

"If you decide it's something you'd like to do, I could work around it." Robert shrugged. "Last year they did a recital, plus some community performances. For children's charities and to benefit the center, things like that."

"Hunh." Ange bent over the box of priced German ornaments, lifted out several to replenish the Christmas tree. He'd left the carousel on, the tinny music playing its dreamy tune as the horses revolved. When he shifted to the other side of the tree, which had him half-facing Robert, the multi-colored lights reflected in his thoughtful eyes. He had an interesting set to his mouth, not necessarily pleased or displeased. Just...hard to read.

Robert left it alone. He'd let it roll around Ange's mind and see what he did with it.

After they finished up, they headed for the house. Since Robert had some calls and paperwork to handle, he encouraged Ange to do whatever he'd like while he went into his home office.

As he worked over the next hour or so, he heard noises above and below that suggested Ange was doing some more interior décor adjustment. Then it got quiet. So when Robert was done, he went looking for him. He wouldn't have been surprised to find him napping on the couch in front of the TV or even more pleasingly, curled up in Robert's bed, but he found him out on the rooftop deck.

Ange was sitting on one of the cushioned outdoor benches, positioned for optimal gazing at the neighborhood tree canopy. He was slouched down in a relaxed pose, upper body sunk deep into one of Robert's heavier coats. His long legs were stretched out, athletic shoes braced on the fire pit.

Robert took a seat next to him, thigh brushing Ange's leg. When Ange gave him a serious look, Robert draped an arm behind him. "All right?"

"Yeah. I think so. Can I ask you something?"

"Anything."

"Do you want me to keep working with you at the store?"

"Absolutely." Robert squeezed his neck. "I love having you there."

When Ange's shoulders relaxed at the immediate, emphatic answer, Robert reinforced it with the simple truth. "Before you, I didn't think there was a single person I could be around almost 24/7 and not get tired of it."

"I feel that way, too." Ange lifted a shoulder, looked away. "I want to be there for you, whenever you need me. You're my Master. And more than that."

"You're my submissive, Ange. And more than that, too." Robert touched his jaw. "Which means your happiness, your contentment, seeing you become all you want to be? That's you serving me, too. I want you to know you have choices. Whether it's teaching at the community center, or pursuing your dancing or any other dreams you have, in whatever way you want, I want you to know that's not going to impact how I feel about you. You have my complete support."

"Okay." Ange's jaw flexed beneath Robert's fingers. Then he straightened and brought his feet down to the ground, turning his body to look at Robert. "But promise me you aren't doing your 'old guy' thing."

"What?" Robert's brows shot up. Ange flushed.

"That thing you do, like when you were setting me up on dates. As if you're this doddering old relic that expects I'm only in your life because of my problems. A bird whose wing you'll fix and then I'll fly away."

Ange surged up from the bench and paced away, leaving Robert frowning after him. But Ange wasn't done. "I can see it in my head. You smiling that stiff smile you do, trying to hide your heart breaking because you don't want to let me go, but you think that's what's best for me."

Robert's second attempt to respond was thwarted once more as Ange pivoted and faced him. The unbanked heat in Ange's flashing eyes startled him.

"When you look at me, my knees get weak. When your hand closes around the back of my neck, I want to fall on my knees, be anything you need me to be. I feel your strength and power, and it surrounds me, keeps me safe, even as I want to show you just how high and strong I can leap and dance. For *you*. Because of you. That's how *you* make me feel, because I know you're there, watching. I'm not just saying it as a spontaneous thing, driven by my cock or because of how you've helped me. You are my Master. My life isn't over, the journey isn't over, because I chose you. It's just beginning, *with you*.

Ange's passion was a sword wielded by an unfaltering, powerful will. And the words kept coming. "You're thirty-seven years old, Master. Maybe those couple years you took care of your parents, you got pulled into that feeling of sickness and death and being old, so that somewhere along the way you started feeling old, too. But every time you embrace your Master side, all that falls away and you're every bit of what you really are. A Master, a man in his prime, able to kick ass and take command of me and your life, and take care of others. Everyone knows that about you. Charlie, Sully, our customers, all the people you help. Including and especially me."

Robert had been thinking so much about Ange these past couple days. How to do things for his sub, help him, actualize him. His submissive had been doing the same thing, only his focus had been Robert. And it was clear a key number of Ange's thoughts had been following the same tracks as Robert's own these past few days.

Now Ange stood before him, strong, beautiful and proud. Showing his love, even as he tossed out the kind of challenge that goaded a response from a Master.

Robert knew the sure way to lose a fight was by holding parts of himself back, refusing to be all-in. Ange was saying in a hundred different ways that he was all-in. Robert owed him the same. This kind of relationship—any relationship worth keeping—had to have that kind of two-way trust. A belief that the two people involved knew what they wanted, for themselves and each other.

As Ange spoke so determinedly, Robert's hand had curled into a half fist on the chair arm. The pounding of his heart had increased, and fire rushed through his blood.

No more fantasizing or mulling it over. He was taking Ange to Patriarch. He'd put his resurrection in a public venue to confirm it, declare it, in the best way possible. It would celebrate what he and Ange had, solidify it. He'd immerse himself in the experience of claiming his sub in front of others who knew exactly what it meant.

It was a damn relief to make the decision, own it.

Robert rose, moved toward Ange. He knew what Ange was seeing in his face, because after the flash of joy, there was a satisfying bit of terror. The kid was smart enough to lower his gaze, change the defiant body language to something more deferential by the time Robert was right up on him. He stood chest to chest with him, with a slight offset so he could more easily speak right into Ange's ear. "What makes you think you can talk to me like that?" Robert asked with sensual menace.

"Nothing, Master," Ange said, his voice full of warmth, healthy fear, and love. "I apologize."

"Uh-hunh. I've decided you and I are going to Patriarch for the Christmas Eve party. I'll show you just what kind of Master owns your ass."

"Yes, sir," Ange said. The sidelong glance he sent toward Robert showed eyes shining with desire and need. His fingertips grazed Robert, high on the thigh, and it was all the encouragement Robert needed.

Being a dancer was second nature for Ange. So much a part of who he was, there was no need to think about it. It took over when called, the way it should.

Just like being a Master did for Robert.

He gripped Ange's wrist, the one attached to the hand that had just touched Robert. Swift and sure, he turned it, pivoted and put Ange down on one knee at Robert's feet. He had his other hand on the back of Ange's neck, just like his sub had described.

"Did I give you permission to touch me?"

"No, sir," Ange said, his body quivering under his hold.

"We're going inside so you can take care of my hard dick with your overly talkative mouth. But you're not getting any relief until Christmas Eve. And that's only if you show me you know how to behave."

"Yes, sir," Ange said, his fingers curling against the ground, right next to Robert's foot. It conveyed his strong desire to touch, without actually doing so. The boy always did learn quickly, picking up on the shift in the balance of power. He was damn good at reminding Robert of the power he had over him, in ways that made him a sub worth keeping.

He changed his mind and didn't take Ange inside. Instead Robert took him around behind the bar as he had before. Put him back on his knees and opened his jeans.

Out here in the cold and still melting snow, on the mostly covered deck, Robert gripped his thick erection, held it in front of Ange's attentive face.

"You want this?"

"Yes, Master. Please."

"You want my cock stretching your mouth? Gagging you,

because I have no interest in being gentle. You can take it, can't you?"

Ange's lips parted, his breath making his chest rise and fall fast. Robert had taken things up a notch, and Ange registered it through the appealing quiver of his body, his hands resting on his knees. "Yes, sir. I can take it. I want it."

"You know the drill. Just your mouth. Keep those hands locked behind your back." Ange quickly complied, shooting satisfaction straight through Robert's balls. "When you're done, I'm going to play with your cock long enough to get you begging for more. Then I'm going to keep you that way every minute possible. If you come, I'll be punishing you at Patriarch in ways you've never even imagined." He sent Ange a threatening look. "I'll probably be doing that anyway."

His mind was overrun with the possibilities. Which was part of feeling fully alive.

❧

On Christmas Eve, Ange didn't need to be reminded of the event that would dominate the night ahead. From the time he'd woken that morning, he'd felt it in the electricity between him and his Master. Ever since Robert issued his sensual threat, that charge had only been strengthening. He'd lived up to it, way beyond expectations.

At the store, Ange was used to Robert's eyes falling upon him often. He counted on it, hoped for it. The new way he looked at him, now that what was between them had been put into the open, made it an even more exhilarating pleasure. Yet his Master had done more than accept what Ange had offered for so long. Robert had taken the tether of Ange's offered submission, tossed it aside and replaced it with a chain.

Robert had shifted from acceptance to full possession.

Every time Ange moved, the braided collar buckled on his

throat reminded him of that claim, as the edges brushed the tender spaces between his neck and collar bones.

It made Ange long for tonight, for when his Master would take that new feeling between them, the power and heat of it, and transcend even Ange's wildest imaginings about it.

He was certain Robert would. Because he'd all-out challenged Robert to throw off any doubt about their relationship. Ange had been frustrated with it, needing Robert to understand how much he wanted that full claim, no turning back. Robert's response had been a glorious, full neon flashing sign that said *careful what you wish for.*

Careful was the last thing Ange wanted to be.

When Robert had put him on his knees in that decisive move on the rooftop deck, Ange's heart had leaped, his cock had sprung to attention, and everything in his mind had stopped. Thought wasn't necessary. Only serving his Master's will, his desires, bringing him approval and joy. Pleasure.

Since then, Robert had done plenty of things to keep Ange suffering from the strongest waves of desires he'd ever felt without jerking off. At the house, throughout that afternoon and evening, all the way up to bedtime, Robert had played with Ange's cock whenever he wished. Stopping Ange in the middle of doing whatever to open Ange's jeans, reach in and grip his cock. His Master had tugged and stroked, growled his demands while kissing Ange's mouth, biting his neck, until Ange was helplessly rubbing up against him. Then Robert pulled away, carefully zipped him back up and sent him off on another task with a firm slap to his ass.

Then there'd been yesterday morning, before the store opened. Robert had been doing stuff on his computer. He'd had Ange strip out of everything but the collar, then put him on his knees next to his stool, behind the store counter. As he worked, Robert curled his fingers under Ange's collar, idly tugging on it as he made some calls, typed one-handed on the keyboard.

When Robert raised his hand a couple times, Ange assumed

he was waving to passersby. It made Ange's erection agonizingly hard, knowing those people had no idea the toy store proprietor, in his tidy bow tie and suspenders—and those sexy damn wire-framed reading glasses—had a naked sub kneeling at his feet.

Getting dressed and ready to work before opening hadn't reduced his erection in the slightest. With a wicked grin, his Master had tossed a black store apron at him. Ange had to wear it all day.

Today was Christmas Eve, which meant a shortened workday. As far as Ange was concerned, it could have been a double shift, the way the hours crawled by. His imagination about tonight kept him agitated, only his Master's firm direction helping to keep him focused.

Yet when they finally closed up the store, found some dinner and went back to Robert's place, Robert still wasn't cutting him any slack. Soon as they were in the door, Robert made him visit the bathroom, strip, then put him on the guest bed, in the room with the cheerful sunflower motif.

He tied Ange's hands and ankles spread eagle with festive Christmas ribbon, a loose tie that wasn't about keeping him helpless, but willingly bound. Then he clicked on the TV and put the remote next to Ange's hand.

"I have some things to do before we get ready for tonight. I'll check on you, but you lie here and wait on your Master's pleasure."

With a heavy-lidded look, Robert bent down and took Ange's cock to the root in a heated, sucking, tongue-swirling move that had his hips jerking up and a rough groan tearing from his throat. Robert gripped his balls tight and twisted, making Ange freeze in place. His Master offered a vibrating chuckle against his shaft and played his mouth over him another minute or two before releasing Ange and giving the inside of his thigh a stinging slap. "Be a good boy."

Another eternity of time, otherwise known as about ninety minutes of sheer hell. Ange didn't change the channel. When

Robert came to get him, he shot him an amused look that made Ange realize it had been on some Lifetime chick flick movie he hadn't even registered. Robert untied the ribbons, letting them float to the floor as he helped Ange to a sitting position. Then he guided Ange up the stairs to the master bedroom. He stayed just behind him, steadying Ange with a hand to his waist and his palm clamped over a naked buttock.

"Stand in the middle of the room."

Robert disappeared into his closet. When he came out, he had two items. One of them, something that looked like a leather jockstrap, he put on the bed. He handed the other to Ange.

Black ballet tights. Ange remembered the errands Robert had handled while Sully was doing his fitting, and wondered if that was when he'd picked them up. He wasn't going to ask his Master about his shopping habits at the moment, though.

"Put those on."

Robert took a seat on the edge of the bed, legs stretched out, knees spread, arms crossed. The position stretched his slacks over his muscular thighs and emphasized the wideness of his chest and shoulders in his dress shirt. He'd removed the bow tie, the shirt open at his strong throat.

His dark eyes stayed focused on Ange. Was it Ange's imagination, or had they become laser-sharp in the past twenty-four hours, the planes of Robert's handsome face even more like carved granite, implacable and relentless?

His Master was revealing a scary, irresistible part of himself Ange had sensed, but that Robert had kept mostly hidden. Until right now.

As Ange stripped down, that piercing gaze lingered appreciatively on the swollen state of Ange's cock. "Got you hurting for it, don't I, kid?"

"Yes, sir. Thank you, sir."

Robert's expression reflected approval of Ange's gratitude. As well as the way the tights fit over the erection, concealing nothing. When Robert revolved his finger, much like that kid who'd wanted to see the carousel in action, Ange pivoted slowly.

"You have the finest ass for fucking I have ever seen."

Robert rose, withdrawing his pocketknife from his slacks. Ange couldn't help noticing his Master's equipment was straining against the trousers as well, and licked his lips.

"You'll get that eventually. If you're good. Stay still."

Robert had closed the distance between them. As Ange watched, barely breathing, Robert slid his hand inside the tights. His knuckles pressed against Ange's bare cock. Though holding still when Ange was hurting this bad for it was the kind of torment only angels and demons knew, the touch was functional. And protective.

Robert slid his knife in between his palm and the front of the tights, cutting a slit. That extra care made Ange's erection worse, because when it came to the things his Master did to him and for him, his heart was directly connected to what was between his legs.

Robert gripped Ange's cock fully, causing Ange to suppress another groan as his Master pulled it out of the cut opening. Then he returned to the bed to pick up the leather jock. It had straps, buckles, metal pieces. Ange's cock was likewise threaded through a hole in the front, so it bobbed bare and free before him. Robert ran the slender strap between Ange's legs and threaded the back strap through it, before he cinched everything to fully secure the jock.

As his Master caressed the curves of Ange's ass through the ballet tights, Ange felt the pressure of the strap between his buttocks. If Robert cut that free, opened up the back of the tights, he'd have full access to Ange.

Though Ange could vividly imagine it, Robert didn't do that right now. Instead he turned his attention to putting two silver padlocks where the straps buckled at the hips. Robert clicked the locks closed with a satisfied look that said no one would be taking them off but him.

Ange swayed, overcome. Robert steadied him, though his voice remained smooth, cruelly unconcerned with Ange's agitated state. That indifferent Master's voice that could keep Ange impossibly hard.

"This jock comes with cock straps." Robert rolled a black condom over Ange's erection, then gripped those three straps, sewn to the front of the jock. He wrapped them over Ange's cock at the base, the middle, and right under the head. They held Ange's dick securely against his body, pointed upward to display it. Through the translucent condom, he could see the fluid blotting the tip.

Robert gave Ange's cock a light slap that sent tingles shooting all over his body. "Put your jeans on over it. When we get to the club, you'll take them off and wear the tights, jock and your collar, and that's it." He gave Ange a thorough look. "Got a problem with that?"

"No, sir." Ange was used to performing, but being in front of a full audience like this, for this, was new. His face must have shown that worry, because Robert put a hand on his collar, tugged. "You know what this says?"

"That I belong to you."

"It sure the hell does. You're going to get eye-fucked to death, no question, but not a single hand gets laid on you other than mine unless I say so, and I don't share, Ange. Beginning and end of that story. Keep that in mind if your eyes linger too long on any other Master's dick."

"No, Master. I'd never..."

"I know that." Robert's tone held stern reassurance. "But it's human to look. I'm just warning you not to linger, unless you want me to cut a hole in the back of those tights and shove this plug into you."

He returned to the closet and emerged with a plug that had Ange's eyes widening.

"That's not...anatomically possible."

"You'd be surprised how much the anus can stretch. You

could take two dicks in there." He leaned in, gave Ange a look that shot straight to his balls. "Or my fist, if I was of a mind to put it there, and you'd beg for it. But if I feel like I need to keep your mind off other Master's dicks, I can make putting this in pretty damn uncomfortable without causing permanent damage. Got it?"

"Yes, sir," Ange managed, enough of a squeak to his voice to win Robert's amusement.

"Good boy. This next thing I'm going to say is important. Are you listening?"

"Yes, sir. Always." Ange met Robert's gaze briefly to prove it, and saw his Master was as serious as he could be.

"My attention will be on you every moment that we play, Ange. But I'm sure you know about safe words. Give me a slow-it-down and full-stop word. Meet my gaze when you say them, so I'll see you'll use them when you should. Nothing's more important to me than us both enjoying tonight, getting the most out of it."

The hand he had on Ange was at his waist now, kneading, massaging. A reassurance and a promise that he meant it. Yeah. Ange's heart and his cock weren't separate things when it came to Robert. Not ever. Ange's gaze slid past him to the dresser.

"Baker for slow down. Chimney for stop."

Robert glanced over his shoulder at the Lehmann toy and smiled. "Got it. Now go put on your clothes. Meet me downstairs."

When he went to the guestroom, Ange found putting jeans on over his erection was a cautious affair. He tugged a heavy-weight black T-shirt over that. Since Robert had left it draped over a chair in the guest room, Ange deduced it was his Master's preference for him. Robert had also left him a pair of black laced boots, slightly higher than the ankle, with thick treads, and a pair of matching short socks.

Coming downstairs, he saw his Master had an opaque garment bag over his shoulder. He also had the sizeable case he'd pulled out of the safe a few nights ago. The one that had held the padded collar and cuffs, as well as the collar Ange wore now. He wondered what other things Robert was carrying in it. Normally Ange could have walked *en pointe* down those steep stairs, but he found himself holding onto the banister to keep from stumbling. Robert's gaze glinted with satisfaction.

"Just the way I want you. Off balance and looking to me to keep you steady." In a tender contrast, he brushed his knuckles along Ange's jaw, tugged his hair. "I love you, kid. You know that, right?"

The surge of warmth, competing with all the physical and emotional responses, had Ange's eyes getting suspiciously wet. What the hell? Now he did sway, but his Master's hand was on him. Robert had dropped the items he was carrying to circle Ange's waist, lift and shove him against the wall in an unexpectedly forceful way. His Master devoured his mouth, his tears, put his lips all over his face, until all Ange could do was hang on, blissed out from the attention. Robert pressed his strong, burly body against Ange from chest to hips, letting him feel the power of the cock that wanted him.

When Robert at last stepped back, he kept a hand on Ange until he was sure he could stand on his own. Then he picked up the garment bag and case again. "Keeping you off balance is just how I want you. Don't hold anything back but what I tell you to. Come on."

CHAPTER ELEVEN

*O*n the way there, Ange had his head propped on the seat back, his hand firmly in Robert's clasp, resting on his Master's thigh. The world was a blur of melting snow, Christmas and city lights decorating the world, giving it a festive, anticipatory air. He was floating in a zone of lust and vibrating anticipation, so he was barely aware that thirty minutes had passed before Robert pulled into a parking lot.

The club was in the predictably crappy area of town. The access door was an unremarkable portal, except for the name of the establishment, done in an elaborate gold calligraphy with a ruby red shadowing around it.

Patriarch – Members Only.

Robert swiped a key card over the security access to unlatch the door. He held it for Ange, and directed him up a short flight of stairs. At the threshold of the scarred wooden door at the top, Robert took the lead. However, as he put his hand on the latch, he stopped. Ange, on the step just below him, waited, sensing that Robert's head had gone somewhere.

"It's been awhile," Robert said at last. "Just taking a breath."

Ange pressed against his back, not an impropriety. Just moving as close as he could, to let him know he was here for him, too. After the meeting with Helena, Ange understood. Even a welcoming re-entry into a world could be a bit over-whelming, especially when the path traveled since the last visit had re-shaped the person. Would it feel the same? Be the same? Better or worse?

Robert tilted his head to give him a look over his shoulder. "Okay," he said. Then he opened the door.

As Ange had predicted, the welcome wasn't in doubt. As soon as Robert came down the short hallway and into view of the holiday party in process, a rousing call of welcome came from a chorus of male voices, including one Ange recognized.

Charlie's face was wreathed in a huge smile as he closed the distance between them. He shook Robert's hand, gripping his upper arm so warmly it was a near hug. "So good to see you here, Robert." He looked toward Ange. The warmth was still in his gaze, but something different, too. Charlie wasn't looking at him as a host, Ange a guest at his house. Here Charlie was another Dom, addressing his greeting for Ange directly to his Master. "And we're very glad you brought your sub with you."

As others came forward to express similar welcomes, Ange glanced around to get a sense of the place. Warehouse style, stark, with plenty of concrete and metal scaffolding, hung with convenient chains and straps. Key spotlighting mixed with shad-ows. Scattered equipment had been positioned in ways that would give the players their space and observers a good view.

There were two levels. The floor space upstairs was also open to view behind metal pole railings draped with Christmas deco-rations. Gold and silver tinsel garlands fluttered from the move-ment of large ceiling fans and a couple of mounted black industrial fans, their low roar adding to the club atmosphere. The air movement kept things comfortable, without dissipating the lingering odors of male sweat and need this much sexual intent and anticipation could create.

Where Ange and Robert stood now, a small socializing area had been created, including a table loaded with potluck offerings of hors d'oeuvres, sugar cookies, and a Yule-themed erotic centerpiece. It had cake pops shaped like dicks, with red and green icing cock collars, as well as sugar cookies decorated with glittering handcuffs made with sprinkles and silver icing. Similarly irreverent but cheerful decorations filled in the bouquet.

"Where are the queens?" Robert asked Charlie.

"On their way back from Virginia Beach. Dallas said for sure they'd be home before midnight. Don't want to miss gift-giving in the morning." Charlie grinned, his brindle moustache bristling. "Billie DeeLite talked them into doing a last minute fill-in on a charity benefit. Theopolis calls it trotting out the fossils to make them feel useful. Total bullshit. If Billie could coax them out on the road with him, he would. He has them doing a performance on Valentine's Day at the Wonder Theater. You'll have to come. They've worked up some new routines that put Vegas productions to shame."

"We'll look forward to it." Robert turned to Ange, put a familiar hand high on his ass, his thumb caressing his lower back. "Take off your jeans and shirt in the sub locker room." He gestured toward a narrow corridor. "I'm going to go change in the Dom area. Find me in the dedicated playroom."

He nodded to a wide archway, across the room from where they were now.

"Yes, Master."

Robert was obviously well-regarded here, so Ange hoped he'd do his Master credit. The best way to do that was being obedient and responsive, which was what he wanted anyway. He wanted to prove just how good he could be. But he was a little nervous, which his Master acknowledged with an additional ass squeeze.

"Don't forget what I said."

No one would touch Ange but him. It was a helpful reminder, because while Ange was comfortable with Charlie's attention, there were plenty of others taking that eye-fuck Robert had mentioned. And Ange hadn't even taken off his clothes yet.

When he entered the sub changing room, he found it had open space for that purpose, as well as two enclosed bathroom stalls. A shower area allowed for clean up before or after sessions. Several subs were in the room and nodded to him. A couple were chatting, obviously unattached and here to be picked up, if things worked out that way. The ones he thought already had Masters were quiet. Like him, they would be getting into their headspace, focusing on what their Doms would require of them.

One of those wore latex shorts and a collar. He stood at the mirror, applying dark liner around his expressive brown eyes. The latex strained over his buttocks as he leaned forward. Another man nearby was strapping his dick in a cock harness. It was all he wore below the waist, though he had on a tight-fitting leather shirt.

Ange removed the boots Robert had provided him. He took off the jeans, coat and T-shirt, put them in a locker, and pulled on the boots again. The simple acts settled him deeper into the anticipation, but they also heightened his nerves. When he approached one of the mirrors for a quick check, he told himself he was looking at a sub ready to serve his Master. His cock was cooperating, straining against the trio of straps, and his collar twitched against his throat as Ange swallowed.

He'd thought he had his feet back under him from the emotional roller coaster of the past couple days, but he noticed his eyes looked too big for his face. Despite his attempt to run a casual hand through his hair, tousling it further the way Robert liked, his heart accelerated at the things he saw reflected back at him. In this stark light, in this new environment, that fragility was still there, like a cracked porcelain angel glued back together.

His hand descended but didn't drop to his side. It landed on his stomach, over the permanent evidence of the two bullets that had nearly killed him.

For a long time after that pivotal day, his sleep hadn't been good. He'd routinely bolted out of it, covered in cold sweat, chased by nightmares of Clarissa dying in his arms. Leo's cry of surprise, then of agony, then nothing. The confusion and fear in his eyes.

No one should ever watch anyone die a violent death.

Crap and fuck. Why had he let his head go there? The room swam and Ange dropped to a squat, bracing himself with splayed fingertips on the tile floor. Not here. Not now.

Please don't do this to me. He didn't know who the plea was aimed at, but he'd known this could happen. New environment, a lot of excitement and change. He was particularly vulnerable at this time of year. While the past few days had held so many wonderful things, it couldn't seem to stop his fucked-up head from digging the event out of his subconscious.

"Hey, man." The sub in the shorts had capped the eye liner and turned, was kneeling next to him. "Okay?"

He didn't touch Ange, but he was close enough to do so. He had a Marine haircut and Semper Fi tattooed over his heart. His shrewd glance at the bullet scars said he might understand a little more than most what was going on with Ange.

"I can go get your Dom if you need him," he said quietly. "Just say the word."

"I always need him. But I can go to him. Thanks. I'm Ange." Steadier now for having the obvious support, Ange managed to meet the calm eyes, hold the lock.

"Okay. Chase is my scene name." The man nodded. "See you on the floor. Or not. Sometimes we don't see much once our Masters start to work us over, right?"

"If it's done right," the other sub said, the one who now had his cock thoroughly tied up in straps and chains. He'd been watching, obviously ready to lend support, too. Now he gave them both a wink. "See you on the other side of heaven and hell, darlings."

As he exited, Ange made it back to his feet. He gave Chase

one more nod, confirming he was okay. The man's gaze swept him, a quick evaluation, but he returned the nod and left Ange.

He was now alone in the locker area. Ange closed his eyes. Trying to fight it would make it worse, so he focused on what would do just the opposite.

Robert loved him. Robert knew him, knew his strengths and weaknesses. If Ange couldn't do this tonight, he'd be more than okay with it. He wouldn't give a damn what anyone thought. And Robert had the type of friends, like Charlie, who understood what a Dom/sub relationship was supposed to be.

Ange had spent these past months learning about that himself. He now knew what a safety net could be, when your Dom loved you, put your well-being over anything else.

That thought, the truth of it, reduced Ange's anxiety over blowing this up. Christmas miracle of Christmas miracles, the episode started ebbing away. He could do this. Not just because he wanted to please Robert, but because he wanted to be claimed by his Master here, in this space. All he had to do was reach for that truth in his mind, and it would take the lead.

He took a couple deep breaths and imagined the details of it. Robert's hands, his voice, his presence. He needed and wanted those things.

He just had to get his ass out of this room and go find them. He thought of how incredibly hot Robert had looked in what he'd worn to the theater last night, the black shirt and gray suit, and wondered what he'd be wearing tonight. He'd said he was going to change in the other locker room.

Ange thought of the masculine smell of Robert's aftershave, inhaled to remind himself of it. He could do that, because he'd used some of it himself after his shower, just to have Robert's scent on him.

His heart was thumping harder for the right reasons now. He was ready.

When he emerged, he headed straight for the wide archway, hoping Robert was dressed and waiting. As expected, he heard a burst of sharp whistles and lewd comments. Nothing unexpected, given the environment and him wearing only boots and a leather jock, his cock out and strapped.

But he was wearing a custom-made collar, too. Not a generic service one. Yeah, he felt exposed, vulnerable, nervous, but not in a bad way. Robert had said no one would touch him. Robert wouldn't bring him to a place where people couldn't be trusted. Robert had always taken care of him.

Every step toward the archway made Ange's body heavier with need and want. When he saw what lay past the threshold, that feeling increased threefold.

The dedicated dungeon area was a bigger version of the area with the food table. More equipment, scaffolding, tall dark cement walls. But no Christmas decorations. This place had one purpose, no distractions from it. The dim constant lighting was enhanced by a trio of spotlights that continually swept over the scenes in process.

One older man was getting worked over by his Dom, a slim younger man wielding a flogger with enthusiasm. The sub was tied spread-eagle to a spot on the scaffolding, his red ass flexing. With every strong blow, he made a short, involuntary cry.

Another Master was enthusiastically pounding his cock into a man bent over a spanking bench. It was the sub wearing the cock harness. Ange licked suddenly dry lips, his stomach somersaulting. The guy's Master must have ordered him to bend and spread them and gone at him right away, no foreplay. Though with this environment, foreplay was hardly needed—it was merely another torment for cocks already straining for attention.

The sub held onto handles on the floor, his arms stretched out, hoarse grunts coming from him.

Two couples were dancing to heavy metal rock, the bass thumping a gritty contrast to the Christmas music in the other room. The couples were so close together they were obviously a foursome, at least right now. The Doms were indulging in a lot of touching, gripping and stroking of their two gyrating and grinding subs, who wore nothing at all. A jeweled plug between the buttocks of one of them caught the spotlights.

A trio of Doms sat together on black vinyl lounge furniture. The middle one had his arms stretched out behind the other two. All three looked toward their spread knees, where subs were kneeling, enthusiastically sucking dick. One of them bore an ass plug that had been embellished with a horse's tail. It went with the hoof boots covering his feet and calves, and a partial head mask that had pointed ears. The forelock sewn into it became a mane that followed the back of his skull and trailed down the valley of his spine, stopping at his shoulder blades. A bold black tattoo of angel wings, one on either side of the mane, made Ange think of Pegasus.

The sexual energy hit Ange like a wave, fed by those scenes as he took in the details, but they were passing impressions. Like Chase had said, a sub really only saw his Master. That was the only thing that mattered. Ange kept his eyes moving, looking for what he wanted and needed the most.

He didn't find Robert on the first couple sweeps of the area. Maybe he was still in the Dom changing room. Ange wasn't sure what to do with himself, though. There were men clustered along the walls and other appropriate viewing areas who had noticed him standing there. While none had approached yet, he was considering what spot looked the most removed from every-thing, a clear message that he was waiting for a particular Master.

His attention passed over the room again. A non-alcoholic bar offered refreshments. It was also a display area, two subs locked in tall narrow cages at either end. Their cocks were chained and held out between the bars, on display for whatever play their nearby and watchful Doms would allow.

Several men leaned against the bar, watching the scenes. Ange saw Charlie standing next to a tall, intimidating Dom. The man was staring at Ange like the pull of a chain wrapping itself around his throat.

Ange knew those dark eyes.

Holy Tom from Finland fuck. It was Robert.

Only not as Ange had ever seen him—except maybe in some very deep-in-the-night wet dream fantasies.

His Master was turned out in full leather. Tight as sin pants and a broad collared jacket, with metal studded shoulders and lapels. The jacket was open to the waist to display the fitted leather shirt beneath. A cop-style hat was pulled low over his Master's stern brow. He was leaning against the bar, jack boots crossed one over the other, a short whip of some sort stuck in the top of one and strapped to his calf.

Now he knew why Robert, normally so meticulous in his personal grooming, hadn't shaved this morning. The stubble added to the dangerous look.

Ange's cock, which he hadn't believed could get harder, bucked against its restraints. His stomach flopped in delighted terror. All the teasing Robert had done to him came together in one big surge of need. His Master was in the mood to bust his ass, and Ange wouldn't stop him. He wanted the ass kicking. Wanted to be used, fucked, completely broken down into a mindless cock and ass for Robert to take however he wanted it.

He lowered his gaze so he wasn't disrespectfully looking right into Robert's glittering eyes, but he couldn't take his hungry gaze lower than the stern, straight lips. Only one man here could demand anything of him, and he could demand everything.

When a fully gloved hand—oh fuck, could he get any hotter? —rose and beckoned, Ange was already on his way to him. At the toes of those boots, he dropped to his knees.

Robert caught his collar on the way down, so when Ange landed on his knees, his chin was jerked up, the strap biting into the back of his neck. Robert twisted the gloved fingers in the strap, briefly constricting it before he eased that hold and gripped Ange's shoulder. Ange moved his jaw and cheek against all that leather, strength and heat.

Robert dropped to one knee, curved over Ange as Ange

curled beneath him in submission, dipped his head, his shoulders. His Master closed the leather-clad hand over Ange's jutting cock.

He knew how to control himself, he did, but not with all this stimulus. The second Robert gripped him, he lost it. With a strangled cry, Ange bucked forward, forehead bumping Robert's shoulder as his cock convulsed, pumped shamelessly into the black condom.

Desperation strangled him. His garbled apology was one step above gibberish. Robert moved his other hand down around to his ass, worked him against his grip as Ange humped air. Whistles and catcalls came from around him, egging Robert on. It was visceral, male, a dark lustful hunger pushing in on all sides. Ange imagined dancing for the demons in hell as they commanded him to keep going, keep going...

He had experienced overwhelming climaxes before, but this one almost pulled groin muscles. He knew he hadn't had permission, so though he was still having little spurts into the condom, his hips twitching, he struggled to sit back on his heels, assume a proper submissive stance. Robert put an end to that, making a reproving noise that kept Ange still and in place. He ran his gloved hand over the bare curve of Ange's faintly perspiring back, the protrusion of his spine, his other hand still milking his cock with easy squeezes. "Good boy," he murmured. "That's my good boy."

He tilted his head, a motion Ange felt rather than saw, since he had his face pressed down, his crown to his Master's chest as Robert continued to fondle his hair, his nape. He had his other hand wrapped over Ange's back, keeping him in place, curled beneath him and in his arms.

"You love your art history, Charlie," Robert said. Despite a rough edge to his tone, the words were deliberately casual. He'd raised his volume to be heard over the music and fans, so the deep power of it stroked over Ange's flesh. "Tell me what that reminded you of."

"The Rape of Proserpina." Charlie offered a sharp, sensual chuckle. "Pluto taking Proserpina to Hell. Or Hades taking Persephone, if you prefer."

Charlie spoke the way Ange thought he would have when teaching students. It fit in this place, where Masters like him and Robert held total authority over the subs attending them.

"The title of the sculpture is unsettling in its translation, but the original Latin, *raptus*, simply meant to seize, or a taking," Charlie continued. "Which fits what I just saw. With him wearing those lovely tights, your strong fingers, biting into his ass, looked remarkably like Pluto's fingers pressing into Proserpina's marble flesh."

Seized and taken. Ange agreed.

Robert fondled Ange's hair, then let him go, rising in front of him. Ange's eyes couldn't help but follow the track of those leather encased thighs, the prominent bulge of his cock triangulated between them.

"Want to suck my dick, do you, boy?" Robert's voice became a growl again, mean as Ange had ever heard it. It sent chills through him, raised gooseflesh.

Ange nodded vigorously. "Yes, sir. Yes, Master."

"Gotta earn that with some pain."

"Anything, Master."

"Follow me."

Ange scrambled up, too fast. But Robert's hands were on him, making sure he was good on his feet before striding away, leading Ange across the room. Past the flogging, the cock sucking, all the ways subs could serve their Masters. Robert brought him to a spot on the scaffolding where a padded mat had been strapped against the metal pipes, like a canvas waiting for an artist.

Charlie had followed, and he carried skeins of red rope. Another sub had joined them; Chase, the Marine in the locker room.

Robert put a hand on Ange's shoulder, a firm leather grip

that commanded his attention. "I want you to warm up, like you would before you plan to dance."

An unexpected request, but looking at the scaffolding and the rope, maybe not.

Ange started most days with some stretches to accommodate his random and spontaneous desire to dance, leap or twirl as the mood took him. But since he expected Robert was about to demand a lot of his body—a thought that sent an eager surge of need through him—Ange did a couple basic stretches and then some of the more extreme ones to ensure he'd be ready.

He did a standing modified spine stretch, then sank into a split, reaching forward and back. The moves verified that his muscles were already pretty loose, in good shape. He wouldn't have to keep his Master waiting long. He rose and executed a standing second position stretch, his hand on the scaffolding while he lifted his leg up to his side, toe pointed straight toward the ceiling while he clasped the sole of his foot.

Since he was doing all this in the jock strap and with a full erection, Ange was glad the leather at least was reasonably flexible. Shifting his grip on the scaffolding, he leaned forward, extending his leg behind him and up, as close to ninety degrees above his head as possible. Then he changed legs and did the process again.

"Holy fuck," Charlie muttered. "My tongue just rolled out and hit the floor, Robert."

"Roll it back in or I'll stomp on it," Robert advised.

As Ange held the position, his Master ran his hands along the deep dip of Ange's back to his hip bone. His other hand moved beneath the point of Ange's extended rib cage. For a second, Ange imagined Robert lifting him. His Master had more than enough strength to do it.

He and Leo had lifted one another at the apartment to practice form, build the arm strength required to raise their lighter female partners.

God, Leo.

Fortunately, he was distracted from that lower belly wrench of grief by Robert's next question.

"What's this called?"

Ange managed a slight, nervous smile. "An attitude stretch."

The handsome lines around Robert's eyes creased. Ange lowered the leg, squatted, straightened, rolled his shoulders and head on his neck. "I'm ready, Master."

"Good." Robert looked toward the vertical mat. "We're going to lift you off your feet. Once we do, I want your front leg bent and the back leg stretched out. A stag leap."

One of the moves that brought that floating feeling, which could take him toward euphoria or darkness, depending on the situation. Nerves shimmered through Ange.

"Charlie is going to tie you to the scaffolding in that position," Robert continued, eyes locked on him. "There should be no painful pressure on your joints, or damaging strain on your muscles. You'll tell me if you feel any."

Robert cupped Ange's face in a strong hand, the look in his eyes tolerating no evasion. "I want to hold you in the air, Ange. In that suspended moment, only this moment is going to be entirely different. It's going to take over all the other moments like that, good and bad. That's my intent. When bad things come, you can go back to this moment. You understand?"

His words plowed up the sediment of his nightmares, but reminded him of what Robert had told him, in so many ways. Ange wasn't alone with them. It made him respond the only way he could. "Yes, sir."

"But if it gets to be too much, you'll tell me. I'm not trying to push you into a repeat of the other night."

"Yes, sir."

"Good, then. Put your arms above your head, and then tell us where to put our hands to lift you the right way."

Ange did. Robert took the upper torso, his palms curved along Ange's hip and side. Chase handled his legs. As they lifted him, Ange felt that ascension inside as well as out. He bent the knee in front and extended his back leg.

Robert and Chase put him against the vertical mat, and Charlie moved in with the red rope. He began to secure Ange, using an overhang of scaffolding to hold Ange's arms above his head, and the frame pipes extending past the edges of the mat to maintain the leap form.

Charlie was experienced at this, not hesitating except to consider his choices for each wrap or knot, how to hold the position Robert was wanting for his sub. Robert and Chase followed his direction, adjusting their grips as needed.

Though Charlie had Ange make slight adjustments to protect and support him properly, the Dom was able to keep the spirit of the leap. As Ange was bound in that position, the yearning feeling, complicated and simple at once, built into a tempest. It spiraled wildly inside a tight frame, drilling down into his heart and soul, bringing so many memories with it.

They'd attracted an audience, men drawing closer to watch. But Ange was less and less aware of them as he locked onto Robert's attention, a lifeline for everything happening in that storm. His Master was registering everything; if Ange was aroused, uncomfortable. If he was getting agitated by what was going on in his head. When Charlie tightened bindings between thigh and ankle, holding that bent knee in place, Ange's cock flexed in its straps, and Robert caught that, too.

The position was about freedom, soaring. The contrast messed with him, his balls aching, his cock hard, his heart thundering as his gaze clung to Robert's face, his ruthless looking mouth. Ange's eyes swept over the resilient body in leather. He wanted him so badly. Every inch, and he wasn't just talking about his Master's thick cock, or the strength of his body surrounding him, subduing him, inside and out.

"Such starved eyes," Robert purred. Charlie stepped back, done. A generous several strides of space separated Robert and Ange from their audience. Any conversation happening among them was muffled by the roar of industrial fans and the head banging music. The mix was background static as far as Ange was concerned. The only sound that could hold him would come from his Dom.

Robert leaned an elbow against the mat as he stroked Ange's hair back from his face, played his fingers over his lips. Ange wanted to taste him, but everything about Robert said Ange better ask for permission for anything, even the right to breathe or exist. And Robert wasn't in a permission-giving mood. So he waited, but when Robert finally pushed one of his fingers in his mouth, Ange moaned with relief and greedily sucked, making his Master's eyes darken.

"Look at you, ready to do anything your Master demands."

"Yes, sir. Anything."

"Good." Robert backed off to look at him from stem to stern, lingering on all the places in between. The audience took his cue and melted back even further. Some re-settled at the bar, or straddled one of the metal chairs scattered about, the legs making harsh scraping noises against the concrete floor.

Robert drew the whip from his boot, released a tie on the handle and shook out an attached tassel of slender strips. The tips of them glittered.

"I have another jock like what you're wearing, only it doesn't have a hole in front." Robert dropped his attention to Ange's groin. "It has a front panel lined with tiny spikes, so when it's buckled up, your cock is pushed against them. When I tease you so much even those spikes can't make you behave, I get to watch you squirm. Hope for mercy."

He threaded the tassel through his fingers and studied Ange thoughtfully. "I have a strong urge to do something, Ange. You know what it is?"

"No, Master." Ange didn't know how he was even forming words, except his Master was expecting an answer and some part of Ange would figure out how to respond, even if he had no voice or functioning brain cells at all.

"Punish you," Robert said, with a fierce, dark-browed look. "Thank me for that."

"Thank you, Master." Ange stared at those strips, sliding over Robert's knuckles. The glitter came from flat metal pieces. Ange's lower belly contracted.

"Punishment is a reminder. From here forward, your main job is caring for yourself, keeping yourself healthy and well for your Master. Serving his interests, because you belong to me."

Robert's brown eyes were tinged with flame. "You're the toy I value the most. I'd give up all the others to keep you."

Ange swallowed. "Even if I'm broken?"

He didn't know why he said it, except everything was coming to the surface, every fear and feeling. Fuck, he wished Robert had gagged him.

Robert's expression flashed dark and dangerous. Yet his words came out thick, almost tender.

"We're all broken. It's how love gets a foot in the door and comes home to stay."

Ange couldn't move much, but his body strained. "Please..." he said, not really sure what he was asking for. But his Master knew.

Robert closed the distance and brought the whip down on Ange's hip. The faint sting made him jump, but Robert was already moving onward, playing the tassels over Ange's body. The next targets were his abdomen and nipples, making him wiggle some more.

"Please, what, Ange?" His eyes were hooded, shadowed. Ange wanted to bite the cruel mouth, feel Robert's hand on the back of his neck, shoving him to the ground at his feet. Holding him there. He wanted Robert to allow him to kiss his thighs, his knees, his boots. The handle of the whip. Worship him until mindless bliss took over.

"Please...punish me, Master. Teach me what I need. I want to serve you."

Robert cupped his face, rubbing a thumb along his cheek.

Then he gave Ange's collar a quick tug before he let his fingers trail over his chest, his nipples, his abdomen. In between those caresses, he snapped the tassels along his inner thighs, his side, over his dick.

He kept going until Ange was panting, shuddering in his bonds. Then Robert tucked the whip under his arm and unstrapped Ange's cock. He removed the used condom, disposed of it. He pulled another wrapped one out of an inside pocket of his jacket, but before he rolled it on, he dipped and closed his hot mouth completely over Ange's organ, taking it all the way to the root.

"Oh..." Ange jerked hard against his bonds. He really was soaring, arms reaching up for the heavens, body swaying away from the mat, trying to take as much of Robert's mouth as he'd give him. Robert sucked on his cock with just the right amount of uncomfortable force and eye crossing pleasure.

He was helpless, entirely at his Master's mercy, but Robert wasn't offering any. He kept alternating fast and slow on Ange's cock, tongue lashing and flicking. He'd change rhythm or force if Ange was on the cusp, knocking it back down a couple notches again.

When Ange really got too close, a desperate plea breaking from his lips, Robert backed off. He rolled the condom on him, re-strapped his cock, tightening the one on the base so Ange knew he intended it to act as a cock ring, helping him obey his Master's will and only come at his command.

Then Robert started working him over with the whip again. This time he was intent on delivering the pain he'd promised, all those tiny metal pieces stinging Ange's flesh. Robert did it with more precision, weight and focus as he went on, reminding Ange of how expertly he'd wielded the buggy whip at the store.

His Master liked whips.

The pain grew, burned over Ange's skin, made him go from grunts to cries, to begging. Not for Robert to stop. At the primal base of his submission, Ange knew begging was the food a Master's soul most craved, that plea for service, sacrifice and salvation.

He wanted to give Robert that. He wanted to give him everything. Fuck, he was hurting. But pain had never felt so good. Robert shed the coat. The tight leather shirt beneath was short sleeved, showing off his biceps, the powerful body Ange wanted to overwhelm him. He'd felt that way ever since he'd first experienced the strength in Robert's hands, touching him as he lay in the alley bleeding, not just from his body but from his soul.

"Please..."

"Keep begging, sub. I want you hoarse before the night's over. From begging, from taking my come down your throat, from begging some more." When Robert turned away to drape the coat over the back of a chair, the thin leather of the shirt creased over his broad back.

As Robert resumed the flogging, Ange lost time, place, everything but sensation. Pleasure, pain and an excruciating, unforgettably punishing level of denied release. Robert's gruff voice, his commands, were all that penetrated. When Ange's pleading became involuntary cries of agony tearing from his throat, the agony of holding back, of enduring everything Robert demanded, Robert wrapped his fist around Ange's re-strapped and latex-covered cock. While that bottom strap was helping Ange maintain some control, he was seriously wobbling on the edge of that cliff.

"You are so beautiful," Robert said. "You're making everyone here want to fuck like rabbits. That's driving you, too, whether you realize it or not. Shut your eyes. Listen."

Ange obeyed. After several ragged breaths that helped him get past the noise of industrial fans and heavy metal music, he heard it. Groans, thrusting, the sounds of equipment clanking, wood creaking. Cries, grunts. Slaps. He inhaled the scents of sex, leather, metal. "Master," he breathed. "Please..."

"What do you want?" Robert said, coming close, because his breath was on Ange's face. "Keep those eyes closed, and you better not reach for my mouth. You have zero permission to do anything I haven't explicitly told you to do."

Ange let out a sound close to a whimper, increasing the ruthless satisfaction in Robert's voice. "You're getting it now. Just how cruel I can be. How much I can demand from you. Remember that, next time you risk anything that's mine, put down something that's mine, doubt something that's mine. You are *my* angel, Ange. You can soar to the heavens, but you'll remember you wear my collar, won't you? You'll remember who owns you, body and soul. I won't let that binding break. You'll never fall. I've got you. Always."

Tears stung Ange's eyes. "Yes, Master. Yes. Please..."

"What do you want, Ange?"

"To do anything that pleases you."

"This pleases me. To do this all night long."

That produced another groan and a spike of terror through Ange's gut, but it came hand in hand with total willing submission. It was as Ange had thought when he was in the locker room. He would accept anything Robert wanted to demand of him. He just wanted to belong to his Master, be used and fucked by him. To love him, be kept by him, serve him...be together forever. Always.

He was speaking, mumbling things like that. Robert's hand was on his face again, his thumb moving over Ange's lips, taking in the words through his flesh.

"That's what I want, too. You have only one focus right now. Serving me. Accepting and absorbing what I'm doing to you, everything it means. You control nothing. I have all of it."

As his Master spoke, Ange was aware of his hands moving over his body, his shoulders and hips. He'd done it several times, checking on Ange's well-being. Things were aching, but nothing was unbearable. Nothing but the feeling in his heart, so explosive and large he feared the organ couldn't take it. But it would. Just like the rest of his body.

Until his Master said they were done.

"All right, then," Robert said, stepping back. "Here we go."

And so it went. Time and place were seized and taken from Ange—*raptus*, as Charlie had said. His Master was the center of everything. He played with Ange's body, his property, with hands, whip, mouth. Called forth pain and pleasure, stroked Ange's dick. He dragged over one of those metal chairs, stood on it and brought his own dick to Ange's mouth. He had him suck and play a good while, rocking relentlessly into Ange's stretched mouth before he withdrew. Then he stepped down and went after him with the whip again, for being too damn good at giving head.

A Master's perversity, which, if Ange survived this, would make him smile somewhere in the dark corners of his heart, where Robert was.

Robert was in every part of him, dark and light.

When finally Robert put the whip away, Ange was barely aware of it. He had no thoughts. He was all feeling. He was still pleading, but all his stripped voice could manage was a whisper.

Ropes loosened as hands took their place. Charlie and Chase were helping him down, then giving him over to Robert's care. Ange slid bonelessly into Robert's grasp, his legs unable to bear his weight. The only thing that had any rigidity to it was the organ between his legs that Robert had teased and teased and teased, but had commanded Ange to keep in that state. No release until his Master said.

Which meant they weren't done.

Robert practically carried him to a spanking bench, and Ange was leaned over it. His Master wrapped his limp wrists in Velcro in front of him, knees propped on a padded step and strapped down. Ange's heart somersaulted in gratitude as Robert employed his knife again, in just the way he'd hoped. He cut the slender strip running between Ange's buttocks and ripped open the back of the tights. His Master used his strong fingers to finish the job of pulling the fabric out of his way, exposing Ange's bare ass to the heated air of the club.

Lube trickled in as Ange quietly moaned, a sound of need and hope. When Robert thrust into him, hard enough Ange was pressed against the side of the bench, he cried out in a relief so great it was a guttural shout.

"Come for me, Ange."

His body bowed up and then jacked out violently, a rasping shriek breaking from him. No hesitation, just instant capitulation to his Master's command. Yet the spurts of his ejaculation seemed to go on forever. Even when that was done, his body was still dry humping, caught in the power of the release. He'd never felt a climax like it. Tears were running down his face, his muscles burning.

But Robert kept going. As Ange gasped and groaned through it all, at the bruising grip of his Master's hand on his ass, the rough pounding of his cock, he realized this was an additional punishment, intended to reinforce the lesson Robert had dished out tonight.

He was his Master's favorite toy. The one he'd give up everything else to keep. That was what he'd said. And Ange would damn well care for himself, so he could give his Master everything he demanded; tonight, tomorrow and always.

Robert at last started to release, those fierce thrusts becoming even more demanding. His climax went on for a long time, too. The idea of how much come was being jetted into his ass thrilled Ange, down to the soul. It confirmed how aroused his Master had been.

When Robert finally finished, Ange's cheek was pressed flat to the bench's deep red upholstery, his tears making it slippery. His hands were curling and uncurling above the straps. Robert had his lips on the back of his neck, large hands stroking down his shoulders, his back, over his ribs and hips. The touch said the same thing over and over, in different ways. The same things Robert was whispering.

Good boy. Love you. Good sub. You did well.

Ange had no strength to do anything, but his Master made it clear his only requirement was to be still. The straps were removed from his wrists, and Robert adjusted him so Ange was draped over the bench rather than stretched across it.

For the next little bit, he was cosseted, muscles massaged, sore places rubbed with a soothing lotion. The jock was removed, and an oversized white T-shirt was put on him. He was shirt-tailing it, everything hanging loose beneath, just as his Master wanted it.

Robert had an arm around his waist, and was helping him to his feet. They didn't have to go far. Just to the nearest couch, where Ange was pulled down into Robert's lap, his legs sprawled out over the cushions. As he drifted in and out, he heard Robert's voice, Charlie's and others.

Gradually he came back to himself, enough to become aware of his surroundings. Robert's hand was beneath the T-shirt. With relaxed frequency, he'd been stroking Ange's limp cock, his upper thighs and the curve of his ass. Ange's long legs were stretched out, his feet resting against Charlie's thigh. Charlie's hand was draped over his ankles.

Charlie was giving Ange's toes a look and grinning in Robert's direction. "You're lucky it's me down here. Theopolis would have these things painted a festive Christmas red with green sparkles."

Robert chuckled, the sound rumbling through his chest and vibrating against Ange. "Good thing it's you, then. Though I doubt he'd notice. Think he's as spaced as a sub can get."

"I'm here," Ange said. "If it's okay to say so, Master."

"It is." As Charlie turned his attention to conversation with another couple of Doms, letting them have their aftercare privacy, Robert touched Ange's face, drawing his eyes up again. "Hey there, kid. Welcome back."

Ange wasn't sure if he really was all the way back, but his Master knew that.

"The club you visited, with the Dom that mentored you that night. Was that club like this one?"

"Sort of."

"Tell me about it. In detail."

Ange fought the clumsiness of his thoughts, sorted through them to answer. He understood Robert had asked the casual question to help ground him, bring him back to earth. Yet somehow his answer morphed into far more intimate info. Like how this experience with Robert was so very different. And how the more Ange opened up to Robert, his Master did the same with him. And he was so glad for that. For everything his Master gave him of himself.

He couldn't stop the flow of words coming from deep in his head, expressing his desire to be so inside of each other that they could almost anticipate one another's thoughts, a connection so strong nothing could break it. They already had some of it, but he wanted it to be that way on everything.

He never would have said such things to Robert, to anyone, figuring they'd think he was crazy. But right now, in this space, it felt like it wouldn't bother Robert. He'd understand.

Robert's gaze never left Ange's face. When Ange simply ran out of words, Robert's expression said he didn't need them anymore, anyway.

He'd understood from the first.

Ange's fingers were playing with Robert's free hand, resting on his thigh. "Love you, Master," he said sleepily.

Robert held him closer, brushing his lips over his forehead. "Same goes," he said.

Ange sent him a look under his lashes. "The leather was seriously hot."

"Tell us about it," Charlie interjected. "Robert, when you come back to the fold, you do it with serious fucking style.

Maddie would have loved it. She'd have expressed her approval so enthusiastically it would have earned her a major spanking."

Robert smiled. However, his intent dark brown eyes hadn't left Ange, and Ange understood the message there.

It was time to be together, just the two of them. His Master was ready to go home. They both were.

CHAPTER TWELVE

*T*hey spent some time in the tub, then moved to Robert's blissfully large bed. He kept Ange right up against him, draped over his body, his hands moving over him. First to reinforce the aftercare. Then because he wanted him again. He pushed his sub onto his back, pressing Ange's thighs open and up, and fucked him, a slow, languid thing. He stared down into Ange's face while the kid shuddered and came apart, came on his abdomen and chest. Then Robert cleaned him back up and returned to the bed, pulling him into a boneless drape over Robert again.

The room held a heated mix of his and Ange's scents, the additional spice of post-coital sex and faint sweat. Robert liked it.

He let them doze awhile, but he had something on his mind, a question he wanted answered. When he asked it, he kept his tone mild, a rumble in the tranquil darkness.

"I want the full answer this time, from your heart. Why don't you want to dance professionally again?"

Ange slid his hand across Robert's chest, fingers threading through the mat of hair. He traced circles on Robert's pec before he spoke.

"You remember when I had that moment with Helena, when I came off the stage? I told her I didn't wish any of it had happened, but if I hadn't bolted, I wouldn't have found the man I love. I know you'll say I sound stupid."

"You don't tell me what I'll say or why I'll say it," Robert said, injecting a firm note of reproof. Even as he tightened his arm around Ange. "And remember what I said. I just want to be sure that you know loving me doesn't mean you have to limit yourself. I suggested the community center because you're so good with kids. But I'm not going to push you toward something you don't really want to do."

"I know." Ange tilted his thoughtful gaze up. "I think it's a great idea. I've also been thinking of something else. Adult dance classes are usually about ballroom dancing, or shag, things like that. I thought I might offer to teach adult ballet. Something along the lines of 'yeah, you didn't get to take ballet as a kid, but you can do it now, have fun with it.' We could do a video of me showing you a couple moves."

"I'd choose someone who actually has some dance aptitude. Like Charlie. He and Amos used to do the *dissssco* together." Robert returned Ange's quick grin, adding, "Lumbering grizzly bears have better dance skills than me."

"Well, your last name is Bauer."

Robert squeezed him. "That actually means peasant or farmer."

Ange's gaze slid to the dresser, drawing Robert's attention to the Lehmann toy. "Fournier means baker in French."

Robert brushed his lips across his forehead. "You are so insanely irresistible."

Ange chuckled, then sobered again. "My dreams have changed, Master," he said slowly. "They changed...that day. I don't need to dance at professional level anymore; I don't want to. The desire is gone."

He took a breath. Robert increased his hold around him, sensing the words came painfully. "That day on stage, I saw a side of the world I can't ever unsee. It wounded my heart, broke it."

After something like that, life changed, perspectives changed. Robert got it.

Ange propped himself on an elbow, stared down into Robert's face. "I put it back together, with you, but it has a different shape now. It wants different things. It wants you. That's the most important thing, the thing I love even more than dance. Or as the center of the dance, if that makes sense."

Dance wasn't about a stage to Ange. He'd found a different place in the world, a different purpose and way to nourish his heart. The flower had gone back to earth through the cold winter and was pushing back up for a new spring, a new season.

I was able to fix you...

"Ange," Robert said, his voice thick.

As he caressed Ange's well-sculpted jaw, let his hand drift over the round of his shoulder, Robert knew it was official. He'd no longer try to buffer himself against the grief or loss that change could bring. If he was being offered the gift of this man's desire to belong to him, he would grasp it with both hands, leaving behind any safety harness.

"That moment with Clarissa and Leo told me how much genuine pain there is in the world," Ange continued, his green eyes brilliant, even in the semi-darkness. His mouth was curved in a bittersweet way, his next words echoing Robert's own thoughts. "Anything that lessens it, helps the heart survive it, is a gift. You did it for me, and then you gave me the honor of letting me do it for you."

He shot Robert an impulsive smile. "Dance lifts the heart. I like the idea of bringing that gift to people at the community center. And I definitely want to go back to the queens' house, dance with them again. See Amos. Did that answer your question, Master? I mean every word of it."

Gazing into Ange's beautiful earnest face, Robert nodded slowly. "Yeah. It does."

His sub had learned what Robert had. The uncertainty of the world could only be balanced by faith in something far less uncertain. Love, reinforced every day, in ways as limitless as the dance of life itself. Or what could be explored between Master and sub.

He drew Ange back down to him, holding him close. "Get some sleep. I'm making you breakfast when we get up."

Ange glanced over at the clock, which showed an hour well past midnight. "Merry Christmas, Master," he murmured, settling his head down on the pillow. When he crooked an arm over Robert's chest, he combed through Robert's chest hair, those sensitive fingers caressing a nipple. It sent a wave of pleasure through Robert's body, tightening it. Damn if he wasn't likely to take his beautiful danseur again before dawn.

He couldn't think of a better Christmas gift to give himself.

"Hey, in the morning?" Ange's voice was sleepy again, yet insistent. "Let's make that cake."

"Absolutely not. We're having a healthy breakfast."

But Robert smiled in the dark and pressed a kiss to Ange's brow. Maybe a healthy breakfast, then cake.

It was Christmas, after all.

∽

WANT MORE? Joey writes a wide variety of BDSM relationships, but **if you particularly love M/m stories**, check out her award-winning title, *Rough Canvas*:

Marcus taught Thomas to embrace who he is, a sexual submissive who responds to the touch of only one Master. But when Thomas's father died, his North Carolina family needed him, so Marcus let him go.

Now he knows he made a mistake. Since Thomas abandoned a promising art career in New York, Marcus offers Thomas a way back into it. On one condition—Thomas must spend a week with him in the Berkshires.

Marcus knows he can be a selfish bastard. And he won't hesitate to use that to give his submissive everything Thomas truly needs.

CLICK HERE TO READ NOW
ROUGH CANVAS

Reading this in print format?
Look for it at your favorite book vendor!

ABOUT THE AUTHOR

Having penned over fifty acclaimed BDSM contemporary and paranormal titles, which includes six award-winning series, *Joey W. Hill* has been awarded the RT Book Reviews Career Achievement Award for Erotic Romance. A submissive herself, Hill brings authenticity to her intensely emotional love stories.

She is grateful for the support of a wonderful and enthusiastic readership, which allows her to live on her beloved Carolina coast with her even more beloved husband and menagerie of animals.

- On the Web: https://storywitch.com
- Twitter: https://twitter.com/JoeyWHill
- Facebook: https://facebook.com/JoeyWHillAuthor
- Facebook Fan Forum: https://facebook.com/groups/JWHMembersOnly
- MeWe: https://mewe.com/i/joeywhill
- GoodReads: https://www.goodreads.com/author/show/103359.Joey_W_Hill
- BookBub: https://bookbub.com/authors/joey-w-hill
- Amazon: https://amazon.com/Joey-W-Hill/e/B001JSCIW0

ALSO BY JOEY W. HILL

Natural Law

Ice Queen

Mirror of My Soul

Mistress of Redemption

Rough Canvas

Branded Sanctuary

Divine Solace

Worth The Wait

Truly Helpless

In His Arms

Ignition Sequence

Naughty Bits Series

Naughty Bits

Naughty Wishes

Vampire Queen Series

Vampire Queen's Servant

Mark of the Vampire Queen

Vampire's Claim

Beloved Vampire

Vampire Mistress *(VQS: Club Atlantis)*

Vampire Trinity *(VQS: Club Atlantis)*

Vampire Instinct

Bound by the Vampire Queen

Taken by a Vampire

The Scientific Method

Nightfall

Elusive Hero

Night's Templar

Vampire's Soul

Vampire's Embrace

Vampire Master *(VQS: Club Atlantis)*

Vampire Guardian *(VQS: Club Atlantis)*

Vampire's Choice

Non-Series Titles

Chance of a Lifetime

Choice of Masters

If Wishes Were Horses

Medusa's Heart

Make Her Dreams Come True

Snow Angel (short story)

Submissive Angel

Threads of Faith

Unrestrained

Virtual Reality

Printed in Great Britain
by Amazon

60967195R00141